OPERATION TOLLBOOTH

OPERATION TOLLBOOTH

K I P C A S S I N O

ARCHWAY
PUBLISHING

Archway Publishing books may be ordered through booksellers or by contacting:

Archway Publishing
1663 Liberty Drive
Bloomington, IN 47403
www.archwaypublishing.com
844-669-3957

Scripture quotations marked NKJV are taken from the New King James Version. Copyright © 1982 by Thomas Nelson, Inc. Used by permission. All rights reserved.

ISBN: 978-1-6657-7153-5 (sc)
ISBN: 978-1-6657-7154-2 (e)

Library of Congress Control Number: 2025900550

Print information available on the last page.

Archway Publishing rev. date: 01/22/2025

CONTENTS

ACKNOWLEDGEMENTS

This book, and every word I write, is dedicated to my true love and life partner Helen. She was my rock and my compass, pulling me from the hell of PTSD and guiding me to achieve a meaningful life. She is gone far too soon, but that is the way with angels. She will always own my heart. We will walk together soon, my darling.

I must also thank our wonderful daughter, Charlene. She and husband Mike opened their doors and hearts to a sad, tired old man after Helen passed and COVID blanketed the land. They have made a place for me in their family, and I am blessed to have it.

As usual, the help of my son Christopher must be acknowledged. He's a busy, successful engineer with a big family to take care of. Still, I wouldn't write nearly so well with out the time I steal from him for guidance.

Recognition also to an old companion from my days in Korea, Dick Bosa—the best S-3 I ever served with and a good friend. I recently learned he passed on in 2006, though his grandson played in the most recent Superbowl.

Other books by Kip Cassino
The Narrow Man
Buddies
OLDOGS
Incident at Aviano—The Story of a Very Brave Man
Gleaners

AUTHOR'S NOTE

In 1968, I was a young Army lieutenant stationed at Camp Pelham, South Korea—not far from the demilitarized zone which still marks the armistice line between that nation and the totalitarian north. At the time, my battalion was one of a few nuclear-capable artillery units there. Because of my advanced security clearance, much of my time in the land of the morning calm was spent working with this "special weapons" ammunition.

As spring began to thaw a brutal Korean winter, my unit was visited by an unusual and anonymous group of soldiers, sent to us for training. These officers and their men were already quite familiar with the howitzers we used. They had come, we were told, to learn how to employ the nuclear rounds they could fire. Soldiers talk, and a few of us knew some of the men who had arrived. It soon became clear they had come from artillery batteries in South Vietnam. Their presence and mission had to remain highly classified.

It did, and after weeks of intense training the men left, as innocuously as they had arrived. I never heard anything more about them, nor did I see the men again. Apparently, any plans to use nuclear artillery in southeast Asia never found fruition. Still, after more than half a century, the writer in in me asks "what if...?" What if such a plan had gone forward? Where and how could nuclear artillery have been used in Vietnam? Possible answers to these questions lie in the pages before you.

Please be aware that some of the technical explanations given in the book have been purposely altered or obscured. There's an appendix in the back of the book that explains more about our nuclear artillery rounds, as well as a glossary of military terms, slang, and Korean words.

The Author
Harrison, New York, 2024

PROLOGUE
The Skies Above South Vietnam, 1967

A silver jet bomber flashed high above cloud cover that thoroughly masked the ground below it. Hidden beneath lay the clear, shallow waters of the Sepon River, where the borders of Vietnam and Laos meet. The pilot needed no landmarks to tell him where to drop his bombs. An intersection of two radio beams was all he required, and that was coming up. "Constant Farmer zero-six, this is Cabbage Picker two-zero, over," he transmitted, glancing momentarily at the clouds boiling beneath his wings.

"Picker, this is Farmer, go," came the immediate response.

"Starting my run, wait," the pilot replied calmly, as he aligned his plane with the intersecting beams on his scope. The big jet bled speed and altitude in a barrel roll, which arced into a graceful dive. The pilot reached for switches, awaiting the signal to release his bombs. In the meantime, too late detected, three telephone pole-like tubes appeared above and behind him. Alarms blared in his earphones. "I got SAMs," the pilot reported, commencing a steep dive to evade the missiles he now knew stalked him, ejecting radar-confusing chaff. "Going low ..." he continued, but the sentence—like his mission—was never completed.

"Pilot error?" The Navy Captain asked. "He came in very high."

Across the conference room table from him, deep in the Pentagon, the Air Force Colonel shook his head. "Hemmer was one of our best. Followed the mission profile perfectly," he said. "High or low, it makes no difference. We go in lower and slower, the guns get us."

"Some get through."

"Yeah, some do ... but not enough. Even one loss, if it's the wrong plane, is too many. My boss, your boss, and the guy running Happy Harry here won't accept that outcome." The Air Force Colonel nodded to his left, at a man who had yet to speak but wore a broad grin.

"My turn, gentlemen?" the Army Colonel asked. "Now that we've talked about what hasn't worked, let's discuss what will. Let me present artillery, the king of battle."

The three men, each a senior aide to his respective chief of staff, were discussing what, on its surface, seemed like a simple arrangement—even though the weapons to be used made it the first of its kind. The Soviet Union would allow the U.S. to take out a target vital to her interests using nuclear weapons. The U.S., in turn, would allow the Soviets to do the same. Only one target could be chosen by each side, and both strikes had to be equally deniable. Simple.

The Soviets had already made their choice known: the Chinese nuclear testing facilities at Lop Nor, on the eastern edge of the Tarim Basin. Their motivation was apparent. Since the Chinese exploded their first atomic bomb in 1964, the Kremlin had become uneasy. By 1967, when they detonated their first thermonuclear device, Soviet discomfort had become alarm. A schism had evolved between the two Communist giants. Border disturbances along the Ussuri River and in Zhen Bao had become firefights. Mao was purging lieutenants who showed pro-Soviet inclinations. It was high time to teach the Chinese a lesson, and retard their nuclear weapons development in the process. Privately, the Soviet leaders fretted that waiting much longer might make their "lesson" impossible to carry out.

The Johnson administration, dealing with the Soviets through "hot line" secure calls and clandestine ambassadorial meetings, found itself amenable to the arrangement—at least in principle. Neither Johnson nor his top advisers had any love for the Chinese Communists. Seeing Mao's nuclear ambitions thwarted would ease world tensions, they agreed. As a secondary effect, heightening Chinese enmity against the Soviets might be good for the U.S. as well. Beyond all else, Johnson liked to make deals. His whole political career was built from them. Perhaps one like this would lead to others, and slow down or stop the ruinously expensive arms race both nations were locked in now.

After agreeing in broad terms, the administration's senior advisers and military leaders ruminated over potential U.S. choices. Finally, they agreed that destroying the Ho Chi Minh Trail in Laos was the best alternative available. Strangling the trail would force North Vietnam to negotiate seriously for peace, and stop the corrosive unravelling of Johnson's political support at home.

The President had never thought of himself as a globally-centered politician. He had Rusk, McNamara, and their subordinates for that. The Great Society, the War on Poverty, Medicare and Medicaid—these were what Johnson wanted Americans to remember about his presidency, not some ugly little war in southeast Asia. Yet the war made headlines every day. Cronkite and others filled the nation's living rooms with its horror and frustration. Too many of the heartland's young men came home in body bags. The generals and the diplomats could do nothing to help him. Maybe this single act of ultimate destruction would. "Do it," he told his most trusted counselors. "Close the deal. Let's make the motherfuckers wish they'd never been born."

The diplomats got to work. Meetings were held ostensibly for other purposes. Classified codicils were secretly presented, reviewed, and approved. By September, planners had begun turning Johnson's decision into reality. Our military had plenty of nuclear weapons, of every size, yield, and description. How would the weapon of choice be delivered? Missiles, in the 'sixty's, were out of the question—too easily tracked, and far too inaccurate. Aircraft made the most sense, except for a proviso insisted upon by Johnson's key advisors: there could be no evidence left behind—no possibility of any nuclear technology transfer due to the attack. Tests flown above the actual target proved that some aircraft would likely be shot down trying to deliver their bombs. The probability for North Vietnamese salvage of an unexploded nuclear bomb was judged too great by McNamara's slide rule gang, much to the anguish and dismay of Air Force and Navy planners alike. That left only one option for Ho Chi Minh Trail destruction: the use of nuclear artillery.

Once the first atomic bombs were constructed, the scientists and technicians at Los Alamos and Berkeley quickly began work on improvements—new bombs for new purposes. Atomic weapon yield could be "boosted," it was quickly found, even before the Mike Test of Operation Ivy demolished Elugelab Island in late 1952, as Teller and Ulam's enormous seventy-four ton "gadget" ushered in the era of thermonuclear bombs. Their device was quickly weaponized, made compact enough for bombers to lug international distances. Nuclear bombs were getting bigger and more powerful.

They were also getting smaller. The Navy and the Army both clamored for atomic weapons of their own. The Navy wanted nuclear torpedoes, depth charges, and anti-ship weapons. The Army wanted nuclear artillery, landmines, mortars for infantry, and even man-carried devices that could be deployed behind enemy lines by agents on foot. All of these applications would require lighter, more compact weapons—nukes that could be lifted by individual soldiers or sailors in some cases, and stored on trucks or ships. Theodore ("Ted") Taylor, a brilliant nuclear scientist, headed a group that responded to their mounting requests. In fairly short order, he designed weapons small enough to be fired from Army cannons, launched from submarines on the tips of torpedoes, and even carried as backpacks. Most saw production and at least some distribution, though almost all were removed from service inventories by the late 1960's. Notable exceptions were the nuclear artillery rounds, which remained available until 1992.

The Ho Chi Minh Trail veered close to the border between Laos and South Vietnam's northern-most Quang Tri province, well within the range of the army's nuclear-capable field pieces. U.S. artillery could easily reach targets twenty kilometers from that border without firing from Laotian soil. Protected by sufficient security, the artillery would be in little danger of North Vietnamese interdiction. Vital logistic routes in the area could be effectively demolished within a matter of days, leaving craters far too deep and wide for even an army of workers to fill without months of labor. In the meantime, supplies needed further south would be choked off. North Vietnam would be forced to negotiate, or watch her forces starved into surrender. If unanticipated progress to open the trail again was discovered, a few more nuclear rounds would erase its promise.

The nuclear round chosen would be fired from an eight-inch howitzer—guaranteeing a yield sufficient for the job. There were plenty of units using that weapon already in South Vietnam—several battalions in the northern province where the mission would be carried out. Their crews had plenty of experience. Familiarity with the nuclear round itself was far less widespread, but there were proficient units in relatively close-by South Korea to instruct those chosen for the task.

A W33 atomic round[1], fired from the exceptionally accurate M110 self-propelled eight-inch howitzer[2], was selected for this mission—which by now had been coined "Operation Tollbooth." Taylor and his team had created a weapon design masterpiece, using technology evolved from the very first atomic bomb—the "Little Boy" that evaporated much of Hiroshima in 1945. To keep the weapon's weight down, "Fleegle" (Turner's nickname for the design) shot two subcritical masses of uranium oralloy toward one another through concentric gun barrels within a titanium-sheathed artillery shell. When the accelerated slug met the annular ring in which it fit, the chain reaction took place. His design reduced the necessary weight of the round by a factor of eight (to 243 pounds), and made it a feasible weapon for cannoneers to handle and load. An intricate triple-deck time fuse was used to initiate the explosion, which promised to unleash between two and four kilotons of hell on any target chosen. There was no need to test the weapon. The W33 had been in Army inventory for years, and had already been detonated as early as 1957, during the Plumbob series of above-ground tests in the Nevada desert.

All was in place—the target and weapon selected. Now the men who would bear the spearpoint of extreme U.S. policy needed only to be chosen and directed to their mission.

---

[1] See Appendix A.
[2] See Appendix B.

BOOK ONE
BUTTER BAR

CHAPTER ONE

THE KOREAN BATH

The brand-new lieutenant sat alone at the big semi-circular bar, his duffel bag beneath his feet. He calmly sipped his scotch and water, even though the sun was high in the sky. Frowning soldiers in combat gear strode past him outside the windows to his rear from time to time—on what seemed to be important errands. Joint wargames with the South Korean Army were in progress, leaving no one at Camp Pelham to take charge of a newly minted junior officer fresh from Officers Candidate School and the replacement depot. The newbie was told to wait at the officers club until someone found time to take him in tow. So the sidelined young man found a stool, ordered himself a drink from the Korean behind the bar, and quietly toasted his own birthday. The date was August nineteenth, the year was 1967, and Xabier Brede was now twenty-one.

The ride from the replacement depot had been uncomfortable, dusty, and pungent. The discomfort began the minute he and others descended from the Boeing 707 that had flown them to Korea from McChord Air Force Base, near Seattle—days ago now that he'd crossed the international date line. He and the other officers from the plane had been led behind a hangar's partition to be given gamma globulin injections, for protection against hepatitis they were told. He was asked how much he weighed by a nearby medic. "One-forty-two," Brede answered, still groggy from the long flight—which had touched down briefly in Alaska and Japan before reaching Kimpo. At that news, the medic produced an incredibly large hypodermic as he told the young lieutenant to lower his trousers. The injection seemed to take minutes, until he was finally allowed to pull up his khaki pants once again. "If I'd known it was by weight, I'd have told you ninety pounds," he told the medic with a weak smile.

"Sit down if you need to, sir," said the medic, who was already sliding away toward his next victim. Brede felt well enough, though tender and a little surprised, so he wandered beyond the partition to see the enlisted men who had been on the plane with him. Unlike officers, they were offered neither privacy nor chairs—lined up instead in rows facing away from the offending medics approaching from behind. Several gasped when presented with the huge hypodermics meant for them. A few fainted dead-away to the hard concrete floor when their shot was administered. After far too little recovery time, the whole group was told to gather their belongings and board the bus waiting outside the hangar doors.

South Korea was still in late summer, so the air outside the hangar remained still, hot, and humid. All the windows of the dark green bus the men entered were open, to catch whatever breeze might drift by. Everyone got to their seats quickly, piled their luggage wherever it would fit, and waited for the trip to the replacement center at nearby ASCOM City.

The bus moved through Kimpo Air Base's gates to a road that passed near the fields and rice paddies of several local farmers. Those within were immediately overcome by the heavy pervading stench, much like the smell of an ill-tended open sewer. Some gagged. Others looked wildly around the bus, trying to locate who among them was responsible for the fetor. Seeing this, the bus driver laughed. "It's none of you!" he announced gleefully. "This is the way Korea smells, all summer long. Farmers here use their honey buckets for fertilizer. In the winter it smells the same, 'cept frozen. You'll all get used to it, in about a month." The man laughed again and continued driving. His passengers shrank in their seats and tried to avoid breathing deeply.

ASCOM City, as he travelled through it, seemed to Brede like a random collection of large warehouses, Quonset huts, and other assorted structures—all humming with activity. Very little grass and no trees could be seen. The bus rolled up to a large hangar-like building, and the driver opened the front door. "Everybody out," he said happily. "Don't forget your gear. Go through the doors to your right. You'll get assigned here. Welcome to Eighth Army!" He laughed, closed the bus door and pulled away from the men, who were left standing on rough asphalt in front of the building's double doors. They shouldered their belongings, trooped inside, and formed a ragged line in the large entry hall. An army clerk was there to meet them, clipboard in hand. "Sing out when I call your name," the Spec-four boomed forcefully. He called a name and rank, got an answer, and checked a line on his clipboard, nodding with satisfaction when his list was completed. "Officers and NCOs follow me," he announced. "The rest of you wait here. Smoke 'em if you got 'em. There's ashtrays around. Don't put your butts out on the floor—unless you want to clean them up." With that, he led twenty-five sergeants and officers through the swinging doors into the typewriter staccato of assignment.

Brede spent much of the next several hours sitting in outer offices and waiting areas. Luckily, he'd brought along a book to read, some new science fiction by Jack Vance. Eventually, orders in hand, he was directed out of the building to another bus, which took him to his quarters for the night. "Be where we let you off at oh-six-hundred tomorrow morning, gentlemen," the old sergeant at the front of the bus announced. "Your mess hall's right across the street. Please don't leave the base tonight," he said with a weary smile. "There's nothing beyond these gates you need to see."

Naturally, instructions like those motivated several newly commissioned officers and gentlemen to put their bags away, wash up, get some chow, and search for the fastest way off base as soon as they could. Brede found himself among a group of six brand new lieutenants walking quickly through a base gate as afternoon fell into evening. They led each other to a large structure less than a block down the road, from which the thump of music issued and heavy in-and-out traffic marked the doors.

"I hear these Korean girls are the best in Asia!" a new armor lieutenant crowed as he led the other five inside.

"I just want a drink," a dour, slight infantryman beside him muttered.

Inside, the place was less than glamorous. Rows of rough wooden tables filled the large windowless room, poorly lit with glaring fluorescents. The air was filled with cigarette smoke and the jarring beat of unintelligible wailing music. Their table was none too clean, its surfaces sticky to the touch. An odor of stagnant beer and cheap liquor overlaid the already foul reek from surrounding farmland. Still, some of the young men had never experienced bars to compare to this one. Those who had found this place not so different from the joints they'd visited around bases in the states. Others didn't care, as long as their basic needs were met.

Short, active-eyed Asian men wearing aprons and carrying trays ranged up and down the aisles between the tables, stopping briefly by those occupied to take drink orders. One stopped at the table Brede's group had chosen. "What you want?" he grunted in partially discernible language, looking from face to face.

Four of the young men wanted beer. The infantryman ordered whiskey and coke. Brede asked for scotch and water. "Okay, okay!" the man said, nodding. "I get! Cost you five dollar American." He held out a grimy hand.

The infantryman, whose name plate read "Collins," rose slightly. "No American," he said, shaking his head. "You take MPC. You bring, then we pay."

"MPC cost more!" the scowling waiter complained. "Okay, you wait." He turned and quickly disappeared into the gloom.

"American money is worth a lot more to these guys than the MPC we're supposed to spend here," Collins explained. "If we'd paid him first, we'd never see his ass again."

"Sounds like you know your way around here," one of the other butter bars at the table said. "You been in Korea before?"

Collins nodded. "Last time through I was a corporal. Just got out of OCS. Why they sent me back here I'll never know. Everybody else in my class went to Nam. The Army works in mysterious ways. Anyhow, hide any American money you have left on you. Just use the MPC they gave you today. You'll be better off."

The little man returned quickly, with four bottles of beer and two cloudy mixed drinks—one darker than the other. "Here you drink," he said proudly. "Now you pay me ten-dollar MPC."

Collins shook his head. "Here's five," he said, handing out some garish paper MPC notes. "That's all you get. I give you one more, you promise to come back."

The server, who said his name was Joon, was as good as his word—as long as the tips kept flowing. As the young men at the table began their fourth round of drinks, he offered them a suggestion.

"Maybe you like girls," Joon said, his eyebrows raised. "Good ones, clean. You want, come with me."

Collins shook his head. "Half the girls he'll show you have clap so bad it will melt your dick off," he said. "They'll steal every cent you have on you while they're at it. Wait till you get where you're going if you need to get laid."

Brede hadn't said much the entire evening, but now he spoke out. "I want a Korean bath," he said, rising from his chair. "I'm going with Joon."

His desire was not absolutely sexual in nature. Brede had read about Japanese baths, and seen pictures of them: large porcelain-tiled pools full of steaming water, with winsome Asian women swimming or wading in them. No one with any clothing on at all, of course. The concept had crept into his dreams since he had learned about his upcoming assignment. He found it appealing, certain that Japanese and Korean baths had to be similar. He intended to find out.

Joon led Brede down a dark hallway to a dimly lit, low-ceilinged room set with several small tables. On the far side of the room, Korean women sat on a long bench. Directed to a chair at one of the tables, Brede was told to wait. "I get you somebody." Joon told him.

The young lieutenant sat at the table, losing himself in thought. He was slim, of medium height, with dark hair, grey-blue eyes, and a prominent Gallic nose. Sensitive of his age, he had grown a mustache since graduating Artillery OCS, but kept it close-cropped within regulation.

There was movement across the table from him. Brede looked up. A small, plump Korean girl wearing a short, revealing dark dress swished by him and sat down. Dark hair, a round face enveloped by a big smile, and large dark eyes confronted him. "I'm Kimmee," the woman said, "you want good time?"

He hardly knew how to react. There were so many inputs to sort through. The girl was pretty—in a dusky, Asian way. Her costume left little to his imagination. She was certainly well-endowed for her size. Eager too, with no pretense. Her scent was exotic, sour-sweet, like no other person he'd ever been near. "I want ... I want a Korean bath," he was eventually able to blurt out.

The girl looked at him in wide-eyed bewilderment for several seconds. "You want Korean bath?" she finally echoed, brushing hair from her forehead.

Brede nodded.

Kimmee made up her mind. "Okay, *jung-wi*! Okay! I get for you. First, you buy me drink!"

Brede nodded dully. The drinks he'd already had were catching up with him. Kimmee's smile broadened in triumph, as she raised a plump arm and called for a waiter. "*Makkoli,*" she shouted.

Joon was back at the table in a flash, two beer-like bottles in his hand, along with spotted, streaked glasses. "MPC is forty," he rattled.

The new lieutenant reached into his pocket. "I don't think I have that much," he said with a frown. "All I've got left is U.S."

"U.S. good!" Joon exclaimed, grabbing a ten-dollar bill from his hand. "This enough!" He quickly scuttled away.

Kimmee, still grinning enormously, poured herself something that looked like beer from one of the bottles Joon had brought. "Now we drink!" she exclaimed. "You very cute. What you name, *jung-wi*?"

"Xabier," he told her, concentrating hard to form the words. "When do I get my Korean bath?"

Kimmee evaluated the *nbyeong* across the table. He was hardly more than a boy, and smelled like burnt meat—as did all his kind. Soon he would fall asleep in front of her. No more money then! She decided to do them both a favor.

"Ess-a-buh," she told him—trying her best to pronounce his name, "you gimme ten buck American. Get up, come with me now."

"Are we going to the Korean bath?"

"Yes, yes!" She said, rolling her eyes, rising. "We go now. You follow me." He stood unsteadily from his chair and handed her a Hamilton, his last—but who cared! She took his hand and led him from the room through a side door. Once outside, he doggedly followed her a short distance down a dirt path, which led to an area surrounded by a fence constructed from what appeared to be wooden shipping pallets. She opened a gate and led him inside, to a group of huts.

Kimmee stood Brede against the slats of a pallet-fence. "You stay here," she told him. "Take off you clothes. I back soon."

Under a big full moon, the night was bright. he eagerly stripped off his khaki's and underwear, combining them with his shoes in a neat stack which he placed to his side—his drunken lethargy overcome by anticipation. He looked around the bleak compound, wondering where a big, porcelain pool could possibly be hidden. As he peered about, he heard a sound, then a giggle, after which his back and shoulders were showered with cold water. Stiffening, instantly sobered, he turned in confusion to be drenched from head to toe by the continuing torrent. Wiping his eyes clear, Brede saw Kimmee a few yards away in the dark, confronting him with a garden hose which continued to spray him with tepid water.

"This you Korean bath," she said between gales of tinny laughter, "Same as I take." Seeing his frown, she dropped the hose and skittered away in the darkness, leaving him wet and alone.

Brede stepped from the muddy puddle that surrounded him to drier soil, then bent to retrieve and don his damp clothing. Angry when he began, by the time he'd put on his pants and shirt he was smiling ruefully. As he stood dripping in the dark, he began to laugh softly. He remembered a line from a John Wayne movie he'd seen once: "People should do what they want to do ... and get what they deserve," The Duke had said. Brede's introduction to Korea certainly proved that. Sighing, he left the enclosure and walked back toward the base gate. As he trudged down the path, he looked at his watch. Two o'clock in the morning. Still time to change clothes and get a nap in before the bus arrived. He tried to light a cigarette, but the pack in his pocket had been soaked.

CHAPTER TWO

THE PLACE WITH NO TREES

The next morning, after far too little sleep, a wilted Xabier Brede boarded the bus which was there to take him to his home for the next thirteen months—somewhere within the area assigned to the Second Infantry Division, the "Indian Heads."

After a long drive over increasingly rough roads, Brede's first stop was division headquarters, where his paperwork was taken and soon replaced with an even larger stack, and he was directed to a smaller vehicle. The "deuce and a half" (two and one-half ton) truck he and others were loaded into took him further north over even more tortuous roads to his final destination for the day, "Div Arty,"—Division Artillery—where his specific assignment would be determined and processed. He would spend the night at Camp Stanley, near what had been a pivotal stop for the North Korean Army heading south to assault the rest of the peninsula in 1949—the railroad junction at *Ujeongbu*.

Here Brede and four other brand-new lieutenants were assigned to their battalions for the remainder of their stay in the land of the morning calm. They were introduced briefly to the distracted colonel commanding artillery for the Second Infantry Division, treated to a perfunctory dinner with his chief of operations, and led to a sweltering barracks by a sergeant, who told them to be ready for chow at oh-six-hundred, after which they'd be transported to their battalions.

"Why the fuck does everything in this place start at oh-six-hundred?" a man named Ruddell whined, rubbing his forehead. "I got jet lag."

Brede knew Ruddell as well as he knew the other three men in the room with him. All had gone through twenty-two weeks of OCS in the same class, which had started with more than one hundred thirty candidates and ended with less than forty graduates. Ruddell and the others had been in different platoons, in a different building or on a different floor of his barracks. He didn't know them very well, nor did they know him. The overwhelming majority of their class had been sent to Vietnam. A handful got stateside or European assignments. The five who slept that night near *Ujeongbu* had no idea why they weren't in Saigon.

"It's an alphabetical thing," a man named Parant decided. "Has to be. The Army's too dumb to be subtle. Some computer sorted all our names, and randomly chose us to miss the fighting."

"So you'd rather get your ass shot off?" The butter bar in the next bunk asked. His name was Gimbel.

Parant smiled. "Don't get me wrong," He said, collapsing on his bunk. "I'm happy as hell to dodge it. I'm just trying to understand how it happened, so I can clue in my son when he's eighteen."

"When your kid's eighteen, it'll all be done with robots," Ruddell said, shaking his head as he lay on a duffel bag pillow.

The patter continued. Brede kept his thoughts to himself. He knew in his heart that as long as nations practiced war, they'd want young men to do the fighting for them. His grandfather had fought, as had his father and most of his uncles. He saw no reason to believe the world was going to change. Sighing inwardly, he fluffed his stony pillow and settled down for the night.

The lights went out a little while later, but Brede was still unable to sleep. As he stared at the stained ceiling above him, his thoughts drifted back to the day he'd joined the Army in the first place.

He'd been in Lubbock, Texas—stranded there by a blown transmission on his little British car, while on his way to meet his parents in Arizona. He wasn't looking forward to the reunion. They had left him in Europe, his father retiring after a career-culminating assignment as an Air Force Colonel. He had been expected to finish a third semester at University of Maryland's Munich (Germany) campus, and then fly home to meet them before transferring to the main campus at College Park. There he would finish his four years and graduate. Instead, Brede had blown out of college a week after they'd left, and spent most of the next several months hitch-hiking around Spain and France with his German girlfriend and a group of other dropouts. Dad had sent him money to get home. He'd worked his way back on a cruise ship instead, and used most of the money saved to buy his little car. Now he was stuck in Lubbock, with dwindling funds and no prospects.

He'd tried looking for work, but no one was interested in hiring a kid with a 1-A draft card. He'd tried selling the car, but nobody in this part of Texas showed much excitement over a foreign ride. His choices boiled down to begging the old man for some more money, or finding some other way out of the mess he'd so carefully constructed for himself. Explaining the last several months to Dad was going to get ugly. He was sick and tired of college anyway. So Xabier Brede decided to join the Navy and avoid both.

Bright and early the next morning, Brede walked from his shabby mo-tel room to the nearest recruiting office, just four blocks away. The Navy petty officer there was happy to see him, glad to let him take the service exam. "What kind of a Navy career did you have in mind?" he asked, after looking over the test results.

"I thought maybe nuclear propulsion or sonar," Brede replied.

"Both possible," the recruiter said, still beaming. "Your scores are very good. Leave me a telephone number where we can reach you. We should find a slot for you in a month or two."

"I can't wait that long," Brede told him as he hurriedly left. He walked a few steps down the block to the Army recruiter, entered, and was confronted by a young staff sergeant with exactly the same bright smile as his Navy counterpart. There he was given the same tests he had taken up the street, as far as he could tell.

When he saw the Army recruiter again, the man's smile was even wider than before. "There are all kinds of Army opportunities for a young man with your test scores," he told Brede. "I'm thinking ASA. We'll have you in by next week."

Brede shook his head. "Let me be honest," he told the smiling young man. "I'm out of clean underwear, money, and time. I can't wait that long."

The sergeant thought a minute, his Cheshire Cat grin widening even more. He slapped his desk. "In that case," he said, "we'll have you in tonight!"

That afternoon, Brede was able to sell his car to the mechanic working on it for $200. With that funding he was able to pay off the motel, buy himself some dinner, and get a cab to the airport with money to spare. There he caught an Ozark Airlines flight that would end up at Fort Leonard Wood, Missouri the next morning. His Army experience had begun.

Brede awoke feeling better than he had in several days. His persistent hangover had faded, as had his sensitivity to the stifling aroma of the land around him. Both remained pervasive, but less overwhelming than before. "If I stay off the sauce a few days," he thought to himself as he dressed, "I'll feel human in another week or so." He straightened his least wrinkled khakis, ran a damp towel over his corfam shoes and his brass, adjusted his service cap, winked at the latrine mirror and pronounced himself ready to meet the day. He shouldered his duffel bag and proceeded out the barracks door, to stand with his four companions awaiting breakfast and transportation to his final destination—the piece of Korea where he'd spend the next thirteen months.

As he approached the others, Brede noticed someone was missing. "Where's Ruddell?" he asked the group in general as he joined them.

"Already gone," Parant told him. "Rolled him out of the sack around four. Surprised it didn't wake you up. Told him he's got a long drive ahead of him. The driver wanted to get it done before it gets too hot. Boy, did he whine."

A jeep pulled up near them. The driver, a young PFC, stuck his head around the windshield. "I'm looking for somebody named Breed," he announced as he shifted his ride to neutral, cigarette dangling from his mouth. "That one of you?"

"That's me," Brede answered, walking toward him. "What's your name, soldier?"

"Garvin," the puzzled driver answered.

"Well, Garvin, PFC Garvin, you have started my day the wrong way," Brede told him, shaking his head. "Turn off the jeep, get out of your seat, and get that smoke out of your mouth. Report to me. Is that clear, PFC Garvin?"

The now wide-eyed driver quickly hopped from the jeep, ground his smoke out under his boot, and raised his right hand in a very, very tentative salute. "Sir ..." he murmured.

"That's right, PFC Garvin: 'sir.'" Brede continued, now standing close to the enlisted man. "I'm an officer, like the others standing near me. When you address us, you'll show some respect." He threw his duffel bag in the jeep's back seat, then climbed in himself. "Now, get back in this vehicle and drive me where I need to go."

"Yes, sir," said the driver, scrambling into his seat, starting the motor, and swinging the jeep back onto the dirt and gravel road. A few minutes later they were outside the camp, driving through the bumpy, dusty streets of a nearby village.

"You gonna report me, lieutenant?" the driver asked Brede, his eyes still wide. "You gonna tell the first sergeant?"

"No," Brede answered, shaking his head. "I'm not going to cause you trouble. Just get me where we're going in one piece. If you see me again, remember I went through six months of hell to get here. Try to show a little courtesy, that's all."

The jeep continued on a potholed, unpaved road past miles of rice paddies and fields, kicking up a rooster tail of dust behind it. The disturbed dust didn't settle quickly in the heavy air. It hung above in an orange-brown cloud, ready to cloak subsequent travelers with a layer of adhesive Korean dirt. Low hills surrounded the road on both sides, but there was no apparent movement on them. Brede looked in every direction, but could see no trees. Bored, he lit a cigarette. "Want one?" he asked the driver.

"Do you mind?"

"No, Garvin, I don't mind. Just put it out when we get near wherever we're going."

"Camp Pelham, lieutenant. North and west of where we are now. It's only about eight miles from the DMZ, around the corner from *Munsani*. We've still got another hour or so before we get there. Can't go much faster than twenty-five on these roads."

Brede nodded as though anything he'd heard made sense to him, then settled back in the hard seat and continued to look around the bleak country they passed through. The sun was already bright, the air hot and oppressive.

"Where are the trees?" he asked after a while.

The driver grinned and nodded. "Damned if I didn't ask the same thing when I got here. I'm from Minnesota. Plenty of trees there. The old sergeants say the Japs ripped most of 'em out. They used to own this place.

Any that was left got blown up in the war. Nowadays, it's against the law to knock down a tree—put you in jail if you do. Imagine that."

By now the country around them showed more life. Huts appeared regularly. As they drove over a railroad track at the top of a hill, Brede saw a very large village spread out before him.

"Munsan," the driver said. "Big ville. This's where most of us go on pass, lieutenant. Not much to it 'cept bad beer and whores, but it passes the time."

Munsan had few structures made of wood or plaster. Those that were stood out from the vast majority around them, which were huts comprised of a variety of materials. Some were mostly repurposed scrap lumber, while others flashed corrugated metal, and some seemed to be mostly sodded or mud brick. Almost all were low and tinted similarly by the dust in the streets around them. The single, striking exception was a large church, with a white steeple several stories high that overshadowed the rest of the makeshift village. The building below the steeple was brick and boasted a shingled roof. The edifice looked as if it had been plucked whole from southern Alabama and somehow transported here.

"Wow," Brede said.

Garvin nodded. "Some church ain't it?" He said, chuckling. "Them missionaries put the whole town to work building it. At least, that's what the old sergeants say. There's some in other villes too, but not this big."

"Korea is a strange place," Brede commented, shaking his head.

"Never seen nothing else like it," Garvin replied, nodding in agreement. "Never been in a country full of foreigners before."

By now the jeep was making its way through Munsan, exciting interest from children of varying ages—who ran beside them, asking for candy or cigarettes. Garvin cried, *"Domang-gada!"*—actually pushing some away. He drove faster as the crowd around them swelled. The jeep hurriedly emerged from the press and passed beyond the edges of the ramshackle village.

"What was that all about?" Brede asked. "You could have hurt somebody."

"Slicky-boys!" Garvin told him angrily. "If I'd gone any slower, they'd have been in the jeep. They'd have got your duffle, my spare tire, and anything else not welded on. They can steal a radio and leave the music!

Just ask Lieutenant Jackson. Well, we're through them, and no harm done that I can see."

There were more structures on the edge of the road now, and these seemed more solid, of wood or corrugated metal construction. Some seemed to be bars or shops, while others had less obvious purposes. All sported large signs printed in what Brede would find out was *hangul*— the written language of Korea. The jeep soon turned off the main road, climbed a gentle rise, and stopped in front of a pole barrier manned by soldiers in an adjoining guardhouse. The area around the road was barred with barbed wire-topped chain link metal fencing, ten feet high. A sign above the road read, "Camp Pelham, 2nd Infantry Division," in white on a red background.

"Welcome to your new home, lieutenant," Garvin said, as he stopped the jeep until the barrier was raised by a guard. He then gunned the vehicle forward onto a broad, unevenly paved street with prefabricated metal structures on either side. He parked in front of one.

"Here you are, sir," he said. "Battalion headquarters, Sixth of the Thirty-seventh Field Artillery. The S-1 is right inside the door. He should be expecting you. Good luck." With that, the driver executed a fair salute, which Brede returned as he climbed from his seat.

"Thanks, Garvin," he said, grabbing his duffle bag, which he placed on the pavement by his side. He looked up to say more, but the jeep had already backed away. Brede shouldered his bag and climbed the steps into the building. Pushing his belongings through the door, he shut it behind him and looked around. He was in a long, narrow hallway, floored with green vinyl tile. The door to his front was stenciled "S-1, Lt. Gilliam." It was shut, so he knocked.

"Come in," came a muffled response. Entering, he found himself in a small room, backed by file cabinets, facing a chest-high counter. Behind the counter, a bespectacled enlisted man labored at a desk overwhelmed by military file folders. He looked up, and recognized his visitor's rank.

"You weren't supposed to be here today, lieutenant," the man said, shaking his head. The nametag on his fatigue-shirt breast read "Carter."

Brede had been in the military less than two years, but he had already learned to appreciate the loopy irony that applied to many Army situations. "Everybody has to be someplace, Specialist Carter," he said. "The Army brought me here today. I had no say in the matter. I guess I need to see Lieutenant Gilliam."

"That's the problem, sir. Lieutenant Gilliam is not here. War games are still going on. He's over at the TOC—the tactical operations center. You'll have to wait."

"Okay," Brede replied, shrugging. "I can wait. Tell me where to sit."

"No place to put you. Not right now." The man thought for a few seconds. "Tell you what," he finally said. "I'll take you over to the Officers Club. That way, at least you can get something to eat and drink while you wait. Maybe Kwan can fix you up with a hooch, even. Sorry, sir, but you may be waiting a while."

"Just show me where to park myself, Carter."

CHAPTER THREE

SCORCHED COFFEE

Several hours went by. Brede quietly sipped his scotch and read the dog-eared paperback he'd kept with him since leaving the states. Eventually, as the sun began to redden and sink in the west, the Korean bartender signaled for his attention. "Lieutenant Gilliam want see you," he said, nodding to the glass doors that led to the bar's patio. A large man in fatigues and steel pot loomed there, wearing a flak jacket and a web-belt with a .45 pistol holstered on his hip. The man gestured for Brede to come to him.

As he approached, the man opened the patio door and stuck out a hand, which Brede shook. "You must be the new guy," the soldier said with a strong southern accent. "I'm Will Gilliam. Sorry I'm so late. Can't come in, either. I'm armed, so if anybody saw me I'd have to buy the bar. Come on, let's sit you over here where we can talk." He led them to a nearby picnic table and sat heavily—then removed his helmet, releasing a mop of thick, dark hair.

"Woo-wee!" Gilliam exclaimed as he ran plump fingers through his scalp. "Good to get that damn thing off my head! Feels like it weighs fifty pounds or more! We've all been in this gear for three days now. Damn Koreans want everything by the book. Thank Christ it's over tonight. I'm going to drink about a quart of bourbon tomorrow, and that's before dinner!"

Brede could think of no response to the outburst and wasn't sure one was needed, so he kept silent—observing the man in front of him. Gilliam, he decided, was a collection of fruits and vegetables. His head was melon-shaped, with close set ears and features compressed toward the center of his face. His body resembled a pear—more massive at the hips than at the shoulders. His low, booming voice issued from a full-lipped mouth set below a pug nose and small, close-set eyes, over the jowls of a double chin.

Gilliam stared at the new officer for a long minute before speaking further. "I'm the S-1 here," he explained. "Can't do much for you today, Lieutenant Brede. 'Xabier,' with a 'b.' That's a new name on me."

"It's Basque, I think," Brede told him. "My grandfather's people were out of Idaho."

"Basque. I'll be damned. Never heard the like. What do your friends call you?"

"Most of them just call me 'Ex.'"

"Well, you can call me Will. Now listen, Ex. These war games won't get over until twenty-two-hundred or later. We're all eating c-rations at the TOC tonight. Hell, might as well feed us cardboard. Do me a favor. Go get that bartender Kwan and bring him out here. I'll have him fix you up with quarters, and get you some dinner from behind the bar. How about a hamburger? That sound about right?"

Brede agreed that it would. He wasn't particularly hungry, but knew he should eat. Finding a place to get off his feet for the night sounded very good right now. He'd get some rest and let the morning take care of itself. He brought the Korean out to Gilliam and stood aside while they conversed in low tones. After a few minutes Kwan went back inside the Officers Club.

"Okay, it's all worked out," Gilliam told him. "I'm going back to the TOC now. You go see Kwan. He'll rustle you up some chow and show you where to sleep. Come see me tomorrow, at oh-nine-hundred—no reason to show up sooner. Bring your paperwork. We'll get you squared away then." The big man rose and replaced the steel pot to his head. "Good meeting you, Ex. Welcome to the Thirty-seventh." He nodded and hurried away.

Brede followed instructions, ate a surprisingly good hamburger, and followed Kwan from the bar to a cluster of interconnected corrugated metal Quonsets, all painted a dreary mint green. They passed through a grove of tall trees on their way, the first he had seen since landing in Korea. Large, raucous birds hopped about high in their branches. Brede would come to know they were Magpies. Entering the structure before them, Kwan stopped at a locker to pull out bedding and towels, then directed Brede to a door halfway down a low hallway.

"This you hooch," Kwan told him. "Mama-san take care of laundry, make bed. Shine boots too. Latrine down hall. Here you key." The Korean handed him a large brass key, put the bedding in his arms, turned and left. Sliding his duffel on the concrete floor, Brede struggled to open the lock, pushed his way inside the door and looked around.

He stood between two metal-frame beds fitted with mattresses. The room arched before him, highest only in the middle. To his front, halfway down the long semi-tubular space, sat a device that looked like a stove of some sort—a wire caged drum topped by a chimney that reached the ceiling, with a five-gallon jerry can emptying into it. This, he would learn, was a space heater, his only source of warmth during the winter to come. Small, dusty windows let in dim light, overmatched by the harsh neon tube hanging a few feet above him.

Brede threw his bedding on the righthand bunk, left the room and proceeded further down the hall—where he found sinks, toilet stalls, and a communal shower in a large room floored in bare concrete, walls painted the same sad mint green as the building's exterior. Satisfied that he knew enough of his location for the present, he returned to his room, unpacked and hung up his clothing in a grey metal wall locker, and stashed the rest of his belongings in a wooden chest of drawers nearby. He made his bed of choice—with military precision, out of habit—then kicked off his shoes and lay down to read for a while. Growing tired, he stripped to his underwear, went to the bathroom, showered, and returned to settle down for the night. He hadn't heard any noise from within the building since Kwan had left. The place seemed to be empty. He soon fell into a dreamless sleep.

Brede was awakened by muffled voices, noises, and footfalls in the building around him: his neighbors arising for the day, he was certain. Rather than get in their way, he decided to lay back and wait until his watch told him it was eight AM. By then, the racket in the hall had subsided. He rose, quickly made his bed, donned clean underwear, starched fatigues, and polished combat boots. He took his shaving kit to the now-empty communal latrine, where he shaved, brushed his teeth, and combed his hair. Inspecting himself in the mirror, he pronounced himself ready to meet the day, grabbed the thick sheaf of his orders and forms, donned his fatigue cap, and made his way back to battalion headquarters to meet Lieutenant Gilliam—a five-minute walk. He was standing in front of the small office's counter, facing Carter—who looked like he'd been there all night—at oh-eight-fifty. He was ten minutes early, just as he had planned.

The clerk blinked at Brede owl eyed, as though seeing him for the first time. Then recognition dawned. "Lieutenant Bread, er, Brede, sir," he stammered. "Lieutenant Gilliam's not here. Not yet. He's in a staff meeting, with the Battalion Commander."

Brede smiled and shrugged. "I'm a little early," he said. Hefting the fat sheaf of paperwork he'd been carrying, he handed it to Carter. "Here's my orders and the other forms you'll need to get me processed. I'll just hang around here until your boss shows up—unless you want to put me someplace else."

"No place better than here," Carter said with a wan smile. "I was just going to get myself a cup of coffee, sir. Get one for you too, if you want. How do you take it?"

"Black with one sugar and thank you, Carter. I promise I'll stay out of your hair."

Ten minutes later, as Brede was finishing his coffee, Gilliam exploded into the cramped room. "Damn if I don't hate staff meetings!" he exclaimed, as he swept his fatigue cap from his head.

He looked over the counter at Carter, who had buried himself in file folders once again. "What's going on, Carter?" he boomed. "Glad to see me back, I know. Any coffee left?" Looking to his right, Gilliam now noticed Brede, in the corner of the room, coffee cup in hand.

"Hey, buddy," he said, smiling slowly. "Right on time, I see. Come on in my office. Carter, get me this man's folder. Let's see what Div Arty sent us."

Gilliam opened a door on the room's left wall that Brede hadn't noticed and held it, gesturing. Brede, who had been leaning on the counter, straightened himself and moved through the door, which was then slammed shut. Gilliam collapsed behind a desk which took up most of the little room. He motioned his new guest to a chair facing it, as Carter hurried through the door—file in one hand, coffee in the other.

Gilliam grabbed the file and threw it in front of him as he took the coffee cup in both hands, loudly gulping a swig from it. "Man," he said with a grimace. "The only thing worse than this coffee is not getting any."

The S-1 turned his attention to the file before him. "Now let's take a look at you, Mr. Ex," he said, flipping its pages back and forth. After a few minutes, he looked up.

"I gotta call Ricci about this," he said excitedly, picking up the receiver of the field phone on his desk as he cranked it.

"Get me to S-3," he said as he held it to his ear.

"Ricci," he bawled into the phone when he was connected, "get your ass up here! Looks like we struck gold!"

Puzzled, Brede looked around him as a series of loud noises approached the room he was in. Then the door flew open and a very large man stuck his head through it. "Why are you bothering me, Will?" the giant who had made the racket bellowed, in what might have been a Boston accent. "You know I'm busy!"

The wide-shouldered man in the doorway was at least six feet four, with short cropped brown hair above a square, chiseled face. His prominent hawk nose perched below a wide forehead, between predatory, shadowed eyes with heavy brows, above a sensual mouth. He was scowling darkly, obviously upset. Brede had no idea who the man was, but made up his mind to stay out of his way.

Gilliam remained calm, took another sip from his coffee cup. "Look at all the hubbub you're making, Bob," he said mildly, "trompin' up the hall like that. Probably scared this young man half to death. I called you 'cause it's important. Wouldn't have done it otherwise. Now meet our newest officer, Lieutenant Xabier Brede … who has a top secret clearance. Already! Background investigation all done, don't have to wait."

Ricci's face transformed, as his scowl became a wide smile. "We'll start training him today, right now!" he exclaimed. "Let me go get Rausch!"

"Now hold on," Gilliam cautioned. "Hold on a damn minute. The man still needs to get processed, needs to see the colonel, needs to get assigned. You can have him tomorrow, but not before. I just wanted to give you the good news. Get back to what you were doing."

The big man bobbed his head up and down as he retreated through the doorway. "Okay, okay," he said nodding. "Just get him to me." He turned and left the room, the din from his departure echoing down the narrow hall. Carter quickly closed Gilliam's office door.

"What was that?" Brede asked, settling himself in his chair once again.

"That was Lieutenant Ricci, our battalion operations officer," Gilliam explained. "Certain things excite him. Your arrival certainly did. None of us were aware of your security clearance. Normally, it takes months of time and paperwork before a top secret clearance comes through. We have to jump through admin hoops to get waivers. You showed up with one, Ex. Any idea why?"

Brede thought for a moment. "When I joined up, it was for ASA—Army Security Agency. A background investigation was required for that. Plus, my dad was in the service. He had a high clearance. Maybe all that helped."

"Whatever the reason, it's a blessing," Gilliam said, shaking his head. "We're short about three slots that need a TS clearance. You'll probably fill them all, for now anyway. One thing you'll notice in Korea—not a lot of captains and majors around. Most of them are in Nam or Europe. We get by with lieutenants in their places, or NCOs when the officers run short. I'm filling a captain's slot myself. Ricci's desk would normally seat a major. Lots of on-the-job training going on. Thank God we've got a lot of old sergeants to help us."

"I keep hearing about these 'old sergeants,'" Brede said. "What's that all about?"

Gilliam smiled widely. "Korea is like heaven on earth to some of these senior NCOs," he said. "They were young during World War II, stuck around for the Korean War and all the other little fights we've had since. Several have seen Vietnam duty. Now they've been through the mill, got no families to speak of. The Army has become the only home they've got. Korea treats them nice. Cheap, plenty of young gals, the work's not tough—it's a good place to fill out those final years before retirement and the old soldier's home, or some cousin's attic. You'll see a lot of old sergeants around here."

Brede nodded as though he understood what Gilliam told him, even though he really did not. While he'd grown up in the military, most of the noncommissioned officers he'd met were younger men. They were the muscle and sinew of the Air Force his father had served in—maintaining the planes, running the airmen, the supply rooms, the offices—doing most of the actual work. His dad had told him, "A good sergeant is worth his weight in gold. Take his counsel. Don't try to run his troops. He can do that." It was advice he intended to follow.

"I'll need about an hour to get your assignment straightened out," Gilliam said, glancing through Brede's personnel folder once again. "Can you stand some more time in the outer room, or do you want to go back to your hooch?"

"I'd just as soon stick around," Brede said, "as long as Carter doesn't mind and there's coffee left."

The S-1 nodded, and stood from his desk. "Fair enough," he said. "Once we're done throwing the paperwork around, I'll get you in to see the colonel. You act older than you look, Ex. You're going to do just fine here."

Gilliam opened his office door. "Carter, damn your hide!" he hollered. "Get this young lieutenant a place to sit for a while, so you and I can get him processed."

By the time Gilliam trooped from his office with Carter behind him, just over an hour had passed. In the meantime, Brede's nose had led him to the scorched odor of a coffee pot on an electric burner in an alcove down the hall—just inside a heavy double door labeled "Tactical Operations Center—off-limits to non-designated personnel."

Using military logic, Brede reasoned that needing coffee—on which the Army ran—was sufficient designation for him to enter and get himself a cup. So he did, twice. No one seemed to notice, nor was the door secured. The coffee was, of course, vile—almost thick enough to chew, obviously far past its intended operational life. Still, that was standard operating procedure in many Army places where he'd found himself since joining up. He drank the brew with equanimity, and a single sugar—slamming his system with a jolt of caffeine sufficient to wire him for the rest of the day to come.

Gilliam finally called him back to the tiny office and explained his new assignment. "We're going to make you the S-2, battalion staff for intelligence and security," he said with a smile. "The slot's been open for over a month, ever since Jackson left. All we've had is Sergeant Overshaft and a clerk to cover us. Don't worry. The old sergeant knows all the in's and out's. He's been at this more than twenty years. You'll do fine."

Brede could only nod. He'd expected to become a forward observer on some Vietnamese hill when OCS had ended. Battalion-level staff jobs were supposed to be years and promotions in the future.

"Of course, you'll have some other duties," the S-1 continued, looking at his notes. "We need a Comm Officer, and that slot needs a TS clearance, so you're it. We need a Survey Section Officer, and you'll get that too—but Sergeant Heilt pretty much handles things there himself. Oh, and it's come time to get a new KRAC Representative. That's the guy who meets with the village leaders, the Korean Relations Advisory Council, to give them assistance and listen to their complaints. They always have a bunch. Meets once a month. That will be another additional duty." He smiled.

"I'm going to be busy," Brede said softly, shaking his head.

Gilliam nodded. "Part of it's due to your clearance," he explained. "Part of it's just 'cause you're junior—right now, the most junior. The junior guy always gets a lot on his plate. Naturally, I saved the best for last. Starting pretty quick, ol' Bob Ricci's gonna have you in a bunker learning how to assemble the nukes—the nuclear artillery rounds this battalion fires. That's going to take up a lot of your time, for the next few months for sure. We got a TPI coming up pretty soon, and you're set to play a big part."

"TPI?"

Gilliam nodded. "Technical Proficiency Inspection: TPI. That's where a bunch of warrant officers from CINCPAC, or DASA, or some other god-damn headquarters comes out here and makes everybody's lives miserable for a few days. If we're not damn near perfect in every aspect of our nuke program, all hell breaks loose. Those old boys will get on you like ugly on the ape."

Brede nodded, then began looking around the small office.

"What are you looking for?" Gilliam asked, after watching him for a while.

"I was looking for the other three guys who got this assignment with me," Brede told him. "Can't find them."

The S-1's mouth widened into an enormous grin. "I think I'm gonna like you, Ex," he said through his chuckles. "You'll find 'em soon enough, just like the rest of us did. This place is going to keep you so damn busy you'll meet yourself coming and going." His voice softened. "After a while it gets easier. Just do the best you can. The nukes are the most important thing—right now, anyway. You've got some good sergeants to help you. Let them show you the ropes. The only way you can fail is by trying to push them around." He rose from his desk. "Come on. Let's you and me go meet the man who runs this battalion."

CHAPTER FOUR

ON THE MINUTE

Lieutenant Colonel Ralph Gaboury did not fit anyone's vision of an Army combat battalion commander. He was somewhat under medium height, obviously overweight. His thin, dark hair unsuccessfully attempted to comb over a balding pate. Large watery brown eyes, a massive lump of nose, and fleshy lips perched above his weak chin. He sat slouched behind his desk looking out the windows that framed his office walls—tapping pale, graceful fingers on the edges of his chair as Brede was ushered into his presence.

"Sir," Gilliam said as he stood to the side of his commander's desk, "Second Lieutenant Brede, our new officer—just arrived for duty."

Brede walked forward, stood at attention, saluted. "Sir, Lieutenant Brede reports," he said, trying not to stare at the man in front of him. He had looked forward to this day—the introduction to his first commissioned assignment—through months of constant harassment and hard work. He wanted all to go flawlessly well. He held his salute, waiting for Gaboury to reciprocate.

Eventually, he did—though more with a wave than a salute. "Be at ease, wieutenant," the colonel said, providing Brede with a surprise he could not ignore. The voice of the man behind the desk exactly mimicked a well-known cartoon character—foil of a famous "wascal wabbit." Only self-control he didn't know he possessed kept him from breaking into laughter. At the corner of his vision, he watched Gilliam shift uncomfortably, staring at the floor.

After a very long pause, the S-1 continued. "Sir, because of his advanced security clearance, we're assigning Lieutenant Brede to the S-2 and Comm

Officer slots. He'll also be working with Lieutenant Ricci in special weapons. He's also our new KRAC council representative."

"I wish they'd get us some captains," Gaboury warbled with a sigh. "I guess the sergeants will teach him soon enough." He turned to face Brede. "You have a lot on your pwate, young man," he said. "Can you handle it?"

"I can only do my best, sir," Brede replied, working to control himself. "I don't intend to fail."

"That's the spiwit!" Gaboury exclaimed with a sputtering guffaw. He rose from his desk and extended a hand in Brede's direction. "Welcome to the Thirty-seventh, wieutenant," he lisped, reciting the unit's motto. "On the minute!"

Brede shook the offered hand, which was neither firm nor dry. "Yes, sir," he said, grinning wildly. "Thank you, sir. On the minute!" He saluted again and performed a quick about-face, exiting the room as fast as he could and proceeding a good way down the hall. There he stood red-faced, breathing deeply, hands on his knees—working to regain his composure after what had been a bizarre experience. A few minutes later Gilliam joined him.

"You did me no favors in there, Will," Brede said, frowning. "Why didn't you warn me about the way he speaks? I almost lost it."

"Tried telling people," the S-1 said. "Only makes it worse. You handled it about as well as I've seen it done. Very impressive. Ricci broke right out and laughed his ass off, first time they met. Claimed he'd just heard a joke."

"Look," Brede said, shaking his head, "I can get over the accent. How is he as a CO?"

Gilliam shrugged. "He's not as bad as some I've heard about. No Eisenhower if that's what you're asking. He spent a lot of years at the Pentagon, so he's rusty on the artillery basics. Hell, so am I, for that matter. Leans a lot on his XO. That's Major Rafferty. You'll meet him later. He's out at B Battery for the next few days. Gaboury asks a lot of his staff. He'll give you plenty to do. He's real sensitive about the voice. Real sensitive. Just do your job and don't get on his bad side, that's my advice."

Brede nodded. "I'll try my best. I meant it in there. I don't want to screw up."

"You'll do fine. Just listen to your sergeants. If you have a problem, come see me. If it's really serious, get in front of Rafferty. Don't worry, Ex. A year goes by in a hurry. Come on. Let's go down the hall and introduce you to the 'deuce' section. Sergeant Overshaft is waiting for you. Then we'll go over to Headquarters Battery, and you can meet Lieutenant Elby. Gonna be a busy day for you."

The S-1 walked him down the hall to a door still stenciled "S-2, Lieutenant Jackson." The room beyond was larger than Gilliam's, but overwhelmed with large metal filing cabinets. At first glance, Brede decided Sergeant First Class Overshaft must have been a big man, years ago when he was healthy. Even now he was well over six feet tall with wide shoulders and little apparent excess weight. Still, his fatigues hung on him, as though meant for someone even larger. His face was deeply scored with creases and lines, his blue eyes almost buried in deep, wrinkled folds below bushy brows, his hair a tangled grey thatch. Overshaft moved slowly and spoke in a rheumy, labored rumble—as if each word required effort. "Sir …," he said, ponderously rising from his desk when introduced, "good to have … an officer … in the section again. Grady … our clerk … is running errands. Back … soon."

"I'm looking forward to working with you, Sergeant Overshaft." Brede said, shaking the older man's hand. "I know I've got a lot to learn." So this is what they meant when they talked about the old sergeants, he thought to himself. "How old is Sergeant Overshaft?" he asked Gilliam as they left the building for Headquarters Battery.

"I'd have to check," the S-1 said, "but he's up there. Been in since before World War II. Seen his share of combat. Knows his stuff though. Never had a gig from any inspectors, and we get a passel of them."

The walk to Headquarters Battery took less than five minutes, down a dusty, tree-lined street. "Good to see the trees," Brede remarked.

"Yeah," Gilliam said, "not many around, out in the ville. What the Japs didn't cut down got splintered in the war. This used to be a Turkish compound back then—or so I hear. They liked to keep it shady, I guess."

"What's 'on the minute' all about?" Brede asked, as they continued to walk.

"The battalion motto," Gilliam said. "They must have taught you about TOT in OCS."

"Time-on-target?" Brede nodded. "Yeah, they did."

"Well, this outfit was great at them, back in World War II. Korea, too. All sorts of unit citations. The Belgians loved us in the Great War. That's why we get to wear the fourragere."

"What's that?"

"You'll get one today from the supply room. It's a nice piece of eye candy—red and green braided cord with brass tips. You wear it over the left shoulder of your dress uniform—a unit award from the Ardennes campaign. Better have yours on right for officer's call at the end of the month, or you'll drink from the cup."

"The cup?"

"You'll see." Gilliam stopped and nodded at the wooden building on their left. "We've arrived. I'll make the introductions, then I got to get back to work. Tommy Elby can show you around from here on."

They climbed low steps and entered the structure, into a fair-sized dark room with two desks, facing each other, set behind a waist-high counter. Behind stood closed doors to other rooms or closets. The desk to the left was unoccupied. A large, florid, middle-aged man with E-7 stripes on his fatigues sat stolidly behind the one on the right, staring straight ahead.

"Sergeant Altobelli," Gilliam greeted him. "I've brought along our newest officer to meet Lieutenant Elby. He around?"

The sergeant remained unmoved. "He's around," he said, in a loud, windy voice. "The man can't sit still more than a minute. He's over at the PX getting pogey bait."

"Gotta leave you," Gilliam said, backing through the open door. "Elby will be back soon. See you later."

The room remained silent for what seemed like a long time. Finally, Sergeant Altobelli heaved himself abruptly from his seat—to stand facing Brede. "No need to wait around anymore," he barked. "I can take you over to the supply room."

"Thank you, first sergeant," Brede responded. "I guess there's special equipment I need here."

Altobelli nodded. "For the winter, mostly," he said. "Gets colder than a witch's tit around here in the winter. Warm as it is now you wouldn't believe it, but it's true. Follow me, lieutenant. I'll take you to supply." He walked through the door, Brede in his wake. The two walked around the side of the headquarters building, to a larger structure behind it with a big double-door. Beyond the door stood a high counter, which fronted several rows of shelving filled with boxes and crates. Two soldiers sat behind the counter—an E-5 sergeant and a PFC. They were playing checkers.

"That's enough of that shit!" Altobelli bawled, his face reddening. "You guys have work to do. This new officer needs his equipment. Sir, I'll be back in the orderly room if you need me." He backed out of the building and shut the doors.

Soon, Brede found himself laden with piles of new clothing: two fatigue jackets with liners, a fur-hooded parka with liner, three pairs of long wool underwear, galoshes and "Mickey Mouse" thermal winter boots, heavy wool socks, gloves and mittens with liners, a waterproof poncho, wool field shirts and trousers, fleece-lined field pants, and a pile cap. He was also issued a steel helmet with helmet liner and camouflage cover, a web belt with suspenders, a canteen, ammunition pouches, a field shovel, a mess kit, a backpack, a sleeping bag with air mattress, a .45 caliber semi-automatic pistol with two loaded magazines, a holster for the weapon, and a gas mask. "It's going to take me three trips to get all of this to my hooch," Brede marveled as he signed for everything.

"Don't worry about that, lieutenant," the sergeant (whose nametag said "Dill") assured him. "The only thing you need to carry out of here today is your pistol. I'll have some KATUSAs lug the rest of your stuff over to officer-land for you. Kwan will tell them where to put it all. It'll be on your bunk tonight. I promise."

"What's a KATUSA?" Brede asked.

"Korean Augmentation to the U.S. Army, sir—KATUSA. The South Korean Army assigns us a bunch of their guys, on account of we're undermanned right now with the war and all. You'll see 'em everyplace. The gun batteries use 'em a lot."

Brede nodded, although he had no clear idea what he'd just heard. "Do I need anything else from you, sarge?" he asked, picking up the holstered weapon from the counter.

Dill opened a drawer and reached in. "You'll need some scarves for your winter shirts, sir." He handed Brede four dickeys, two red and two olive camouflage. "And, of course, the fourragere. Better take these with you."

"What about unit patches for my fatigues and winter shirts? Name tags?"

The sergeant shook his head and smiled. "Kwan and the mama-sans will take care of all that," he said. "Your uniforms will be ready by morning, trust me." He moved back to his seat and began to set up his checkerboard once again.

Surmising that his time in the supply room had ended, Brede walked through the door and headed back to the headquarters battery orderly room. He assumed Elby would look for him there. If Elby didn't show up, he planned to make his way to the Officers Club and get some lunch.

After waiting in the dark empty room for several minutes, he walked back to battalion headquarters, into the S-1 office.

Carter looked up from his files as he entered. "Lieutenant Gilliam's not here, sir," he said. "He's in with the colonel."

"That's okay," Brede told him. "Maybe you could tell him I was by, and that I'm going to the Officers Club for lunch." He spun on his heel and walked from the building, not hungry for lunch—just seeking a place to sit down and compose himself for a few minutes.

Gilliam caught up with him on the way. "Glad I found you," He said. "Did Elby ever show up?"

Brede shook his head. "His first sergeant has a very loud voice," he observed.

"Hard of hearing, I think," Gilliam said. "Ornery, too. That ol' boy could start an argument in an empty house. Let's get some lunch. I believe you've got a surprise waiting for you."

By now they had reached the Officers Club. Gilliam led them through the main entrance to a large room set with several wooden tables covered with white cloth. Seated, he looked at the menu before him. "Looks like chicken fricassee today," he said. "It's not so bad. The cooks here do a fair job. It'll sure keep you going the rest of the day."

"Whatever you say," Brede replied. "I'm not that hungry, just wanted to get off my feet for a few minutes ..." then he lost his train of thought, as unexpected visions walked into the room.

Three western women, two somewhat younger than the third, had entered behind them—talking among themselves in low voices. All wore skirted blue uniforms and white shirts. They moved past Brede and sat by themselves in the room's corner.

Gilliam chuckled. "There's my surprise. Bet you didn't expect to see round-eyed gals, this far from home," he said, grinning and nodding toward the singular figures. "They're Red Cross, Supplemental Recreation Activities Overseas. That's SRAO, or just 'Donut Dollies' to the rest of us. Supposed to boost our morale. Based right here, out of Camp Pelham— about twenty of 'em, anyhow. A little bit of home, right in our own backyard. The older woman, the one in the middle, she runs 'em. Her name's Jackie. Jackie Lake. My advice: stay out of her way. She's tough as a nickel steak. Acts like a colonel and gets away with it. If she sits near you at the bar, best move yourself over a few seats."

Brede stared open-mouthed at the women, any thought of the steaming chicken and sauce over rice just served him erased from his mind. "Right here ...," he managed to mutter.

"Put your eyes back in your head," Gilliam told him. "If you want to see a Donut Dolly, all you have to do is sit at the bar tonight. They'll float right by you—the ones looking for a man to take home with 'em, anyhow. Keep your distance for a while, Ex. Most of those gals aim their noses so high they'd drown in the rain. A year goes by fast around here. Your short timer calendar will be mostly colored in before you know it. If your glands can't wait, there's always the ville."

Brede laughed. "I've gotten more good advice from you before lunch today than I normally hear in a month, Will. Don't worry. I've never been much of a lady's man. When I tried it I got nothing but trouble. That's how I ended up in the army. You guys have given me plenty to do. I doubt I'll have much time to chase skirt."

"Good plan," Gilliam agreed, and stopped talking to dive into his lunch. Neither man had much to say for the next ten minutes.

"How'd you like your first solid meal here?" Gilliam eventually asked, putting down his fork.

"Not bad," Brede said, nodding. "Not home cooking, but not bad."

"The Koreans do a good job here," Gilliam said. "We could do a lot worse. Nice sharing lunch with you, Ex. I've got to get back to work. What are you up to?"

"I thought I might check in with your friend Ricci," Brede told him. "He seemed anxious to see me this morning. Once that's done, I'm going to find out more about S-2 and try to learn something about the comm job."

"Hell, you don't need me to guide you around," Gilliam said, slapping him on the back as he stood from the table. "Though I doubt Bob will let you out of his sight before the end of the day. You may want to do the other things first. He'll come sniffing around for you soon enough, believe me."

"More good advice?"

"Free advice," Gilliam said, turning to leave. "Worth what you pay for it."

CHAPTER FIVE

SOIXANTE QUINZE

B rede spent most of the rest of his day huddled with Sergeant Overshaft and his clerk Grady in the crowded confines of the S-2 office. He was gratified to see that someone had stenciled his name on the door during the morning. The S-2 function, as Overshaft explained it, had three major aspects. First, they filed and cared for the classified materials in the battalion's possession. This included destroying them when necessary, making sure all access was controlled and logged, and assuring all were properly documented and secured. Second, the S-2 supervised all physical security within the battalion—including weapons and documents stored at the firing batteries. Third, the S-2 was tasked with informing the battalion commander and his staff concerning enemy threats and capabilities.

"All these file cabinets contain materials somebody thought had to be classified," the sergeant told him. "That's why they're all bolted and locked. Most of them are over-classified, but that's not our job to decide—unless they're generated here. We keep a mimeograph for that purpose. Our job is to protect them, store them the right way, and destroy them if we're told to do so. It's a librarian's job, for the most part. Do you like to read, Lieutenant Brede?"

When Brede nodded, Overshaft smiled. "I thought I saw that in you," he said. "Lieutenant Jackson didn't read, not a lot anyway. Took him a week to get through 'Playboy,' when it came in. Liked the comic books, though. Didn't look at much that didn't have pictures." He spread his big hands, taking in the cabinets around him. "This battalion's bible and our compass sits in these files—what we'll do if a war breaks out, what we'll do if the South

Koreans stop being our friends, direction for all the other 'what if's' that might happen. They're all right here, locked up tight. Colonel Gaboury has read a lot of the files. That's to his credit. The man before him never did."

"What can I do to help this place run better?" Brede asked him.

"You don't have time to learn all the rules, all the in's and out's of filing," Overshaft said. "Leave that to me. I'll answer any question you ask me, but a year's not enough to learn it all and the Army keeps changing the rules. Leave the filing, the handling of the documents, to Grady and me. We won't let you down. You'll need to know what's in the important documents—the op-plans, the SOPs. I'll show you where to look, but you have a lot of reading and studying to do—if you want to keep current."

"I don't mind the work," Brede said.

"Good. If you do that, handle the battery inspections—I don't travel so well these days—and help me with the document destruction, sir, we'll do just fine."

"That sounds great, sergeant. Show me where to sit, and start throwing those files at me."

They led him to a small desk around a corner of the room, obscure behind yet another wall of file cabinets. There was a field phone on the desk, which was empty—save for an old, dog-eared copy of 'Playboy.' He tossed that in the trash can, placed the holstered pistol he still carried in a drawer, and began reading the first of a stack of document files Grady placed before him. After a few hours of reading, his eyes grew bleary. The coarse, mimeographed pages were filled with acronyms, abbreviations, and references he did not understand. He asked for a pad of paper, and began noting what he could not decipher to discuss with Overshaft later. He put the pad in a desk drawer, and carried the files back to Grady. "Please put these away until tomorrow," he said to the stocky, red-haired specialist, whose wire-rimmed spectacles teetered precariously on his large nose.

As Brede stood on the steps of battalion headquarters, the doleful strains of "Taps" sounded over the camp's scratchy PA system, calling him and all other soldiers who heard it to attention and reflection. The sun reddened low in the west. "It's seventeen-hundred," he thought to himself, wondering briefly where the day had gone. "If I go back to my room now, I should have everything put away in time for dinner and a drink." With that in mind, he walked back to his hooch.

All was as the supply sergeant had predicted. His clothing and equipment from the supply room had been stacked neatly on his bunk. The additional sets of boots he'd brought with him were lined up beneath the bed, polished and gleaming, as were his dress shoes. His clothing all had the proper insignia and correct name tags sewn on, and the room had been dusted and cleaned. The used clothing he'd left on the bed was gone, hopefully to be laundered. Brede thought about all the work he'd done in OCS every day to keep his cubicle this clean and organized. "Where were these mama-sans when I really needed them?" he wondered.

He found room in his locker, the bureau, and under his bunk for the equipment left on his bed. He used the combination lock from his duffle bag to secure the pistol in his locker. By the time all was stored it was, in fact, time for dinner. Rather than sit for a meal, Brede decided to head for the bar and order a hamburger—which he would wash down with his first scotch and water of the evening. He had become a heavy drinker in Europe—since laws there permitted teen-age alcohol consumption. Upon joining the Army, he found most stateside bars did not ask for ID from GI's, and graduated to the ugliness of weekend binge drinking. Liquor flowed more freely through American society (and especially through the military) during the 'sixty's, as did smoking and other lifestyle choices later encouraged far less. Brede was no different than many of those around him, though he had perhaps begun to accumulate his bad habits a little earlier in life.

The bar was almost empty when he arrived. He chose a stool at its far right side—a place he'd maintain throughout his stay in Korea—sat and signaled for Kwan, who was nearby polishing glassware.

"Yes sir, Mr. *jung-wi*," the ubiquitous bartender responded, "what I get for you?"

"You and I are going to have a wonderful relationship, Kwan," Brede told him. "You can call me 'Lieutenant Brede' or 'Lieutenant Ex.' Which do you prefer?"

"'Ex' shorter," Kwan said.

"Then 'Ex' it is, my friend. Now, you got me a delicious hamburger yesterday. Do you think I might have another? Put some ketchup on it, please."

Kwan smiled. "Yes sir, Lieutenant Ex, right away! You want drink with that?"

"Kwan, you have read my mind! I'll have a scotch and water, not too heavy on the water, and water for a chaser."

Kwan nodded and moved away. Brede's drink was before him in almost no time. The burger, on a plate overflowing with French fries, followed a few minutes later. Brede slowly savored the scotch as he weighed the day he'd just had. Not bad, all things considered, he thought. No bad mistakes yet, anyhow. The tension he'd felt all day in this unknown place diminished with each sip of his drink. He began to unwind.

By now, more men were entering the bar. Some ordered food, others called for beverages. Some sat at the bar, while others moved to tables placed around the room. Many were probably not from the Thirty-seventh, Brede realized, but from the First of the Fifteenth—a light howitzer battalion also at Camp Pelham.

He'd finished his hamburger and ordered another scotch when a large, heavy hand gripped his shoulder. Turning, Brede recognized Bob Ricci standing behind him, wearing a wide grin.

"I see you've found your way to the bar," Ricci boomed, laughing. He gestured, and Gilliam joined him, along with another lieutenant Brede didn't recognize. All held drinks in their hands.

"This is Jimmy Diamond, the Thirty-seventh's S-4," the big man said, nodding to a slim, shorter Black man with a receding hairline. "Now we're all together—the batstaff!" With that, he hummed a few bars from the theme of the "Batman" TV show.

"Ex Brede, Good to meet you," Brede said, shaking Diamond's hand. He began to say more, but Ricci interrupted.

"Now, some official business!" the S-3 roared, theatrically clearing his throat as the bar quieted. "This being your first evening in the battalion, a ceremony must be observed. In Major Rafferty's absence, I will preside. Kwan! Rustle us up a Thirty-seventh special 'French Seventy-five.'" Kwan smiled and hurried away. Diamond and Gilliam stood back from the bar, watching.

"As you may know," Ricci intoned, "the Sixth of the Thirty-seventh has a long and respected history." At this, hoots from around the bar erupted—likely from members of the Fifteenth.

Ricci held his hands up to silence them. "Jealousy is unseemly among officers and gentlemen," he said. "To continue, this battalion fought in the

Great War—in World War I—with our courageous French and Belgian allies. It was they who passed on to us their liquid tribute to the weapon we all employed against the monstrous Hun, the magnificent *Milimétre Soixante Quinze* howitzer!"

"Hear, hear!" Gilliam and Diamond chorused.

"This potation, the 'French Seventy-Five,' amalgamated by the loving hands of our good friend Kwan, must be imbibed to fold you into our camaraderie. Kwan! The drink, please!"

The bartender slid a tall cocktail across the bar. Brede noticed that it was golden pale and bubbled like champagne. The Korean also handed Ricci an egg, which the S-3 held in his hand.

"Ah," the big man said, "the final ingredient! The *piece de resistance!*" With that, he cracked the egg's shell and dropped its raw content into the drink, where it flowed slowly to the bottom of the glass. "Drink up now, my friend," he said gently as he handed Brede the concoction, "and leave nothing in the glass—not even a speck of yolk—or else we'll have to try again with another."

"Only one way to do it," Brede thought to himself. "Chug the whole thing down at once. Otherwise, I'll choke and leave something in the glass." So, holding the cocktail in both hands, he willed his throat open and did exactly that. It was a trick he'd picked up in college, drinking German beer.

Afterwards, he slammed the empty glass on the bar. "A little light on the gin," he said, "but otherwise okay." In reality, Brede could feel the raw egg as it slid through his digestive tract. He made himself ignore the odd, unpleasant sensation.

Ricci's eyes had grown large as he watched Brede chug the drink. "I've seen a lot of guys go through this," he said. "Never seen anybody do it like that."

"You should have seen him with the Colonel today," Gilliam said. "Never even cracked a smile. Didn't warn him, neither."

They patted him on the back. "Welcome to the battalion, Ex," Ricci said. "I need to see you tomorrow. What time can you come by?"

"I can be there by ten-thirty," Brede replied, as he concentrated to understand what was being said. "I have to take care of some S-2 business in the morning."

"That's fine," Ricci said, smiling. "I've got a feeling you and I are going to get along great. Here, let me buy you a drink."

"I already had one coming when you guys showed up," Brede said, reaching for his scotch. "Then I should hit the sack."

Best intentions rang hollow, soon brushed aside. One drink led to several more. The evening blurred. Even so, Brede retained one coherent memory. Across from the bar, next to a brick fireplace, stood three artillery rounds—examples of each kind of shell fired by the Fifteenth and the Thirty-seventh. An eight-inch shell towered over the others. "Damn thing weighs over two-hundred pounds," Ricci told him, as the big man slapped it. "I've only seen one man lift it, besides myself of course."

"Why would anybody in his right mind want to move it an inch?" Brede asked.

"If you wanted a weekend pass, you would," Ricci told him. "The only way for you to get one in this outfit is to take that shell from where it sits and somehow put it on the bar, in front of witnesses—all by yourself."

Later on, Brede recalled snorting derisively. "That damn round weighs a lot more than I do. Good thing I don't need any weekend passes, I guess." As is so often the case, his words would later haunt him.

CHAPTER SIX

WALTZING MATILDA

The next several weeks flew by, as Brede began to learn the intricacies of one of the nuclear artillery rounds that would be such a big part of his job. He became aware of the mission his battalion was tasked to perform in the event of war with the North Koreans, and possibly their Communist Chinese allies. Every evening ended much the same, with too much scotch at what was becoming his designated place at the Officers Club bar.

There was very little to do at Camp Pelham but work and drink, the young lieutenant rapidly discovered. That was alright with Brede. The work was challenging, but got a little easier to handle every day. The drinking quickly became his evening pastime of choice.

His battalion was part of a tripwire against invasion from the north, Brede learned—after reading some of the documents Overshaft passed to him and talks with Ricci. The eighteen Korean War vintage 155 millimeter howitzers at A, B, and C batteries had targets predetermined around the DMZ—many unchanged since before the armistice. All three firing batteries regularly lobbed shells into that heavily mined wasteland, just to keep in practice. The Thirty-seventh's fourth firing unit—D battery—was equipped with four newer, more powerful eight-inch howitzers. These were self-propelled, very mobile, and had a mission different from the rest of the battalion. If fired in anger, their initial nuclear rounds would try to knock out advancing enemy armored columns before they could ford the shallow Imjin River.

Current operations plans (OP-Plans) from both Second Division and Eighth Army had the Thirty-seventh retreat to a series of set fallback positions during the first week of any foreseen hostilities. By that time, reinforcements and supporting airpower would arrive and stabilize the front, predicted by then to lie somewhere immediately north of Seoul.

The ROK (Republic of Korea) Army, guided by Chaebol intransigence, did not accept even an inch of retreat. Their war plans called for an immediate, massive assault across the DMZ, in order to destroy or push North Korean guns back—beyond their ability to target Seoul and important harbors. War games of that era were schizophrenic, with U.S. forces retreating while the South Koreans surged forward. Large gaps between simulated frontlines of the allies occurred.

Use of nuclear artillery was key to ROK strategy. In every wargame, they asked for—and received—permission to fire U.S. nuclear rounds from their own howitzers. The rounds would be delivered, assembled, and supervised by U.S. officers.

"That will be your job, Ex," Ricci told Brede. "If the balloon goes up, you'll take a deuce-and-a-half up to the SASP at *Gaya-ri*, pick up six rounds from the caves there, and deliver them where the EAM tells you."

"What's an EAM?" Brede asked. The hair on the back of his neck had begun to rise. This casually mentioned mission sounded like a good way to win posthumous decorations.

"An EA M is an Emergency Action Message," Ricci explained. "That's how we get permission to fire the nukes, and where to put them. We have plastic wafers, some call them 'cookies,' kept in one of your S-2 safes. When an EAM comes in over secure teletype, we break open the wafer and match the code inside to what's on the EAM. If the codes match, we follow the message instructions and send you on your way."

"Huh," Brede said, frowning. "So I'll be driving around Korean roads in a truck full of nuclear rounds. What's to stop the ROKs from just killing me and taking the whole truck?"

During his short time in-country, Brede had already discovered that the South Koreans around him were both brutal and aggressive. He had watched the battalion's KATUSA sergeant-major club another ROK soldier unconscious with his fists over a reported breach of conduct. The day before, the ville down the road had erupted with the pitiful howls of dogs before a wedding took place. Women and children had hung the animals from roofs by their hind legs and spent hours beating them to death with sticks. He was told this made their meat more tender. Brede realized men from such a society wouldn't hesitate to murder a young U.S. soldier if they wanted what he carried in his truck badly enough.

Ricci laughed at his question and its implications. "Don't worry," he said. "If they try anything, you'll have a squad of our guys with you for security. Besides, the ROKs have no idea how to set these rounds up, or how powerful they really are. You'll be fine."

Brede remained uncertain. Soldiers he'd seen so far at Camp Pelham didn't seem that tough. The kind of rounds he'd be carrying in the truck— the W48's—were "sealed pit" weapons. Their nuclear materials and detonators were already inaccessibly secured within the shell's titanium casing. Assembly was really only a matter of mounting a fuse to a projectile and setting it. Any experienced artilleryman would probably have no trouble determining how to do that. Each round could deliver the equivalent of more than seventy-two tons of TNT to a target as far as nine miles away from the firing howitzer. He wondered how likely a ROK soldier, pitted against his implacably hated enemy in heavy combat, would be to follow protocol.

Sitting at the bar that evening, he willed himself to shrug off his trepidations. There hadn't been any serious danger of reopening hostilities for years, Brede told himself as he finished his scotch and ordered another. Chances were excellent the unsteady peace on the peninsula would continue long after his tour was over.

By now, his days had fallen into an established routine. In the morning, he'd work at his desk in S-2, and oversee any communications issues Sergeant Barr sent his way. Then lunch, followed by an afternoon learning the intricacies of nuclear field artillery. Here he spent most of this time with Sergeant Rausch. The tall, raw-boned E-5 knew the classified manual for the W48 round backwards and forwards, Brede suspected. That didn't matter, of course. Every step in the assembly and fusing procedure had to be read verbatim from a copy of that manual, turned to the proper page, his index finger on the proper line. Any deviation from what was written or illustrated would incur scowls of disapproval from glowering inspectors at the next TPI—leading to reams of explanatory paperwork and repercussions that could ruin careers.

Every afternoon in the secluded training bunker Rauch would read instructions to Brede and two other soldiers, who would dutifully perform each procedural step announced on an inert training round. Then, after a short break while all components were put back in their original places, the two men would switch roles and repeat the process.

"How long do we have to keep this up?" Brede asked Ricci when he stopped by to observe their efforts one afternoon. "I know the damn manual almost by heart. I think I could do the assembly in my sleep."

The big S-3 chuckled. "You'll do it every day unless something more important comes up—and that won't be often. Every day, Ex. Just like I had to when I was new, and the guy before me, and the guy before him. You'll thank me when those dead-eyed inspectors show up. Once you've gotten through a TPI with no errors, we can talk about lightening things up a little."

"What about the eight-inch round? When do I get trained on that?"

Ricci shrugged. "The W33 is a lot more complicated than the W48 round. Older technology. We'll start you on that around Christmas. Nobody comes around to inspect us during the winter, so you'll have the time to go out to D Battery and learn it."

The month of August ended on a Thursday in 1967, so the Battalion held its officers call on Friday, September first. That afternoon, after the completion of work, most of the battalion's commissioned officers gathered at Colonel Gaboury's quarters for their monthly get-together. The firing batteries and battalion staff were both represented. All present wore dress khakis, which were inspected carefully by the Thirty-seventh's XO, Major Rafferty, for any missing or incorrectly mounted elements. Any who failed his inspection were condemned to drink from "the cup"—a tarnished silver trophy with wing-like handles that could hold over a pint of liquor.

Rafferty, who Brede had recently met, was a phlegmatic careerist with nearly two decades of Army service behind him, including two tours in Korea during the hostilities. His knowledge of the mechanics and tactics of field artillery was encyclopedic. He was respected by everyone he worked with, his direction unerringly correct. Nevertheless, for reasons unknown to any in the Thirty-seventh—save perhaps Gaboury himself—he would never be promoted again. He was one of the "Iron Majors" the Army depends upon, who would finish his active duty and retire at his current rank.

Physically, Rafferty was a small, thin man. He wore his greying hair in a short crewcut, and the large grey eyes set under the heavy brows of his seamed face seemed to see everywhere at once. His disproportionately large, gnarled hands could effortlessly dismantle the most complex equipment, almost as though they had lives of their own. Every evening, around eight, he came to the Officers Club bar for a single Manhattan cocktail—which he sipped slowly before retiring. While he was there, noise in the normally boisterous room muted—though he never requested quiet. Neither Gaboury nor Colonel Nesbitt (his peer at the Fifteenth) caused the same effect.

Now Brede stood motionless as the XO examined his uniform for flaws. He was cautiously confident none would be discovered. He had left work early and used a ruler to place each brass element on his khakis. His ribbons (the three he had) were exactly where they should be. The fourrag-ere perfectly draped his left shoulder. All was per regulation, straight out of the field manual he'd borrowed from Ricci's office.

"Looks like everything was ruler-measured," Rafferty commented. "Well-polished, too. Good job, lieutenant."

Brede let out a long slow breath, began to relax.

"Except for those ribbons, you'd be perfect," Rafferty concluded. "They're on backwards." He shook his head. "Sorry, young man. You'll get to drink from the cup this evening."

As he looked down, Brede immediately realized what he had done. He'd laid the shirt on his bunk facing away from him, so he'd been looking down from the top when he pinned the ribbons on. He'd unconsciously mounted them facing the wrong way.

Several men stood at the cabinet where Gaboury kept his liquor, splash-ing streams from various bottles into the loving cup. "This will be a hell of a pour!" Ricci hollered.

As he was handed the cup, which he grasped with both hands, the chant began.

> "Here's to Ex-o, he's true blue! Thirty-
> seventh, through and through!
> Cannon-cocker, so they say! Tried to get to
> heaven but he went the other way!
> So drink! Chug-a-lug, chug-a-lug, chug-a-lug! So drink ..."

Brede took a deep breath, raised the cup to his lips, took one deep swal-low, then another as the rant continued. The potent admixture exploded in his gut. He briefly lowered the cup to take another breath, then drained it almost empty. The officers around him cheered. He felt light-headed, dizzy, and knew he had to sit down—at least until the loud buzzing in his ears diminished. He staggered to the nearest chair and planted himself, uttering something between a moan and a sigh.

Those around him slapped his shoulders, shook his hand, and laughed congratulations. The cup was removed from his nerveless fingers, rinsed and put away until next month's use. Conversations continued—some of which he may have joined—but Brede remained largely oblivious to what went on around him for the next several minutes.

By then, everybody was standing, as the event concluded. All present began singing the battalion song, with far more energy than melody. As he heard the first lyrics, Brede realized he knew the song well, and quickly joined a forgettable rendition of "Waltzing Matilda:"

Once a jolly swagman camped beside a billabong,
Under the shade of a Coolibah tree,
And he sang as he watched and waited till his billy boiled
"You'll come a Waltzing Matilda with me!"
Waltzing Matilda! Waltzing Matilda!
"You'll come a Waltzing Matilda with me."
And he sang as he watched and waited till his billy boiled
"You'll come a Waltzing Matilda with me."

Down came a jumbuck to guzzle from that billabong
Up jumped the swagman, seized him with glee,
And he sang as he stowed that jumbuck in his tucker bag
"You'll come a Waltzing Matilda with me!"
Waltzing Matilda! Waltzing Matilda!
"You'll come a Waltzing Matilda with me."
And he sang as he stowed that jumbuck in his tucker bag
"You'll come a Waltzing Matilda with me!"

Down came the squatter mounted on his thorough-bred,
Up came the troopers one, two, three,
"Whose that jolly jumbuck you've got in your tucker bag?
You'll come a Waltzing Matilda with me!"

Waltzing Matilda! Waltzing Matilda!
"You'll come a Waltzing Matilda with me."
"Whose that jolly jumbuck you've got in your tucker bag?
You'll come a Waltzing Matilda with me!"

Up jumped the swagman, dove into the billabong,
"You'll never catch me alive," said he!
And his ghost may be heard if you pass beside that billabong
"You'll come a Waltzing Matilda with me."
Waltzing Matilda! Waltzing Matilda!
"You'll come a Waltzing Matilda with me."
And his ghost may be heard if you pass beside that billabong
"You'll come a Waltzing Matilda with me."

The sliver of Brede's mind that remained lucid wondered how the Thirty-seventh came to adopt an 1890's Aussie protest song as their own. He told himself he'd find out some time in the dim future when his brain functioned reliably again.

Now he found himself on his feet, propelled with the crowd around him out the door of Gaboury's hooch and down a paved walkway to the Officers Club, where all sat at tables on one side of the dining room while their CO mounted a low stage set beyond the entry doors. The two battalion commanders and the "head Donut Dolly" sat behind a table and looked out at them once everybody had found a seat. Officers of the Fifteenth and ladies of the Red Cross filled the rest of the dining room. Brede dimly realized that this must be some kind of monthly event, and tried his best to pay attention to what was going on. At this he was unsuccessful. Most of his diminished willpower was used up just trying to remain upright and fight off the urge to close his eyes and sleep.

From time to time, one of the three leaders would rise and speak. Afterwards, everybody would applaud. Brede did his best to take his queues from those around him, and clap when they did. Later on, everybody was served dinner. He was unable to imagine trying to eat, so he looked around the room while everyone else dug in. They all seemed to enjoy what had been served, though he could not recognize what was on the plate in front of him. His goal was to last through the dinner without bringing attention to himself, then retire quickly to his hooch and pass out. The world went away.

When he regained consciousness later, his watch told him the time was about two AM. He rose shakily from his bunk and began removing his uniform. His head hurt whenever he moved. He felt the beginnings of nausea, but didn't think he'd be violently ill—though he knew that would probably be best for his ravaged digestive tract. He wondered if he had any aspirin in his kitbag, and whether he'd be able to find it if he did. Unsure, he contented himself with struggling out of his clothes and laying back on his bunk. Sleep again enveloped him immediately.

Brede was awakened several hours later by the noise of others around him. Every sound assaulted his brain like a hammer, and the thick, oily taste in his mouth was reminiscent of unwashed dishes. He realized immediately that he had to get up, and dimly reckoned that the day before him would be both painful and trying. He forced himself to rise from his bunk, causing waves of throbbing pain to erupt between his ears. He groped for some fresh underwear and a towel, and padded dully to a shower he hoped would clear his head and make him feel more human. Men he passed in the hall smiled when they saw him. A few laughed openly. He ignored them and soaked his tortured head under the shower far beyond the regulation five minutes normally allotted, but felt no relief from it.

Finally, somewhat scrubbed, dried, shaved, and dressed—Brede plodded to his desk in S-2, avoiding light and sound as best he could. The thought of breakfast crossed his mind, instantly rejected. What he needed was coffee, in large quantities. He got little actual work done that morning. The simplest sentence he read required repetition and concentration before comprehension dawned. Speech demanded careful, studied deliberation. Otherwise, only meaningless noise escaped his wooden lips.

Later that interminable morning, Gilliam came to visit him. "Half expected you'd be on sick-call today, Ex," he said, leaning against a file cabinet. "You were drunker'n Cooter Brown last night. It was amazing just to see it. You must own a cast-iron gut."

Even though it hurt his head, Brede looked up. "Don't feel much like iron today," he mumbled, smiling ruefully. "Probably would have gone to sick-call if I had any sense. It's like somebody beat me with a big stick and then marched the Russian army through my mouth in their stocking feet." He nodded, which hurt his head even more. "I feel awful," he concluded.

The S-1 laughed. "Well, as beat down as you are today, you were feeling no pain last night, my friend. Once we got to the bar ..."

"Wait!" Brede gasped, his eyes wide. "Wait! You mean I didn't go back to my hooch after dinner?"

Gilliam shook his head slowly. "Are you kidding?" he said with a chuckle. "You looked kind of droopy through chow, I'll admit. But once we got you up and to the bar, you brightened right up! Must have had a pitcher of scotch after that. Hell, you even danced with Jackie Lake. The old broad looked like she enjoyed it, too! Showed a smile that fit her like socks on a rooster."

Brede held his aching head in his hands. "What else ... did I do?" he whispered.

"Nothing much," Gilliam told him. "You were quite a gentleman, all evening long. Big smile on your face, too! Bet you were fun to party with, back in school."

Brede moaned. "Yeah, fun. That kind of fun got me kicked out of college."

It being Saturday, duty largely ceased by lunchtime. Those who had passes left the camp for the surrounding villes. A few grabbed transport to Seoul. The remainder finished their work and retired to their quarters—or to the bars that served them. Brede dragged himself to his hooch and went to bed, where he slumbered through Sunday morning. He felt better—but still tentative and tender—the rest of that day. By Monday evening, he was back at his seat at the bar.

CHAPTER SEVEN

MOONGLOW

A Technical Proficiency Inspection (TPI) team rolled into Camp Pelham early on an October afternoon, as cooling temperatures and colorful leaves falling from the few trees around announced the change of season. Three commissioned officers, six warrant officers, four sergeants, and ten enlisted personnel arrived in two International Harvester Scouts and a bus. The team commander billeted with Colonel Gaboury, in a spare room set aside for VIP visitors. The remaining officers were assigned hooches in the green Quonsets. The rest of the team took over a Headquarters Battery barracks, forcing Comm and Survey sections to "double up" with neighbors. These inspectors had travelled from Hawaii, at CINCPAC—U.S. military headquarters for the Pacific side of the world. Only the DASA inspection due in the Spring carried more importance.

The long-anticipated event would last three days, Brede was told. The Thirty-seventh had been notified several weeks before—plenty of time to make things ready. After visiting them, the inspectors would travel east to assess the First of the Seventeenth Artillery at Camp Saint Barbara.

Days preceding the CINCPAC team's arrival became strenuous and hectic. Battalion structures were all liberally daubed with new paint, inside and out—standard Army response to any upcoming inspection. Soldiers in general were scrutinized, their boots and brass examined for scuff or tarnish. Vehicles important to the exercise were thoroughly lubricated and maintained, their logbook records perfected. Sergeant Altobelli's windy bellow was often heard, as he exhorted those around him to tasks his immediate focus deemed imperative.

In S-2, Grady and Overshaft worked to make sure all pertinent documents were current and filed properly. Up the hall in S-1, a similarly motivated Gilliam exhorted Carter to ascertain personnel records were pristine. Security clearances for everybody involved in the inspection— from Colonel Gaboury to the newest slick-sleeve private—had to show unblemished perfection. Around the corner, behind the big double doors of S-3, Ricci and his crew reviewed "special weapons" training records and schedules to correct anything out of line, and practiced incessantly to make sure the fire direction center was ready to prosecute nuclear fire missions.

Sergeant Barr thoroughly inspected the crypto and associated communications gear in his trucks. Like the vehicles themselves, all his equipment had to be in perfect order. Any missing parts that couldn't be found and acquired in time became the province of Diamond's S-4 section. Parts remaining on order had to have requisitions clearly passing blame for their absence up the line—time-bending alternative history in some cases. At the firing batteries, the pace and anxiety levels were much the same. This was especially true at D Battery, where the eight-inch rounds and their attendant vehicles had needs not shared with the rest of the battalion.

All this took place under the deific supervision of Major Rafferty and his henchman, Sergeant-Major Bankowski. Between them, the two men unerringly pointed out flaws and gaps in work the lieutenants and sergeants had thought perfect. They seemed to be everywhere at once. Arguing with either one of them made no sense, as they were always proven correct. The battalion staff began calling them "Batman and Robin," after the comic-book characters. Colonel Gaboury himself seldom left his office. The battalion commander preferred calling subordinates to his deskside, gently but firmly interrogating each of them using an extensive checklist he annotated as they conversed. Sometimes, the meetings lasted hours.

The Officers Club bar, normally well-populated with patrons from the Thirty-seventh, became noticeably less occupied. Kwan, who saw the phenomenon annually, dutifully delivered hamburgers to the hooches of tired lieutenants who crept late to their bunks too fatigued to socialize. He knew they'd all be back soon, with a vengeance. Meanwhile, he made sure that the club itself was clean and tidy, liquor stocks in order, plenty of steaks on hand—and admonished the girls in the attached barber shop to be ready for increased traffic. *Yangkiseu* always wanted haircuts before a big inspection.

The TPI team arrived at Camp Pelham's gates on October Ninth, at fifteen-thirty hours local time. Members were directed to their various assigned quarters to unpack, while their commanding officer, Captain Alvin Harper (USN), met with Colonel Gaboury and Major Rafferty in the battalion commander's office. An hour later in the battalion classroom, he briefed Thirty-seventh inspection participants on planned activities during the next three days.

"Tomorrow, we'll examine your records, documentation, and training," Captain Harper explained, as a soldier beside him brought the appropriate sheet to the front of a large, easel-mounted flipchart. Harper was a short bantam rooster of a man, whose unlined oval face and short hair made him look young at first glance. He seemed to bounce rather than rise from any seat he took. Now he strutted across the small stage, peering sidewise at his audience. Those who knew him were aware he'd been passed over during the last promotion cycle, and resented the reality that he'd never make admiral as a personal slight.

"Chief Warrant Officer Braddock will lead the personnel records team," Harper continued. "Chief Warrant Officers Kline and Stanley will inspect training records and classified documents—including filing, storage, and disposal procedures." As their names were called, the Warrant Officers named stood and nodded. Though differing in complexion, height, and hair color, they were all middle-aged, thick-waisted, crew-cut men with blank expressions and flat, dispassionate eyes. They surveyed the Thirty-seventh's representatives in the room with cool, lizard-like indifference.

"On Wednesday, we'll evaluate your weapon assembly procedures," Harper continued, as the flip-chart was ostentatiously folded forward by the woodenly emotionless sergeant at his side—who then retired to his place behind it. "Chief Pryor will assess your Headquarters and A Battery teams, while Chief Yost will do the same at B and C Batteries. Chief Damon will spend the day at D Battery, inspecting procedures there.

"Thursday morning, we'll observe a live training exercise, the details of which will be announced to your commanding officer at that time. The exercise is projected to begin at oh-six-hundred and conclude before noon. Then, after a luncheon break, we'll conduct an exit briefing at this location." The Captain smiled joylessly. "I know you've all trained hard. Our only purpose here is to help you do an important job as well as you must. We'll be wrapped up by Thursday afternoon. Any questions?"

Gaboury stood, gravely serious. "I'd like to thank Captain Harper and his team for their excellent outline of the next thwee days," he said, his voice high and loud. "You're right, sir—we've worked hard to pwepare ourselves for your inspection. I'm sure my officers and men will join me in pwoviding all of you with evewy courtesy and full access to any wecords or procedures you ask to see." He looked around the room, nodded, and sat down. There were no further questions. The inspection had begun.

"Any scuttlebutt about these guys?" Brede asked Ricci as they left the classroom.

The big man nodded. "The guy before me said Pryor is a dick," He said, keeping his voice low. "He'll gig you if you sneeze. I don't know about the others, but they're all cast from the same mold. These guys spend their waking hours thinking up ways to make G.I.'s sweat. They'll always find some reason to write you up, it can't be helped. Just make sure you don't do anything really wrong, and get ready for the RBI."

"RBI?"

"Response by Indorsement—RBI. It's the long report you and I will have to write about how we'll correct anything these bastards find wrong. The more they find, the longer it will get. Let's hope it's not too long, this time around." Ricci gave Brede a long look. "You'll do fine, Ex. Trust me."

From Brede's limited viewpoint, the inspection seemed to go well. His own section passed muster easily, and he heard no howls of anguish from either Ricci or Gilliam. His assembly team made no obvious mistakes, although the basilisk-eyed inspector took several pages of notes as he watched. Problems occurred on the third day, when Captain Harper announced that the truck carrying nuclear rounds had caught fire. Several minutes of uncoordinated panic ensued, as groups of soldiers rushed around the truck—some gas-masked, others not—some trying to extinguish the mock blaze, while others worked to evacuate the practice round to another vehicle or just watched slack-jawed. The inspectors jotted copious notes as they watched—and allowed themselves tight smiles.

The exit briefing was perfunctory. The young men involved had tried earnestly to avoid errors, so of course mistakes were made. All present were relieved to hear that the battalion had met at least minimal standards to continue their mission. Everyone was simply glad the episode had concluded. As the inspector's convoy pulled away, Ricci looked at his watch and then turned to Brede, who stood nearby. "I don't know about you," he growled, "but I have some drinking to catch up on tonight. I don't think I've tasted whiskey for damn near a month. My liver is complaining. Ol' Kwan has probably forgotten my name by now."

Brede smiled widely. "High time to reintroduce yourself," he said, laughing. "I'll be on hand to assist, as a good junior officer should. Just save some scotch for your S-2."

Ricci frowned. "Scotch?" he said. "Never touch that stuff. Tastes like medicine."

"Wonderful!" Brede agreed. "More for me."

At Camp Pelham's various clubs that evening, the scene was blurred and loud—as the men of the Thirty-seventh strode to dissipate tension built during the last three weeks. Beer and liquor flowed, laughter filled the halls. Brede returned to his favorite seat at the Officers Club bar, musing over the drama which had enveloped him during the recent inspection. The anxiety that had pressed him was pointless, he could see now—after two plentiful scotch and waters. By this time next year, no one here would remain to remember what had happened. A completely new group of men would confront the gimlet-eyed warrant officers from Hawaii. The cycle of anxiety would simply repeat itself to a new audience. Little or nothing would have been altered. He laughed out loud as he raised his glass.

"What's so funny?" a low but clearly female voice enquired.

Brede glanced to his right to find a bemused Jackie Lake, turned in her seat, looking at him over her martini glass. How long had she been sitting there? He hadn't noticed her before. He remembered Gilliam's warning to move away from her quickly, but he didn't feel like departing. Anyhow, she didn't seem angry or intimidating—and this was his seat, after all.

Months later, in a very different place, Brede's memory of this moment would remain clear as crystal. The room was brightly lit, becoming crowded and louder as dinner in the adjoining restaurant concluded. Kwan had turned on the radio behind the bar. A forty's standby— *Moonglow*—was playing on Armed Forces Radio. The dulcet tones of Benny Goodman's clarinet filled the air.

He'd never looked at her closely before then. The angular, lightly freckled face he saw tapered from a broad forehead to a cleft chin. Large hazel eyes with strong brows stood above her straight, narrow nose and a wide, thin-lipped mouth that trembled on the edge of a smile. Short auburn hair fell around her ears in a loosely combed pixie cut. She wore no make-up that night, slim in her frumpy Red Cross uniform. About five-five, he guessed. Large hands, the nails man-cut. He figured her age to be late thirties to early forties, based on the fine lines around her eyes and mouth—roughly the age of his mother.

In the back of his mind, Brede realized hazily that a person's features, taken separately, seldom summed to their totality. Taken one part at a time, Jackie Lake would not be considered as attractive as she clearly was.

"I was laughing at myself," he answered belatedly, lifting his glass to her. "At all the drama that's been dancing through my brain for the past few weeks."

She lifted hers in response. "That's quite an inspection you just gave me, lieutenant," she said, tilting her head. "I'd hate to be one of your G.I.'s, hoping for a pass."

He felt his cheeks redden. "Never expected to see many women over here, ma'am," he said. "Still can't get my head around it. My apologies. My name is Brede, by the way. Xabier Brede."

"We've met before, Ex," she said laughing, "though you were probably too drunk to remember. I understand your buddies at the Thirty-seventh had just poured a gallon of liquor down your throat. So you don't have to be so formal."

"Reflex," Brede said. "My apologies again. I was brought up to call ladies ma'am unless we'd been introduced."

Jackie stuck out her hand. "In that case, pleased to meet you, Ex. My name's Jackie Lake—just in case you were unsure."

Brede solemnly shook her hand. "Pleased to meet you—again, I guess—Jackie." He glanced at his glass. "Looks like my drink's done. Yours is too. May I buy you another?"

"I'll take you up on that—but not right now, Ex. I have a meeting with my ladies in a little while, and I'll need a clear head. See you tomorrow?"

"I'm here almost every night—until my short-timer's calendar gets filled in or the colonel puts me someplace else," Brede told her. "I'll save you a seat."

He looked up from a drink the next evening, surprised to find her in the seat beside his again. He had long since despaired she would show up, but keeping the seat free had been no problem—once he told those approaching who had reserved it. Apparently, Jackie Lake commanded serious respect among Camp Pelham's officers.

"Am I still good for that drink?" she asked. Instead of her blue uniform, Jackie wore a maroon turtleneck and knee-length tweed skirt tonight.

"Absolutely," he said, smiling. "Glad to see you. I had just about given up hope. Several people have wanted your seat. Do you want a gimlet, like last night?"

Jackie shook her head. "Let's see what Kwan can do with a gibson," she said, nodding to the bartender. She pulled a cigarette from her purse. "Got a light?"

"Yes, ma'am," he said, pulling a zippo® from his trouser pocket.

As he closed the lighter to put it away, she stopped his hand. "That's some band you're wearing, Ex," she said, examining the big silver wolf's head on his right ring finger.

He laid his hand on the bar so she could see it better. "It's a gift from my grandfather. I'm named after him, and people always said we we're a lot alike. He told me his dad gave it to him, when he joined the Canadian Marines in World War I."

"Obviously hand-made—and very large. It's a wolf, right?"

He nodded. "Kind of a family totem. I've never seen another ring like it."

"It's striking. Adds to your personality."

They talked for another hour about trivia mostly. She explained the trips her group made to the field every day, to see the G.I.'s near the DMZ, how they no longer made their own donuts, the programs and games they conducted with the troops they visited.

"Must be muddy out there about now," Brede observed. "Colder, too. I'll bet those guys are glad to see you when you show up."

She nodded in agreement. "It's tough for the guys north of the Imjin. Anything that reminds them of home makes them smile. I think we do them some good."

During the next few weeks, their cocktail discussions became a frequent, welcome part of Brede's day. He was sure there was no romance on either side, but it was good to have a non-army friend to talk to, from time to time.

"Why do you wear that moustache?" she asked him once. "It doesn't suit you."

He laughed. "You know how young I am, Jackie," he answered. "I guess I was trying to look older when I got out of OCS. Got my ID card picture taken with it, so I've kept it. Believe me, I've thought about shaving it off. Sometimes it's harder than hell to trim right. Come on, didn't you ever try to look a little more mature when you were my age?"

Jackie thought a moment. "It wasn't all that long ago, you know," she said smiling. "Back then, I sure wanted a fuller figure. I was thin, thought I looked like a boy." She laughed. "Nowadays, I agonize if I gain a pound. Funny how things change."

"Your figure looks just fine, Jackie. Believe me, you've got nothing to fret about. You're a very attractive woman."

"You're not bad yourself," she told him. "Why are you spending platonic time with me, with so many young Donut Dollies floating around? I guarantee there's a few who would give you a look."

"To be honest, I'm not interested," he said, lighting them both a cigarette. "Got my fill of girlfriends during my truncated college career. Don't get me wrong, we had a lot of fun and the sex was great. Even so, I wanted something more from the gals I knew. Never found it. Maybe in a while I'll be ready to look around some more. Right now, I'd rather spend my free time talking to you. You're much more interesting. Our friendship is very important to me, Jackie. It makes my time here more bearable."

"Well then, order me another martini, young man," she told him. "Then we can talk some more."

CHAPTER EIGHT

THE IMJIN SUBMARINE

A turgid Imjin River delineates North and South Korea's western boundary. Further east, north of Seoul, the demilitarized zone between the two Koreas moves north of that river. This is where many Second Infantry Division soldiers were placed in 1967. During monsoons which the area endures every year, the Imjin runs deep and treacherous with flood water—but during drier months water levels subside dramatically. Local fishermen cast nets for large carp found in the river, even though these bony fish are difficult to eat and taste muddy to westerners. Brede, who learned fishing from his father, had been to the river several times. He marveled at the size of the carp brought up—really no more than enormously overgrown goldfish, in his opinion.

The Imjin was far from top of mind as he slept one November night, after an evening of too much scotch and too many cigarettes. By now Camp Pelham had begun to feel the chill of an approaching Korean winter. The uniform of the day had changed from cotton fatigues to woolen field shirts and trousers, worn with a pile cap. Brede had already gotten his first fright from the space heater that warmed his hooch. Several days ago, he woke to find it glowing red hot, its crude carburetor set much too high. He had either forgotten to reset it when the room warmed up, or simply passed out in bed before it did. In any case, his error could easily have become disaster if a fire had occurred. He gingerly turned the damn thing far lower, and made up his freshly alert mind to keep it low from now on. Instead, he'd get more blankets from Kwan.

This evening, his slumbers were interrupted by loud and persistent knocking on his door, which he eventually awakened to answer. He looked out in the hall to find Colonel Gaboury's driver standing before him. "Sir," the young corporal blurted, "sorry to wake you up! Colonel Gaboury needs you at his hooch right away. I'll drive you over when you're ready."

Still half asleep, Brede nodded dully. "Okay…" he mumbled, "okay. Be right out." He shut the door and threw on his uniform from the previous day, mechanically blousing his trousers as he laced his boots. He ran his fingers through uncombed hair, gargled some mouthwash, shrugged into a field jacket, threw on his pile cap, then stumbled groggily from the hooch. "I'm ready," he announced, and followed the driver to his jeep.

The drive to Colonel Gaboury's hooch was brief. Brede probably could have walked the distance in less time than it took their vehicle to negotiate its way. He climbed from the jeep and entered, to find his battalion commander in slippers and robe, sitting across from a battle dressed soldier. Incongruously, Jackie Lake was also in the room —wearing a parka, huddled in a corner chair. In the room's dim light, it took Brede a moment to read the nametag on the soldier's field jacket and note the eagle painted on his steel pot. He realized then the man in front of him was Colonel Arthur Wainright, the division's second brigade commander. Wainright sat on a couch, drinking amber liquor from a glass, a malodorous cigar in hand. He looked up as Brede entered the room. "This what we've been waiting for?" he growled, clamping the glowing stogey between his teeth. "A butter bar? Hell, he's just a kid."

"He's my S-2, sir," Gaboury said quietly. "He does a good job for me."

"Then let's get on with it! Every minute we sit here they could be landing spies!"

Gaboury turned to Brede. "Ex, the bwigade commander has gotten an astonishing weport. One of his outposts spotted the perwiscope of a submawine in the Imjin."

"Goddamn right!" Wainright snarled. "A submarine! Those commie bastards are trying to sneak something in. I've already alerted my infantry. I need you guys to plaster the area with artillery fire. ASAP! That means right away, young man!" As he stood, Brede noticed the colonel was wearing his silver-plated .45 pistol—homage to his hero, George Patton. Wainright was a big man, well over six feet tall, and heavy—his spherical gut visibly straining the zipper of his field jacket, jowls welling from his shirt collar.

"Yes sir," Brede responded. "Do you have the coordinates of the sighting, sir?"

"Wha ... yeah, here somewhere. Gimme a second." Wainright searched his pockets. "My guys will have 'em when they call in the fire mission. Why do you need them?"

"To determine which battery has the best shot, sir," Brede answered calmly. "No reason to get everybody up." He turned to his commanding officer. "Colonel Gaboury, do you have your map case handy, sir?" he asked.

Brede sat as he looked through the maps Gaboury handed him, nodding when he found the one he wanted. Propping the chosen map on his knee, he traced the coordinates he'd been given, then placed it on the couch. "You can stand your soldiers down, Colonel Wainright," he said. "The Thirty-seventh will follow your orders of course, sir. Once the fishermen in the area are evacuated and we get clearance, we'll shoot all the rounds you want at that spot on the river—but there's no submarine there, I can guarantee you that."

"Did they teach you about insubordination at OCS, lieutenant?" Wainright asked, walking to stand over Brede, staring down at him.

"Yes sir, they did," Brede replied, rising from his seat. "They also taught me how to read a map. I was at the coordinates you just gave me—or close by—two days ago, watching the Koreans fish for carp. They could walk across the Imjin there, colonel—the water's no more than three or four feet deep right now."

"Then what did my outpost see, lieutenant?" Wainright said with an angry sneer.

"Probably the branch of a tree floating down the river," Brede replied calmly. "That would be my guess, sir."

Wainright was about to say more, when Gaboury intervened. "Thank you, Wieutenant Bwede," he said quickly. "The colonel and I can handle things fwom this point." He walked briskly to the door of his quarters and held it open. "You are dismissed," he said. "Pwease escort Ms. Lake to her quarters on your way back to your hooch." He guided them both through the door, and shut it firmly—muffling the sound of loud voices that now erupted.

In the chilly darkness, Jackie Lake began walking off. Brede stopped her. "Wait up, Jackie," he said. "I've been ordered to escort you."

She shrugged. "I can find my way from here, Ex," she said. "No need to go out of your way. It's late …"

"I may be young and green, but I know how to follow orders. Come on, Jackie—don't make it hard on a butter bar."

She nodded, and waited for him to join her. "I see you're not intimidated by rank," she said. "You stood right up to Wainright."

"My dad wore eagles on his collar too," Brede said, as they walked toward the Donut Dolly quarters. "They put their trousers on the same way I do. Rank deserves respect, but not awe. What's he going to do, get me sent to Korea?"

She laughed. He lit them both a cigarette as they continued walking. "I guess you're wondering what I was doing there tonight," she said.

"None of my business, really," he replied. "Even though Wainright doesn't strike me as your type. Of course, I just met the man. He may be a sweetheart once you get to know him."

"No, he's pretty much what you saw tonight," she said. "All flab and bluster. It gets worse, the more he drinks." She wrinkled her nose. "His cigars stink, too. Thinks he's God's gift to women. He's taken a run at a few of my gals. We all stay away from him as much as we can."

"Then why …"

She rolled her eyes. "He was doing me a favor. I was at Camp Stanley, waiting for a ride back here. Wainright offered me a lift. Nothing more than that. This Imjin submarine thing came up on our way here, and he got excited. I've been stuck in the back seat of his jeep for hours, while he tried to restart the Korean War. Thank God I can finally get to bed."

He stopped and looked at her, as thoughts that had tumbled unconnected through his mind for a while suddenly fell into place. "I'm glad there's nothing between you two," he said carefully.

She laughed. "You're a little young for a chaperon, Ex," she said.

He shook his head slowly. "It's not that, Jackie," he told her. "What I felt wasn't propriety, not at all. It was jealousy. You see, I have feelings for you myself." With that, he caressed her cheek and kissed her gently. To his surprise and tremendous relief, she kissed him back.

"Wow, I'm glad that's finally over with," she said with a sigh, looking up at him. "I've been wondering if you felt what I did." She smiled, eyes flashing, and hugged him closer. "Here, do that again, Ex. It felt incredible. Then let's tiptoe to your hooch and get out of all these clothes."

Their first night was rushed and awkward, often the case with new lovers. Even so, by the time she crept from his quarters—long before a wan sun rose—both knew their time together had just begun.

Now every hour they were apart frustrated both Brede and Jackie. One or both of them had to spend days at a time away from Camp Pelham on various duties. Most of their moments together were too brief and far too public. They found peripatetic intimacy whenever they could—sometimes at her quarters, sometimes at his, sometimes in places guided by frantic ingenuity.

As their relationship blossomed, she found him to be a gentle, caring lover who valued her pleasure above his own. He in turn discovered the depth of her responses to his touch and caress—far stronger than younger women he had known. She taught him how to be a more patient, considerate partner, while he lit fires within her that surprised them both.

"I'm going to be working in and around Seoul the rest of the week," Jackie announced one evening as Kwan served them drinks at the Officers Club bar. "Get a weekend pass so we can have some quality time with each other, Ex. I'll get us a room at the Chosun Hotel. If I can keep my hands off you long enough, we could even see some of the city."

He laughed. "It's tough to get a weekend pass at the Thirty-seventh," he told her. "Ricci tells me it can't be done."

"Am I worth the effort?" she asked, knowing the answer.

"I'll figure something out," he told her.

Two nights later, the club was unusually empty. The Fifteenth was on field exercises—so many of the place's normal denizens had debarked to muddy tents and foxholes, miles distant. Ricci and Gilliam were sitting quietly at the bar, talking and nursing their drinks when Brede approached them. "Bob," he said, with more confidence than he felt, "I'm here to get a weekend pass."

Both men swung around in their barstools. Ricci frowned. "Ex, how much do you weigh these days?" he asked.

"About one-forty-five," Brede answered. "All the great food and drink at Camp Pelham have played hell with my girlish figure."

"Little more than a pup," Gilliam said, shaking his head. "Hasn't anybody told you how heavy that eight-inch round is?"

"Our S-3 tells me it comes in at more than two-hundred pounds," Brede said, nodding to Ricci.

"So how in the hell are you going to move that shell from where it sits to the top of this bar?" Gilliam went on. "Why would you want to hurt yourself like that?"

"I need a pass this weekend. So I gotta make it happen. You two will be my witnesses."

"Ex, anyone your size tries to move that round has got no more sense than a bag of cats," Gilliam warned. "Don't even attempt it."

Brede had already turned from the two men, and now approached the projectile he would have to move—in its place beside the room's brick fireplace. Dark green in color, it stood roughly three feet tall, and weighed less than a standard round since all explosives had been removed. He tipped the heavy shell forward until it fell to the floor with a loud metallic clink. Then he rolled it to the bar, trying his best not to damage the tile beneath it. When it was close enough for his purposes, Brede stopped the round's movement—careful not to get his feet or his hands caught beneath it.

Ricci applauded slowly. "Very good, Ex! Very good!," he said. "Just not good enough. The round has to be on the bar, not under it. Sorry, buddy."

"Not done yet," Brede told him. He grabbed a bamboo-legged bar stool and tipped it over on its back, then rolled and pushed the round into the stool's upholstered, chair-backed seat. "Here's where it gets tough," he said with a grimace.

Bracing himself, Brede levered the stool—working to restore it to its vertical position. He used every ounce of strength he possessed, pulling with arms and shoulders, lifting with his back and legs. Once the stool was again standing properly, he tipped the heavy projectile from the seat to the bar top, as gently as he could to avoid marring its polished wooden surface. There the big round finally sat—fully on the bar! Brede stood quietly, arms hanging at his sides. His gasps for breath were an indicator of the strength he had called up to accomplish the Herculean task.

Eventually, when his heavy breathing subsided, Brede spoke again. "Thank you, Archimedes!" he said. "I'll stand it up if you want, Bob—but I'm afraid I'll scar the bar's wood. So, do I get the pass?"

Gilliam laughed, slapping the bar. "Damn if he didn't do it!" he said between hoots. "You can't say he didn't, Ricci!"

Ricci shook his head, amazed. "I've seen people try a dozen ways to do this—men a lot bigger than you, Ex! Never saw but one man succeed, and he was a giant. I'll be damned! Sure, I'll get you your pass. What the hell is so important that you had to go through all this effort?"

"Some places in Seoul I need to see," Brede said, as he rubbed his sore upper arms. "I'd hate to go back to the states without getting off this camp at least once. Now, If I buy you guys a drink, will you help me put the damn round back where it belongs? I think I'll rupture myself if I try it alone."

Brede was called to Colonel Gaboury's office the next morning. He reported and was told to sit.

"I understand you earned a pass this weekend, young man," his battalion commander said.

"Yes, sir," Brede responded, nodding and grinning widely.

"Wieutenant Wicci has made them hard to come by, yet you succeeded where many others have failed," Gaboury observed. "Wicci says it was wemarkable."

"Thank you, sir."

"That night at my quarters, a few weeks ago—that was pwetty wemarkable too."

"Sir?"

"You saved the battalion a lot of twouble, and prevwented Colonel Wainright from behaving foolishly. Not bad for a second wieutenant."

"Just doing my job, sir. I am your S-2."

"Even so, it's good to get some appwiciation once in a while. My dwiver will take you to Seoul on Saturday. Have a good time, Ex. You've earned it."

Brede found himself smiling a lot the rest of the day.

That Saturday, at a little past fifteen-hundred hours, he climbed from Colonel Gaboury's jeep in front of Seoul's well-known Chosun Hotel, wearing a slightly dusty dark blue suit he'd had made at the little PX on Camp Pelham. He found Jackie waiting for him in the lobby, standing under a large, glittering crystal chandelier (from Louis Tiffany, he later learned) wearing a pretty light green dress that showed off great legs. Left speechless, he mutely reached for her outstretched hand. "Right on time!" she said, flashing a smile that seemed to brighten the room around him.

"Come along. Bring your gym bag with you. Let's have a drink and celebrate a little. Oh Ex, I'm so glad you're here!"

Holding his hand tightly, she guided him to a booth in the nearby bar. She glided to her seat as he stumbled in the whirlwind of her wake. "Aren't you going to say anything?" she asked.

"I'm overwhelmed, Jackie," he replied, looking around, blinking. "Remember, I've been stuck at Camp Pelham since August. All this is a lot to take in. And you—you look terrific! I'm glad we're together, without having to tiptoe around. Sure, let's have a drink. Hell, let's have several. I've been waiting all week to be with you."

A pretty waitress wearing a traditional hanbok approached the table. "Welcome to the Chosun," she said in perfect English. "May I take your drink order?"

Remembering his last off-base Korean drinking experience, in the seedy grime of ASCOM City, Brede had difficulty stifling a laugh. "You probably know what's good, better than I do," he said to Jackie. "Got any suggestions?"

She smiled, nodded, and turned to the waitress. "Two soju cocktails, please," she said. "Soju is the local whiskey here, Ex. I think you'll like it."

The drinks came quickly and they toasted each other—her smile still radiant, his grin still dopey. "So, your first time in Seoul?" she asked.

"First time south of Munsan," he told her. "Unless you count a very forgettable evening at a dive in ASCOM City. This is quite a place," he said, looking around. "I didn't think I'd see anything so impressive here, after the war and all."

She nodded. "I've stayed here before, so I did a little investigating. This hotel was built by German architects, after the Japs took over Korea. All that reddish-brown brick you see is specially made. They put the first elevator in the whole nation here. All pretty grand—except they tore down Korea's most important monument to make room. All that's left is the Hwangudan Shrine. It's nearby. Maybe we'll get a chance to see it tomorrow."

"Tomorrow?"

"Yes, my dear. We're going to spend the rest of today and tonight right here at the hotel. You and I have some catching up to do. First, we'll …"

He interrupted, guiding her mouth to his. They kissed, long and deep, as he held her face in his hands. "I'm hoping that's what you meant," he whispered.

"Mmmm, exactly what I meant," she sighed.

He reached for his bag. "No reason to wait," he told her.

Several hours later, over a delicious dinner in the hotel restaurant, they toasted each other with champagne. "Here's to being here," Brede said, raising his flute. "You have no idea what I had to do to get this pass."

"I've watched men a lot bigger than you try to move that enormous piece of steel … and fail, Ex," Jackie said, suddenly puzzled. "I still can't believe you were able to succeed. How did you do it?"

After he told her, they both laughed. "Even with all the planning, it was no cakewalk," he continued. "My back and arms were sore as hell the next day. Still, it was all worth it. I'd do anything to get next to you, Jackie. You are incredible."

"You're pretty special yourself, mister …" As she started to say more, the band on the dais began to play.

"That's it!" Brede exclaimed. Rising from their table, he took her hand. "We have to dance," he said.

She rose and he led her to the dance floor. "I'm not much of a dancer," he told her, "but this tune is special."

"What makes it so unique?" she asked, confused.

"Back at Camp Pelham—that first night you and I talked, this was playing on Armed Forces Radio," Brede told her. "*Moonglow*. I'll never forget it as long as I live. Whenever I think of you, this song pops into my head, Jackie. It will always be special to me, because of you."

She buried her head in his shoulder and kissed his cheek. "This will be our song, then," she said. "Always."

Later on, they rested on the wide hotel room bed, having penetrated and caressed each other to a contented state of bliss. She lay on her back, as he explored her breasts with tongue and touches. Small, firm, upturned, they showed large areolas and prominent, erect nipples—which he nibbled and sucked gently.

"Ahhh," she murmured, "that's very nice," and reached for him once more.

"They're too small," she said later, continuing to stroke him lazily.

"What do you mean?" he asked, his words muffled as his head rested in her lap, kissing her inner thigh—working his way toward her clitoris.

"My breasts," she sighed. "Way too small. Some of my ladies have much larger."

"Yours are just right," he insisted. "Fit my mouth perfectly. Here, let me show you," and he did, assigning his nimble fingers to complete the journey his lips had begun.

Morning began with the best of intentions, but a shower together led to damp, energetic bed top activity instead. They made it up and dressed on their next attempt to rise, and got to breakfast in the hotel dining room just after nine.

"I'm determined to get you to the Hwangudan Shrine," Jackie said, biting hungrily into her omelet.

"My plans are less ambitious," said Brede. "All I want to do is find a place I haven't kissed you yet, and eliminate the oversight. It's a simple objective that even a butter bar lieutenant can understand."

She licked her lips. "How will you attain this victory, soldier?" she asked, careful to sip her coffee with both hands.

"My forces are already rising to full attention," he told her, grinning. "Two plans present themselves. I can start at the top and work my way down, or start at the bottom and work up." He shook his head. "Neither strategy is foolproof. To make sure I'm thorough, I'll have to do both."

Jackie looked at her watch. "I guess culture will have to give way to military expedients," she said, eyes bright. "We have about three hours before they throw us out of this hotel. You'd better get started." Smiling happily, she led him from the restaurant. As they reached the elevator, she laughed.

"What's so funny?" Brede asked as he punched their floor button.

"I'll confess. I had an idea events might lead this way," Jackie admitted, "so I didn't put on any underwear." She rubbed against him as proof.

He nodded, gently lifting her hand to kiss her palm. "I had the same hope," he told her softly, "so I didn't either."

CHAPTER NINE

CHRISTMAS ELF

During the second week of December, Brede was sent to D Battery to learn assembly of the eight-inch howitzer's nuclear artillery round. While he was there, he was instructed by First Lieutenant Jack Farr, the battery's AXO—who was in charge of nuclear round assembly. Farr, a graduate of University of Chicago, was nearing both the end of his tour and his time in the Army. Tall and thin, Farr's short-cropped brown hair hugged his head like a mat. His dark eyes sat deeply hooded beneath heavy brows, giving his pale, gaunt face an almost Neanderthalic cast. A flat nose over a small mouth, prominent ears, and a long, narrow chin completed his remarkable visage. His irritable nature fit his appearance.

"I hear they like you at battalion, Brede," Farr told him when they met. "That gets you no points with me. They're all assholes—every fucking one of them. Just learn what they sent you here for—as quick as your tiny mind can grasp it—then get out of my hair. Understand? I'm too short for this shit."

Brede nodded and kept his thoughts to himself. Farr got no points with him, either.

"Unlike the W48 you've been playing with, the W33 actually has to be put together," Farr explained early the next morning, outside the assembly vehicle they were about to enter. "Lots more steps to take, lots more mistakes to make—and you'll make them all, Brede. Come on, get your ass in the truck," he said, pulling open the vehicle's back door. "Let's get started."

The W48's technology was similar to the world's earliest atomic bomb—the "Little Boy" dropped on Hiroshima—according to Farr. It was a gun-type device that shot a slug of fissile uranium (oralloy) through an annular ring of the same material. While neither component had enough nuclear material to cause an explosion separately, when the slug passed through the ring their marriage was sufficient. Both the slug and the ring were shot at each other using a "double gun mechanism," minimizing the amount of oralloy necessary—decreasing the weight of the round enough for a gun crew to handle. Precise timing for both shots was controlled by a sophisticated clock mechanism, carefully set when the round was assembled.

"So, assembly has three important stages," Farr went on, standing in the assembly truck. "Inserting the double gun into the round, loading the gun, and setting the clocks. All the rest is just closing things up and putting the shell in the howitzer. Any questions so far?"

"Where do the clock settings come from?" Brede asked.

"They're printed right here in the manual," Farr sneered. "That should be obvious."

"Can the round go off before it's loaded and fired from the howitzer?"

"Damn good question, for a change. I don't get one often. Yeah, it's possible. The double gun can be fired by hand, and the clocks could be set wrong. Unlikely, wouldn't normally happen. Couldn't, if you follow the assembly manual—but conceivable, if you really fucked things up."

"Would that cause a fizzle, or a full detonation?"

Farr shook his head, suddenly angry again. "We're not here to discuss science fiction. As far as you're concerned, Brede, if it's not in the manual it can't happen. Understand me?"

The tempo of his training was much like what he'd previously gotten. Every day, Brede would put the round together as Farr read him directions, verbatim from the manual. Then they'd switch places, and he'd read the manual aloud as Farr preformed the assembly.

One section of the manual enraged Farr, and he vented his anger on Brede. "See that picture," he said, eyes flashing as he pointed to an illustration. "That's supposed to show you how to lift the annular ring assembly out of its container and place it in the gun."

"Okay," Brede replied. "We've done it a million times so far this week, I think. what's the problem?"

"The problem, you asshole, is that you can't lift the damn ring assembly like that—with both hands on top. It's physically impossible. Go ahead, try it."

So Brede did. Until now, he had lifted the assembly with one hand on top of the wrench-like tool holding it, prying with other hand underneath it. It was heavy, but the process was doable. However, his strength did not allow him to lift the same weight with both hands holding the tool from the top. Without leverage, he couldn't move it.

"Huh," he said. "I never noticed that before. Looks like the illustration has an error."

Farr howled in anguish. "You're goddamn right it has an error. Goddamn right! So why do I get gigged for it in every fucking TPI I've been through?"

Brede shrugged. "Maybe they just don't like you, Farr," he said.

To his surprise, Farr nodded. "I've thought about that," he said, his voice suddenly small as he glanced around the assembly truck. "It's the only reason that makes sense."

After that, Brede redoubled his efforts to master what he had to learn and get back to Camp Pelham—convinced that Farr was a loon. Within ten days, he was in his seat at the Officers Club bar, buying Jackie a martini once more.

"I've missed you," she told him.

"I can hardly keep myself from gathering you up and running to my hooch," Brede said. "I know that's not very romantic, but being away from you these days is like being without food or water, Jackie. A world without you just doesn't work very well."

"Calm down, Ex," she said with a smile. "Later on it gets better, for both of us. Anticipation will make it splendid." As usual, she was right.

"Ex, I need your help," she said the next time they met.

"If I can do it, you know I will," he answered grinning. "I'm big on volunteering. Look where it's gotten me so far."

His irony made her smile. "It's gotten us each other," she retorted. "Even if it took Korea to make it happen."

"I'd go anywhere to be near you, Jackie. So, how can I help?"

"There's an orphanage not far from here," she told him. "It's only for Amerasians—kids with G.I. fathers who left them behind. The Koreans don't treat them very well. They're not allowed the education or government services full-blooded Korean children get. It's been a project of mine to help out however I can."

"You never told me about this before …"

"Those of us who try to assist keep it to ourselves. If Korean officials discovered all we do, they'd make it harder on those kids—and they already suffer enough. Anyhow, Christmas is coming. I need a Santa Claus to give out the gifts. It'll take a day or two of your time, but I'll sweeten the pot: we can spend a couple of nights together while we're there. So, what do you say? Are you in?"

"I'd be in if I had to walk home alone both nights, Jackie. I'm not going to make much of a Santa, though—not enough meat on these bones. How about if I'm 'The Christmas Elf' instead? If you can rustle up some green clothing dye, we can put a costume together."

"I can handle that," she said laughing. "You'll have to get Colonel Gaboury's approval for the time you'll spend there. Think he'll sign off?"

The next morning, Brede planted himself in front of Gilliam's desk. "I've got a special request, Will," he said.

The S-1 looked up, frowning. "This ain't one of them last-minute 'home for Christmas' requests, is it Ex? Too late, partner—that dog can't hunt."

"Nope," Brede said, shaking his head, "don't need to get that far. No further than *Ujeongbu*. I will need two days off post, from the twenty-fourth through the twenty-fifth."

"That needs the colonel's approval," Gilliam said. "What's it all about?"

Once the plight of the Amerasian orphans was explained to him, Gilliam became enthusiastic. "Let's go see the colonel right now," He said. "I'm sure I can get you in. Where do you come up with these ideas, Ex?"

"Some nights, when I least expect it, an angel whispers in my ear," Brede answered with a wistful smile. "I never know when it's coming." In the back of his mind, a clarinet played *Moonglow*. At that moment, he realized he had fallen in love with Jackie.

Gaboury was excited by the concept. "Is there anything the battalion can do to help?" he asked.

"You should speak to Jackie Lake about that, sir, "Brede replied. "She knows a lot more about the whole matter than I do. Hell, all I'm doing is playing a skinny Santa Claus."

Later on, at the Officers Club, Jackie was full of news. "Your colonel is the sweetest man," she told Brede. "He's going to arrange a Christmas dinner with all the fixings for the kids at the orphanage, and send some blankets and clothing along as gifts."

"He signed off on my pass," Brede said. "I'll get you a pair of my long-johns, so you can dye them green, along with some socks. We'll make this a great Christmas for the kids."

"You made it all happen, you know," Jackie said, flashing a smile that lit up the room.

"Just shows what a guy will do to get near you, sweetheart," Brede said.

That Christmas morning, the Amerasian children in the orphanage outside *Ujeongbu* woke to find a big Christmas tree in the central room they used to take their meals. Of course, it wasn't a real tree. Instead, Sergeant Altobelli's soldiers had constructed an ingenious wooden frame-work, from which they'd hung paper, tinfoil, and other slapped-together decorations to mimic a six-foot pine bedecked for the special day. Below the ersatz tree lay packages, one for each of the twenty-seven children in the home. The parcels held chocolates, chewing gum, oranges, and other sweets—as well as desperately needed socks, blankets, and clothing. The same truck that delivered the tree had brought along turkey dinner for everyone there—including stuffing, sweet potatoes, cranberry sauce, Christmas ham, and three kinds of pie—enough to overflow the big table from which they all ate.

"I'll be back tomorrow morning to pick up the food containers," Sergeant Dill told Brede as he climbed into his truck to leave. "Please take plenty of photos, sir. A lot of guys worked hard on the tree and the packages. They'll want to see how things turned out."

He saluted. Brede felt slightly foolish returning his salute in the costume he was wearing, but he did anyhow. "You guys did a wonderful job," he said, as the deuce-and-a-half shifted gears to pull away. "Don't worry. I'll get you plenty of film." He waved as the truck left the orphanage courtyard, then turned and went back inside the building.

As he entered, the children were beginning to rise from their pallets and come to the common room. When he looked at them, Brede's heart swelled. Their eyes sparkled with surprise and joy at the sight of the big tree—now lit with twinkling candles. Their mouths hung open in wonder.

This was obviously the first near-western Christmas any of them had ever seen. Each was drawn to the tree when he came into the room, as a moth to a flame. They stood around it, quiet and still. While they did, Brede looked from face to face. The features of the boys he saw gathered in the flickering candlelight varied remarkably. Some looked purely Caucasian, while others had African-American features. Some bore the epicanthal folds of Asia in their eyes, but many did not. Complexions varied from saffron to umber. The group ranged in age from under five to mid-teenage. The only real commonality among the boys was that all were in this dingy room, at this dilapidated place. "Where are the little girls?" he whispered to Jackie, who stood near him.

She turned, fitfully brushing away a tear gathering in her eye. "No girls come here," she answered him. "They're too valuable in the sex trades. Our G. I.'s like girls who look a little western. They're all sold off or taken."

Mr. and Mrs. Bae, who ran the orphanage, gently guided the boys to the big table—now piled high with Christmas fare. They sat, and murmured what was obviously a prayer. Then all dug into the meal before them.

As the boys ate, Mrs. Bae approached Brede and Jackie. "There is so much food here," she said. "We cannot eat it all now. Some must be stored outside for days to come. My husband and I both thank you, though he has no English. You are far too generous." The small woman bowed, then moved away.

After an hour or so, the remaining food was carefully put away—in outdoor cupboards where the bitter winter cold would preserve it. There was plenty left for future meals, Brede was glad to see. Mrs. Bae approached again, and Jackie explained what would happen next. "We've brought along gifts for each of the children," she said. "Tell them to rise when you call each by name, and approach our 'Christmas Elf' (nodding with a smile to Brede, who blushed). He will give every boy his gift."

Brede stood and moved in front of the construct tree, his costume fully revealed to the boys at the table for the first time. He hoped few of Jackie's photos were wasted on him. In his mind, he looked terribly silly. He wore long woolen underwear died a brilliant green, decorated with red and white wool pom-poms. A green sock sat on top of his head, with a very large red pom-pom dangling from its tip. His feet were similarly shorn. Jackie had added insult to injury by painting his cheeks and nose with bright red lipstick. He knew when a snapshot of him in this get-up reached the Thirty-seventh, he'd become the butt of severe derision. He decided he didn't care. The only really important matter was how these children felt on this special day.

He handed each child's packet away as they passed before him. He tried to read their eyes while they received their gifts—usually no more than some candy, some fruit, some clothing that might fit. This part of Korea now endured bleak winter. Wind-driven sleet whipped along the hard frozen ground outside. The room around them was barely warm enough to keep breath invisible, and everyone wore layers of whatever clothing was available. Brede wondered if the gifts he placed in each boy's hands might make the difference between needed warmth and the shivering palsy of chill in this hard place.

Some of the boys—especially those older—looked away from him as he tried to see what was in their eyes. These adolescents would soon have to leave the scant security they'd known at the orphanage, and find their own way in a nation that would shun them at every turn. Without education and the paperwork others their age took for granted, their chances to rise above the meanest levels of Korean society were nonexistent. They would be pariahs in their own country, despised by even the lowest around them, and they knew it. Their downward gaze reflected dawning hopelessness.

The younger children's eyes still shone with hope. Many could remember the love of a mother—a few the touch of a father. Confused by where they found themselves, they were at least content to be part of a place that gave them warmth, care, and companionship. They still smiled, with both their eyes and their faces.

Once the gifts were given, Brede retired to a bench at the rear of the room—where he and Jackie watched the children play and trade their gifts between one another. Little was said. He enjoyed watching her pleasure as the happiness continued around her—the glow of her smile, the joy in her eyes. After a while, he went outside. She joined him.

"I don't think I've ever seen you so happy," he said, lighting cigarettes and handing one to her.

"You have no idea!" she replied, her eyes dancing. "I've been trying to work out some way to help these kids—really help them—for months now. Turns out, all I had to do was get you involved. You're fantastic!"

Brede shook his head, blushing. "I can't take the credit, Jackie. All I did was talk to my CO. This is your achievement, with his help and some hard work from a lot of other people—I played a very small part."

"You were the catalyst that got everything started. Don't try to talk me out of it." Jackie put her hands to her ears, a big smile on her face.

Brede led her to a nearby bench, where they both sat. He reached into his field jacket, brought out a small package, and placed it in her hand. "The orphans aren't the only ones getting gifts today," he said, kissing her cheek. "This is for you, Jackie."

She opened the package to find a small wooden box nestled in the wrapping paper. Within the box was a fine gold chain, with a golden pennant in the image of an angel hung from it. "This is your guardian angel, darling," he told her. "It's very old, been passed down through my family for generations. My grandmother gave it to me, and now it's yours. Someday, you'll give it to someone you decide should have it. Until then, my ancestors' prayers will protect and guide you. Merry Christmas, Jackie."

She held the beautiful pennant in the palm of her hand. Somehow, it seemed heavier than its apparent weight. "This is beautiful, Ex ... but I can't accept it. Your family couldn't possibly want to part with such an heirloom." She started to hand it back.

Brede smiled and shrugged. "Sorry," he said softly. "Once given, it can't be returned. Besides, my grandmother made me swear to make sure it never left the family. I intend to honor that oath."

Jackie frowned, confused. "I don't understand," she said.

"Simple really," Brede said with a smile. "The angel can't leave the family, so you'll just have to marry me. That works out well because I love you so much."

"Oh, Ex," she said, shaking her head. "I love you too—more than I could ever tell you, but a marriage would never work. The age difference ..."

"Doesn't mean a damn thing to me, now that I know you, Jackie. Stop getting yourself upset. Just say 'yes,' and the rest of it will work out. Please make me the happiest elf on the planet."

She put her arms around his neck, and kissed him deeply. Cruel wind whistled around them, but she felt only warmth. She wondered if the pennant was working its magic even now. "You're right," she said, making up her mind. "I say yes. I do love you. I never want to be with anyone else."

Later on, over a dinner of warmed c-rations, Jackie had a question. "What would you have done if I'd said 'no,'" she asked him, the guardian angel now nestled warm against her bosom.

Brede thought for a moment before answering. "I hoped you'd say 'yes,' but I couldn't be sure," he told her. "All I really knew for certain was that I had to ask. When you love somebody the way I love you, you have to try. My feelings for you would be the same, no matter what you'd said. I know you're the only woman in the world I want next to me, Jackie. I'd have been very sad, but nothing else would have changed. You own my heart. You always will."

"We'll need to make some plans ..."

"Yes, we will," he interrupted, "but not tonight, darling. Tonight is for the kids here ... and for an angel who has found a new home."

CHAPTER TEN

COFRAM AND
PASADENA

B ack at Camp Pelham, Brede got work the next morning to find a gaudy envelope lying atop his S-2 in-basket. "Came while you were at the orphanage, sir," Grady told him. "You sure were something in that 'Christmas Elf' get-up, lieutenant. I'm sending copies of those pictures home to my folks. They'll get a big kick out of them!"

"I'll bet they will," Brede said with a sigh. As he sat at his desk he opened the big envelope. In embossed, raised print, the card within it required him to make himself present at fourteen-hundred hours on December 29th **"... at a year-end reception in Honor of Colonel Arthur Wainright, Commanding Officer, 2nd Brigade, 2nd Infantry Division, to be held at the Officers Open Mess, Camp Red Cloud, ROK."** Class A uniform required. RSVP. He immediately took himself to Will Gilliam.

"Yeah, yours matches mine," the S-1 told him. "Every officer in this part of Korea got one. Pretty, ain't it? Gaboury has one just like it. Unless you've got a medic's buck slip or a special assignment, you'll be there with the rest of us, freezing your butt off. It's ridiculous, but what can you do?"

"The guy's a real asshole, Will," Brede said. "Can you get me out of it?"

"Too late, partner. Ricci got duty officer. Nothing else available. Nope, if you're not down with the plague you'll be there, same as me. By the way, loved those photos of you at the orphanage. The colonel liked them too. If you don't make the Army your career, maybe you should head for Hollywood."

He stopped in the long hallway on the way back to his filing cabinet citadel to light a cigarette. Looking up he saw Major Rafferty purposefully striding his way. "Good morning, sir," he piped, hoping any trouble would pass him by.

"There's a convoy of ten-ton trucks coming up the road, lieutenant," the XO told him, looking intently into his eyes, "full of special artillery ammunition—all classified top-secret." He looked at his watch. "It should be here in about twenty minutes. That gives you ten minutes to work up a security plan with a guard-duty roster and get it to me for approval."

Brede nodded. "On it, sir. Can you tell me what this stuff is? Why it's classified so high?"

Rafferty shrugged. "I don't know what it is, Brede. The message refers to it as COFRAM.   We're getting six-hundred rounds to distribute to the firing batteries, plus two-hundred eight inch for D Battery. Until they come to get their shares, we'll have to guard it all here. We'll need to set up a perimeter, surround it with barbed wire, and secure it 24-7. You've used up two of your ten minutes. Better get to work."

By the time he brought his security plan to Rafferty's office, Brede could hear the engines of the big trucks as they labored up the rise to Camp Pelham's main gate. He put the plan, compete with guard duty roster, on the major's desk. Rafferty glanced through it, a scowl growing on his face. "Do you think this is some kind of joke, lieutenant?" the XO said, throwing the hand-written notes across his desk.

"No, sir." Brede replied.

"Then how do you account for the names on this roster? You've got most of battalion staff—including you and me—on this list." He shook his head. "I expected much better from you, Ex."

"Sir, you did say the classification of this ammo—this COFRAM— was top secret, did you not?"

Rafferty nodded, still frowning.

"Sir, there are only twelve people in the battalion who have that clearance—not counting Colonel Gaboury and Sergeant Barr, who have to be exempt, and Sergeant Overshaft, who has a medical waiver. The rest of us will have to pull a four-hour shift guarding those rounds on a rotating schedule, every day. I've outlined the schedule for you, sir."

"This is ridiculous!"

"Unless you can get that ammo declassified, we have no option, sir."

As he stood there, Brede could see the first of a long line of huge trucks unloading ammunition crates in the big, muddy field in front of the S-4 shack.

For a few seconds, nothing more was said. Rafferty glowered at Brede—who stood in formal "at ease" posture and tried his best to remain calm.

"Get out of here," the XO finally said. "I've got some calls to make."

Within the hour, Brede was informed that although the ammunition would remain classified top-secret, Second Division headquarters had reduced the necessary clearance for those securing or transporting it to "classified." He told Overshaft to set up a guard roster with Sergeant Altobelli, and arrange for concertina wire to secure the growing perimeter, as the big olive-drab crates continued to be dumped and piled in the field outside his window. "Another tin-pot crisis removed from my life," he thought—and got back to his normal work, still wondering what the hell that odd COFRAM acronym stood for. In just four months, he would know for certain.

Two days later, under the slate skies of a particularly frigid, sleet-blown morning, Brede joined the rest of the Thirty-seventh's officers in a convoy of jeeps that crept over treacherous, muddy, snow-streaked roads to Camp Red Cloud's Officers Club. Most wore heavy parkas and carefully bloused their Class A uniform trousers into ugly but practical galoshes.

They arrived after hours of slow going, numb from cold even in their winter gear. They parked in a field beside the building, alongside more than a hundred other vehicles from every Army unit in the Second Infantry Division's Second Brigade—a substantial military force now completely incapacitated while its leaders paid respects to their commander.

Brede walked with Gilliam, Diamond, and several others from the Thirty-seventh, through a crowd of infantrymen, tankers, engineers, military police, and others who languished in the slush outside the club, which was closed and locked. Brede looked at his watch. "I guess they're going to keep us out here until fourteen-hundred," he said to no one in particular. "That gives us another ten minutes to acclimate ourselves." He shrugged, reached into his parka for a cigarette.

Others gathered at the shuttered door, including some more senior officers, were far less sanguine. A few circled the hexagonal building, trying to find some way in, to no avail. Some beat mightily on the locked doors, and heard only the echoes of their efforts. Two battalion commanders stormed back to their jeeps to transmit infuriated radio messages concerning the situation, but no responses were received. This would be the perfect time for a North Korean attack, Brede mused as he watched the tableau unfold around him. The whole brigade could be decapitated in one fell swoop.

At precisely fourteen-hundred hours a lone jeep made its way to the building's entrance. A lieutenant emerged from it with a piece of paper in his hand, which he quickly taped to the Officers Club door. His mission accomplished, he left immediately—without having uttered a word.

Those closest to the door immediately converged to read what had been posted. Having done so, they turned and walked away, shaking their heads. Some laughed, while others frowned in jaw-locked ire. Brede moved through the crowd that now pressed to read the typed message, which was brief and to the point:

"Colonel Wainright sends his regrets. He has gained tickets to the Rose Bowl. As a devoted USC alumni he cannot pass them up. He's on his way to Pasadena. Go Trojans! Happy new year!"

Back at Camp Pelham that evening—nestled in his semi-reserved seat by the bar, warmed and relaxed by two stiff scotch and waters—Brede wondered aloud how the antics of a man like Wainright could be tolerated by an otherwise severe military. Major Rafferty, who had come by for his evening libation, heard and answered.

"The Army issues each of us exactly enough rope to hang ourselves," the acerbic major said, as he looked calmly around the bar. "Colonel Wainright's ration is apparently greater than most of us draw, enough for a long drop." He finished his drink and left.

Later that week, Jackie returned to Camp Pelham from an extended DMZ tour with her ladies, as all prepared for new year's eve. Kwan stocked extra bottles of champagne, and brought out the posters of passing year's old man with new year's baby to hang above the bar. A box of party hats and noise-makers, some dating from many years back, was placed where those who wanted them could take what they needed.

The tide of bureaucratic paperwork rose at the Thirty-seventh's headquarters, as year-end reports of all sizes and levels of importance became due. At his small desk in S-2, Brede found himself busier than usual preparing, editing, checking, and signing a pile of paperwork that seemed to grow of its own accord every evening after he and Overshaft left for the day. "Year-end is a busy time," the old sergeant told him, "maybe the busiest we get all year. Don't worry. Either we'll get through it or we'll all die from paper cuts."

The extra workload kept Brede at his desk far past his normal schedule. He didn't see Jackie until after twenty-hundred hours for three nights running. The time they were able to share was focused on her need for planning and clarification. He answered every question she posed with effortless, breezy certitude.

"The future's simple," he told her over a drink. "You'll get out of the Red Cross, and we'll go on together to my next assignment—where I'll make captain unless I really screw up. You'll find a university where you can get your masters in nursing. Once you've done that, I'll bail out of the Army and finish up my college. Then, the whole world will open up for us, sweetheart."

"We can get the rings anytime," he explained on another occasion. "There are plenty of nice ones in the PX catalog, and there's shops in Seoul. Or—we can wait until we hit the states, and you can pick out whatever you want!"

"We'll get married in a little California town I know about—San Luis Obispo, right on the ocean," he whispered as they lay in each other's arms one night. "There's a little Swedish village nearby called Solvang. Great place for a honeymoon."

"You seem to have this all figured out," she said, laughing softly as he stroked her thigh. "I hope it all works out exactly as you see it, Ex. The world has a way of throwing monkey wrenches into all the wonderful plans people make."

He frowned. "You're not getting cold feet are you? Please say no, Jackie."

"No, Ex—no cold feet. No matter how the future treats us, whatever happens, I'll be yours."

January was a dreamy time for the two lovers, who decided to keep their betrothal plans under wraps—at least until the end of Jackie's tour in May, when she'd announce her resignation from the Red Cross. "I'll meet you at the Fairmont Hotel in San Francisco on September eighteenth," he told her, "as soon as I'm off the plane from Kimpo. I'll have a month's leave coming, so we can drive down to San Luis Obispo and get married at the Spanish mission there. You'll have plenty of time to pick out a nice wedding dress. I'll wear my dress blues, of course. My heart's so filled with love for you I think sometimes it's going to burst."

She laughed. "Ex, you are always so upbeat. There's miles of details to take care of between now and then, tons of things to get done. Do you want any guests? How about any I might want? My mother's dead, my father's in a nursing home—but what about your family?"

"Mom and dad divorced, not long after I joined the Army," he explained. "They don't talk to each other, and neither one talks to me. I haven't heard from my sister in a long time. If you don't want any guests, I guess it will just be the two of us. That's fine with me."

The discussions continued, plans and dreams that grew more solid and sure as January progressed. Brede's work at the Thirty-seventh continued, as the battalion prepared for more inspections as well as field exercises in June. Then, on the twenty-first, any semblance of calm disappeared. On that Sunday, North Korean dictator Kim Il Sung dispatched thirty-one special troops to assassinate South Korea's President Park Chung Hee—at his residence in the hills above Seoul.

This was the famous "Blue House Raid." By moving quickly over the mountains that form the spine of the Korean peninsula, some of the North Korean commandos successfully evaded all attempts to interdict them. They got within two hundred yards of the presidential residence before all but one were captured or killed. In the meantime, the entire Second Infantry Division was stirred into a hornet's nest of activity—from which the Thirty-seventh was not exempt.

Every military unit from the DMZ to Seoul was placed on high alert. No one knew at the time whether the raid was a singular event or the harbinger of more generalized aggression. Monday saw Brede in full combat gear, awaiting possible orders to move with his unit to the first of several pre-planned alternative locations. Everyone was tense, and what little news was heard echoed through the halls of battalion headquarters as quickly as it came off Sergeant Barr's teletype. Rumors, firefights, and casualties on both sides continued to be reported through Tuesday. Altogether, four U.S. soldiers and twenty-six South Korean troops were killed before the raiders were stopped. Twenty-nine of the North Korean commandos were killed, while one was captured and another escaped back across the DMZ. Ominously, on the same date, North Vietnamese troops began their attempt to destroy the U.S. combat base at Khe Sanh, in South Vietnam. Planners at the Pentagon wondered initially whether the two assaults were coordinated.

On Tuesday, in the midst of this turmoil, Kim Il Sung's navy seized a U.S. intelligence ship in the Sea of Japan. Commander Lloyd Bucher and his crew of eighty-two were captured and imprisoned. Their ship, the U.S.S. Pueblo, was commandeered and towed to a North Korean port. Later that week, Ricci and Brede were shown the coordinates of the place Pueblo's crew was being held—only sixty tantalizing miles from the DMZ. Could they be rescued with a lightning raid? Contingency plans were under study, and Wainright howled for the opportunity. Still, by week's end calmer heads prevailed. U.S. troops in Korea began to relax as fears of more immediate hostilities declined. Work got back to normal. No one in the Thirty-seventh wore a steel pot to work on Monday.

The following day, the '68 Tet Offensive erupted. As battles raged throughout Vietnam, U.S. forces in South Korea braced again for what might become an aligned assault from the north. When that threat dissipated, Brede and others finally breathed a sigh of relief. Tensions along the DMZ remained high through February, but the imminence of general war on the peninsula diminished substantially.

Brede's butter bar turned silver, as he was promoted to first lieutenant. He and Jackie continued weaving their dreams and plans, cautiously hopeful that world events would not disrupt them. The shortest month ended, and the slowly warming days of March saw the bitter land around them begin to thaw.

INTERLOG
Washington, DC, 1968

On that Wednesday evening in late February, Walter Cronkite looked directly into the eyes of millions of Americans from his news desk, through their television screens, into their hearts and minds. "To say we are closer to victory today is to believe, in the face of the evidence, the optimists who have been wrong in the past," he told them. "To suggest we are on the edge of defeat is to yield to unreasonable pessimism," he continued gravely. "To say that we are mired in stalemate seems the only realistic, yet unsatisfactory conclusion."

President Lyndon Johnson turned off the television monitors that surrounded his oval office desk: NBC, ABC, CBS, all of them. A terrible sadness fell upon him. He saw his political career coming to an end, the victim of a senseless war in an Asian backwater. Much of the good he had accomplished would be pushed aside. He could not run for re-election, to gain the time he needed to finish great programs only just begun. "If I've lost Cronkite," he realized, "I've lost middle America."

The 1968 Tet assaults would cost him his future, Johnson concluded—even though the North Vietnamese and their southern allies hadn't been able to win a single battle or hold a single piece of contested ground. The pure public relations of their fighting was enough, it seemed—for Cronkite and for the nation.

The next day, he called Clifford to his office. Clark Clifford—the man he had chosen to replace a burned out, faltering McNamara—would know what to do about all this. Johnson used to joke about the tall, elegantly slim, careful lawyer who had been a senior advisor to powerful men in Washington since Truman's era. "There's not an edge on him," LBJ would gibe. "He's slick as a goddamn whistle. If Clark was ever the eleventh man in a ten-man elevator, he'd just naturally squirt the fuck right out."

Clifford would know what to do. He would know what levers of power could be pulled to bring this disastrous situation back under control. They met in seclusion. No notes were taken, no others were in the room.

Both men agreed that Johnson's future could not be salvaged. The knives were out. If he attempted to run, Bobby Kennedy would flank him. He might not even win the nomination. His time in office would end next January.

"These bastards, these NVA, they've screwed me, Clark," he growled. "They've ruined my dreams, damaged the country. What can I do to punish them—really hurt them—in the time I've got left, without killing a lot more of our boys?"

Clifford, who had been studying his soon-to-be predecessor's files in preparation for taking over the defense job, raised an eyebrow. "Well, Mr. President, there is Tollbooth. You've been sitting on it since November, hesitating to pull the trigger. It promises severe damage to Ho Chi Minh's plans in a hurry, and should force him to negotiate in Paris from a greatly weakened position. As a plus, it will make the Soviets happy and anger the Chinese."

Johnson looked up. "Oh yeah, that Tollbooth thing," he said—bringing back to mind an issue he had nearly forgotten. "What the hell, Clark. McNamara and the chiefs told me it wouldn't work. Something about the soil being wrong."

Clifford shook his head. "The basaltic, clay-like soil around Khe Sanh is not optimum for nuclear weapons," he said, "that's true. Still, the nukes will take out the Ho Chi Minh Trail just fine, Mr. President. McNamara didn't want to have their use on his conscience." The National Security Action Memorandum was signed the next day.

In the month that followed, Johnson seemed to many who watched him to have recognized the nation's inability to prevail in Vietnam. He denied Westmoreland 200,000 additional troops he'd requested, and signaled through diplomatic channels the nation's willingness to open peace talks and limit bombing. Finally, on the last day of March, he announced during a televised address to the nation that "… I shall not seek, nor will I accept, the nomination of my party for another term as your president."

He would still beat those bastards, Johnson thought to himself after the speech. He would make those commies pay for what they'd done.

BOOK TWO
THE HILL

CHAPTER ELEVEN

STRANGERS

Korea is a place of extremes. The winters are bitterly cold, the summers tropically hot and humid. Heavy monsoons sweep the peninsula in midyear, causing widespread flooding. Still, as the ravages of winter fade and summer's blistering heat has yet to return, the area around *Munsan* enjoys spring respite. It is a time of hope—when new seeds are planted, new enterprises begun.

The men arrived without warning or fanfare, in a nondescript deuce-and-a-half truck. They came to Camp Pelham mid-morning on March fifth, after a long drive from Kimpo and a series of longer plane flights before that: fourteen men, anonymous in brand-new unmarked fatigues, rank badges pinned to their collars. As they dropped from the back of the truck that had brought them, they stretched, grabbed their duffle bags, and formed into two ranks of five men each, with their commanding officer, XO, and senior NCOs standing before them. The teams were called to attention, then ordered to stand at ease. Their leader, who wore the rank pin of a major, addressed them. He was a mid-sized, crew-cut man of stocky build, who looked to be in his thirties. His eyes were his most startling feature—large and emerald-green in his sunburnt face, below thick blonde brows. He had a hatchet nose, a prominent jaw, a mouth that didn't look like it smiled much—nor did it now.

"Your quarters are behind you," he told them, nodding to the concertina wire-encircled tents he faced. "The first sergeant and the XO will get you squared away. Find yourself a rack, settle in, relax. Stay where you are, though—don't try to wander off. The MP's at the entry point won't let you through the barbed wire in any case. While you're here, you must avoid any contact with the local troops, except when absolutely necessary. Call each other by the numbers you've been assigned. There's a reason none of us have nametags. There's no need for anybody here to know my name or any of yours. We're going to be here three weeks. Surely we can all keep our mouths shut that long. If you don't think you can, see the first sergeant right now, or see me. If anyone here finds out who you are, where you've come from, or what you're here to do—there will be consequences. They will be severe. Be smart. Pick a buddy and stay near him. The two of you can help each other keep quiet.

"You men were selected for this mission because you're some of the best at what you do, where we come from. I have faith in every one of you. Don't make me regret it." The major nodded to the captain beside him and walked away, climbed the steps of the headquarters building for the Sixth of the Thirty-seventh Field Artillery, and entered. His first sergeant began lining the men up for entry through the wire to their tents.

Brede saw the men arrive from his office window, and watched them linger at the edge of the big, muddy field in front of the S-4 shack. He had seen Sergeant Altobelli erect the large canvas tents that would house them as February became March: four altogether, closely grouped, all set on pallet floors, a covered latrine pit dug to the rear. He'd wondered what they were for. Two squads of G.I.'s, he estimated—and hoped they weren't at Pelham for some unannounced inspection. He had his hands full as it was, getting ready for the DASA TPI just eight weeks away. Jack Farr had ended his tour—no loss there—but his D Battery replacement was shaky, as was the new butter bar in S-3 who had just begun his "special weapons" training. In the past, Ricci would have stepped in, but the big man's tour in Korea ended before May. So, if neither trainee's work improved, Brede might be forced to work two TPI assemblies. That would be a difficult and perhaps unacceptable solution for the mean-eyed DASA inspectors out of Albuquerque.

The still-new first lieutenant could only shrug. He was doing all he could, trying to help the new men gain confidence about what they were trying to learn. The work wasn't really that hard, but it did require strict attention to what was going on. Both men's concentration waned as the monotonous instructions were read, he noticed. He had watched their eyes glaze over. They lost track of what was read to them, hesitated, and continued to make mistakes they shouldn't have made by now.

Brede made up his mind. He would meet with Gilliam and Rafferty, right away. They'd set up an audition among a bigger selection of the lieutenants in the battalion. The two who showed the most promise would replace those currently in training. If everything happened quickly, there was still ample time to prepare teams before DASA came up. Satisfied, he rose from his desk just as Carter, the S-1 clerk, burst through his office door.

"Carter, that's about as fast as I've ever seen you move," Brede marveled. "What's going on?"

A breathless Carter paused for a moment, then stared at Brede. "Colonel needs you in his office, sir," he gasped, wide-eyed. "Right now!"

"I was going that way anyhow. Calm down and get yourself a cup of water. I think I can find my way alright."

The clerk's head bobbed like a metronome. "Right now, sir! Please hurry!"

"Okay, Carter. Okay. I'm on my way." Shaking his head, Brede walked quickly down the long hallway to Colonel Gaboury's office. He hoped no one was in trouble. Whatever was happening, he wasn't going to get upset—that much he knew for certain. Ever since he'd asked Jackie to marry him, a lot of the tension and confusion in his life had simply ... disappeared. He was a far happier, calmer person these days. He drank less, worried less, slept better, and smiled more. Life was good, and getting better, he thought as he knocked on the door to the colonel's office.

Someone shouted, "Enter!" It sounded like Rafferty was in there already. He wondered what was going on. He pulled the door open and looked in as he walked through. Gaboury was at his desk, as expected. At the long table that fronted the desk sat Rafferty, Gilliam, Ricci, and a man he'd never seen before. That man wore shiny new fatigues with no identifying name tag or unit patches. A major's oakleaf was pinned to his collar.

"Pwease shut the door and sit down, wieutenant," Gaboury lisped. "We have important bwisness to discuss." Brede complied, and his CO nodded to the anonymous major.

"Before I begin, everyone in this room must understand that the matters we discuss are classified top secret," the man said. "No notes or recordings of any kind can be made of what is said, nor can any discussions about it with those not here take place, under the provisions of AR 380-5."

"Understood," Gaboury said, looking around the table from face to face. The others nodded, including Brede. He shifted in his seat. This was becoming weird.

"My name is Jack Caul," the stranger continued. "Until last week, I was XO of an artillery battalion located in Phu Bai, South Vietnam. At that time, I got orders I have just shared with your commanding officer. Lieutenant Brede, when this meeting is concluded you will see to the secure storage of the documents containing these orders, which are classified Top Secret NOFORN. Need to see these orders will be limited to those of us in this room, with no exceptions. Is that understood?"

"Yes, sir," Brede responded.

"Colonel Gaboury, since you have seen my orders, you can understand why no previous announcement about them could be made to you—or to anyone below the highest echelons of Eighth Army. While we believe our secure communications networks to be uncompromised, we cannot be absolutely certain this is the case. So, only direct, word-of-mouth explanation of a project this sensitive can take place below the JCS level. I apologize for these abrupt orders, sir."

Gaboury nodded.

"I have brought with me a team of men, selected from their units in Vietnam for their competence at what they do. Four are trained in fire direction control, including a lieutenant who will act as fire direction officer. Four are designated to become assembly teams, two men to a team—one officer and one NCO each. Two gun section chiefs, a chief of firing battery, a first sergeant, and an XO to assist me are also included. I am glad to see the precursor orders you received were followed, Colonel Gaboury. The quarters you have prepared for us will certainly be sufficient."

Gaboury nodded once more.

"Your mission, gentlemen, is to train me and the men with me in all aspects of the assembly and employment of the M33 nuclear artillery round. According to my orders, we have until March twenty-fifth to accomplish this task. No record of this training or our presence here will be kept. My men have been ordered to remain anonymous to your troops. Fraternization between personnel stationed here and them must be kept to a strict minimum, avoided completely if possible. They will take their meals separately, and remain in their segregated quarters when not in training. My XO and I will lead them in daily calisthenics. Contact between any of us and KATUSA or other Korean military or civilian personnel is forbidden. When we're done here, I'll meet with some of you at this table to work out a training schedule which must begin immediately. Are there any questions?"

There might be a million questions, Brede thought as he left the room later, his head spinning. He'd need equipment, training materials he didn't have. Was some available at the SASP? Nobody knew. The assembly manual was classified top secret, and each team would need one to learn from. Where would they come from? He was guessing everybody Caul had brought with him was security cleared, but he didn't know. He shook his head. That was Gilliam's problem, not his. He had enough on his plate already. It was going to be a long, long day, he realized.

By the end of the first week, most of the biggest problems had been resolved. Brede had figured out a way to train multiple assembly teams at the same time, so only one manual was needed. They found the equipment required at the SASP. Preparation for the upcoming DASA inspection was halted, but that couldn't be helped. The men he trained, who referred to themselves by number, seemed eager to learn. To his surprise, he knew one of them. He had gone through OCS with Lieutenant "3," whose real name he recalled was Majiesky. He'd been in another platoon. Those who knew him well had nicknamed him "Magic." He could see Majiesky also recognized him.

"They still call you Ex?" he asked Brede during a smoke break.

Brede nodded. "Still call you 'Magic?'" he asked, and got a nod back.

"Seen any of the other guys?" Majiesky inquired.

"Five of us ended up in Second Infantry," Brede told him. "The others are up the road from here. Remember Ruddell? He's still whining."

Majiesky grinned. "Fuckin' Ruddell!" he scoffed, shaking his head.

"Man, you've shed a lot of weight," Brede noted. All through OCS, Majiesky had been big and hefty—bearlike. Now he was noticeably thinner. His once-round face was drawn and gaunt.

"Must be the cee's," Majiesky replied with a shrug, referring to the c-rations nobody liked much. "A steady diet of them will get anybody skinny." The break ended, and everybody got back to training. Later that day, Brede reported his knowledge of Majiesky's identity to Major Caul.

"I don't know what you want to do about it, sir," he said.

Caul nodded. "You're in on what's happening anyhow," he said, "so I don't think there's any security risk. How well did you know each other?"

"He was in a different platoon," Brede explained. "We weren't buddies, or anything like that. Even so, when a group of soldiers shrinks from more than a hundred to less than forty, the ones who make it all know each other some. He's lost a lot of weight, but I still recognize him—so I had to report it."

"You did the right thing, lieutenant—but don't sweat it. It's no big deal, as far as I can see."

A minor incident, fully unappreciated at the time, took place as the special training entered its third week. Three soldiers from Headquarters Battery reported fatigue shirts missing from the hangars in their barracks. Sergeant Altobelli suspected a prank. The shirts were replaced from supply. Everyone was too busy to pay it much attention.

Two days later, three of the "special" trainees were discovered absent from their enclosure during morning headcount. They had apparently dug a shallow trench under the wire sometime during the previous evening. Training was cancelled while a thorough search for the men around Camp Pelham and the surrounding villes was conducted. By noon of that day, the missing trainees had still not been found. Majiesky was one of those unaccounted for.

Acting on a hunch, Sergeant Overshaft called Camp Pelham's Military Police Detachment and asked if they'd picked up any soldiers in the ville the night before.

"Sure did," the duty sergeant responded, "but we can't get a line on their unit. They're all wearing stolen uniform shirts, and they refuse to tell us their names. No ID on any of them, either."

"Why are they being held?" Overshaft asked.

"Two for drunk and disorderly," the MP said, "with a charge of robbery on top of that. We got a mama-san who says they strong-armed her for some money yesterday. The third asshole is more serious. He resisted arrest. One of the sergeants who tried to subdue him is hospitalized with a broken jaw and some other injuries. It took four men to bring him down. We figure he's a meth-head."

"Where are they now?"

"Still here, locked up and very unhappy. The truck from Camp Carroll is due to pick them up within the hour. I'll be glad to get rid of them—especially the meth-head. He's kinda scary."

"Don't move 'em yet, sarge," Overshaft advised the MP. "I've got some brass coming to take them off your hands. This is a special situation."

"As long as you've got the paperwork I'll be well shut of them," the MP said.

"Found them," Overshaft reported to Brede, "right here on Pelham. I guess you can't tell me what all this is about, sir."

Brede shook his head. "You probably deserve to know more than most who do," he told the older man, "but I can't. Great job, though. You've relieved minds with a lot more rank than I carry. I don't know what the Thirty-seventh would do without you, Sergeant Overshaft. I mean that."

Later that afternoon, Caul and Brede interviewed Majiesky, who now sat on a hard chair, shackled to a post, in a shed behind battalion headquarters. As he looked at his former OCS companion, Brede realized the fight that took him down must have been brutal. One of Majiesky's eyes was blackened, his face was badly bruised, his stolen fatigue shirt in tatters. When he saw them enter the shed, he pulled at his chains in an unsuccessful attempt to turn away from them.

"You want to tell me about it?" Caul asked him.

"This is bullshit," Majiesky growled. "None of it was my fault. Those other two, they talked me into it, sir."

Caul shook his head slowly. "That won't fly. We already interrogated both of them. Their stories corroborate. You were the brains behind all of this, lieutenant. You thought the whole thing up. The question is, why?"

Majiesky raised his battered head, giggled softly. "Just needed a little," he said. "Just a taste. Enough to last me 'til I got back in-country, back to my stash. Those guys I went out with—dumb as fucking stones. Once they got a little booze in them, they didn't know when to quit. We were only supposed to sneak out for an hour or so … but I couldn't get them to come back in."

"You didn't want the booze, did you, lieutenant? You wanted something else."

"Yeah, so what?" Majiesky snarled. "So fucking what? You sit at your fucking desk in Phu Bai, Major Caul—yeah, I know who you are! Sit at your fucking desk in Phu Bai while the rest of us die out there in the bush! The meth helps … gets me wired enough I'm not scared anymore. It's not like I use that much—just a taste, once in a while." He looked around him, wild-eyed. "It's not like I'm an addict or anything!" he yelled, then caught himself. "I'm not saying anymore," he said, his voice suddenly subdued. "I want to see a JAG attorney."

Caul leaned against the shack's wall, arms folded. "No JAG attorney for you, I'm afraid," he said, shaking his head. "This is a top secret mission, lieutenant. Not a word about it can get out, nor will it. Perhaps you've forgotten the release you signed. There are places where people who jeopardize missions as important as this one are put. You will be sent to one of them tonight. You may be released someday—if the classification of the mission is reduced substantially—but I wouldn't count on that. You're going to a part of the world you've never seen before. You'll be there a long, long time. Look on the bright side: you'll kick your drug habit, for sure—and you may even learn another language." He turned to Brede. "We're done here," he said, and left the shack.

Immediately afterward, as the sun began to set, Caul met with Ricci and Brede in Gaboury's office. "I need your current assessment of training status," he said. "We're down three men—including a full assembly team. I have to send the Pentagon a 'go-no go' decision within the hour."

"The FDC crew is fully trained, ready to go," Ricci told him. "They've all done well, and no more training is needed, in my opinion."

"Everybody, including the three who gave us trouble, has gotten the assembly training down pat," Brede said. "Maybe we can form another team, using your XO and one of the section chiefs. I don't know how else to make up the shortage."

The major frowned. "That won't work. It would leave us short in a critical slot. Any other ideas?" He looked around the table, but found no answers.

"In that case, gentlemen, we've failed," he told the others in the room. "I'm going to have to send a 'no go' assessment to Washington."

Brede had expected this conversation since morning, and he'd given it a lot of thought. He had reluctantly decided there was only one way to save the mission. "I could go," he said softly, cursing himself silently for volunteering yet again.

The others in the room looked his way. "What did you say?" Caul asked.

"I could go, sir," Brede repeated, louder now. "I know everything you need about assembly, and fire direction as well. That way, we'll only be short one man, really. I'm sure we can figure a way to make it work, Major."

"Be careful," Gaboury advised him. "Don't wrush to any decisions, Ex. Take some time. Think things over."

"I've given this decision a lot of thought, sir." Brede replied, his voice stronger now. "I'm not willing to let the mission fail, so it's the only solution that makes sense. If you and Major Caul can get the paperwork straightened out, I should go. Three conditions, though."

"Name them," Caul said.

"First, put me wherever we're going on TDY. When the mission's over, I'd like to come back and finish my tour with the Thirty-seventh."

"That actually simplifies the paperwork," Caul said. "Granted. And the second condition?"

"You'll need Colonel Gaboury's help with this one. I need a chaplain to get me legally married before I leave, sir—and I need my new status on all my paperwork."

Gaboury nodded. "We'll have the cerwemony at my quarters," he said. "I'll set it all up tommowow. I think I know who the young lady might be."

"That leads me to my third condition, sir. When we first met, my opinion of you wasn't high I'm afraid, Colonel Gaboury."

His CO sighed.

"Since then, I've come to know you as one of the finest officers I've ever met. It's been an honor to serve under you. May I ask you to stand up for me at my wedding, sir?"

The older man nodded silently. His full eyes betrayed his emotion.

That evening, Jackie walked into the Officer's Club bar to find Brede already there, several drinks ahead of her, flashing the biggest smile she'd ever seen on his face. He handed her a martini as he ushered her to the seat beside his. "How'd you like to marry me, sweetheart?" he asked, kissing her cheek.

Eyes wide, She looked around the bar as she sat.

"Ex, keep your voice down!" she whispered harshly. "I've already said 'yes'—have you forgotten? Do you want the whole bar to know our plans?"

"No reason to hide it anymore, darling," he told her. "Unless you say 'no' we'll be married tomorrow!" He looked around them. As he'd predicted, others around the big bar paid no attention to them at all, busy with their drinks, their conversations, or playing bar-top dice games with those nearby.

"Tomorrow? What about San Luis whatever-it-is? The plans we made?"

"In this wacky world, plans have to change sometimes, Jackie. I have to go away soon—day after tomorrow, in fact. The whole thing just came up. I'll be gone for a while, maybe a month or more. So, I figured, why wait? This way, you can start drawing my pay right away. It will get you set up and into college until we're back together."

She looked at him sternly, a frown forming on her face. "You've done it again, haven't you?" she said.

"Done what, darling?"

"Raised your hand," she said, shaking her head. "You've volunteered for some insane mission, haven't you, Ex?"

Brede hung his head, then nodded. "I had to. The whole effort would have fallen apart if I hadn't. I only agreed to go if we could get married before I left. It's all arranged. We'll have the ceremony at Colonel Gaboury's quarters tomorrow evening. The chaplain, everything's set up. All that's missing is a 'yes' from you."

Jackie took a heavy sip from her drink, then slowly nodded—a smile forming on her face. She laughed, then reached to hug him. "Sure, why not?" she said, still laughing. "Why not? Everything about our romance has been wild, so why stop now? Ex, I'll marry you tomorrow, or right now if you want! I love you like crazy, you big idiot!" She gave him a long, lingering kiss.

The crowd that had gathered around them by now burst into cheers and applause. Even dour Major Rafferty joined in. The couple's drinks were free the rest of the evening. Everyone smiled. Even so, Jackie couldn't quell disquieting unease—a queasiness at the pit of her stomach she could not shake. She hoped her lover hadn't finally raised his hand one time too many.

CHAPTER TWELVE

RINGS AND
DEPARTURES

The next day was busy, with preparations for departure among some at Camp Pelham. Major Caul gave his men a final half-day's training, so he could closely observe and confirm their readiness for the mission ahead. Afterwards, he told them to pack their gear and get ready to leave. A truck would pick them up at oh-five-hundred the next morning and transport them to Kimpo, where a jet would take them where they were going.

Brede spent the morning going over S-2 business with Sergeant Overshaft and Grady. Gaboury and Rafferty had agreed that his job would be left open until his expected return in about six weeks. He kept himself busy, focusing his thoughts on tonight's ceremony in the Colonel's hooch—marriage to a woman he knew he would always love. Just the thought of it filled him with joy. That afternoon, he packed his personal belongings in a footlocker and returned the clothing and equipment he had drawn from the Headquarters Battery supply room. He took out his class A uniform and prepared it for the evening's ceremony, then sat on his bed and read to pass the time.

Jackie Lake began processing paperwork for her immediate resignation from the SRAO program and the Red Cross that morning. She expected to be on her way stateside by month's end. Reaction to her announcement had been mixed. Some of the ladies in the unit were genuinely happy for her, while others less kind sneered at her for robbing the cradle. She ignored the whispers. They didn't matter. She was joining her life to a man she loved completely. Nothing else was important right now.

"Magic" Majiesky, whose rank was now indeterminate, had found himself awakened in the shack where he was held before sunrise, put in a truck and driven to a nearby helipad, where a small helicopter was waiting to take him ... somewhere. No one spoke to him, and none of his first angry, then tearful questions were answered. The men who handled and shackled him wore anonymous fatigues and kept silent in his presence. After an hour's flight south he was transferred to a bigger aircraft, chained to a seat, and eventually glimpsed water beneath the plane's wings as it continued its journey. The drugs were thoroughly gone from his system now. He began to weep.

Colonel Gaboury's day was punctuated by a surprise visit from the second brigade commander. Colonel Wainright stomped unannounced into his office, demanding the release of three soldiers to his custody. "My MP's had 'em, you took them away," he growled, pacing around the battalion commander's desk, stogey between his gritted teeth. "You had no authority to do that. I've got a sergeant in the hospital, for God's sake! I want those men back, right now! Now, Colonel Gaboury—before I lose my temper and put you out of a job!"

Gaboury remained behind his desk, calm and unmoving. "I can't do that, sir," he said quietly.

Wainright stopped his pacing. "Why not?" he asked, raising his voice, his face now flushed. "You tell me right now why you can't obey my direct order, Colonel!"

"Those men are no longer in my custody, sir. They were wemoved this morning, at oh-four-hundwed hours."

"Okay, then. Just tell me the unit that's got them, so I can go take a chunk out of that CO's ass. You still owe me an explanation as to why they were here in the first place."

"I can't tell you that, sir," Gaboury said softly. "It's classified, and you are not among those with a need to know."

"I suppose you have orders to that effect," Wainright said, his voice dripping sarcasm. "Show them to me. Right now, colonel."

Gaboury shook his head. "I'm sorry, sir—I can't do that. You are not on the distwibution list. Showing you those documents would violate securwity."

Enraged, Wainright hammered Gaboury's desk with his fist. "Then tell me who is on this list of yours, Gaboury! So I can go see them, before I bring you up on charges!"

"Besides a few of my subordinates, there are thwee people on the distwibution list in Korea, sir: Commanding Officer, Division Artillery; Commanding General, Second Infantry Division; and Commanding General, Eighth Army."

Wainright's face purpled. "You think I won't call General Izenour the minute I get back to my office?" he yelled. "It will take me about two minutes to talk with him. Then I'll be back to have your ass on a platter!"

"Be sure to give the general my wegards, sir." Gaboury said calmly. He stood from his seat and saluted. "Always good to see you, colonel."

In response, Wainright rushed from his office, forcefully slamming the door behind him. Gaboury never saw him again. However, notice received a week later announced that Colonel Arthur Wainright had been relieved of his command and transferred immediately to Fort Dix, New Jersey. There he would command a warehousing and logistics depot.

That afternoon, at 1730 hours, Colonel Gaboury and his staff gathered with several Red Cross SRAO ladies at his quarters, in anticipation of the wedding to be performed there. The chaplain was due to arrive half an hour later. Brede and Jackie showed up soon afterward, and everyone waited impatiently for the ceremony to begin. Many took pictures, and Kwan served champagne. The little hooch was filled with smiling people. No one, not even Major Rafferty, could remember such an event happening in this part of Korea before.

The Chaplain Corps major, who happened to be Methodist, showed up in a rickety, noisy jeep a little past eighteen-hundred hours. A chubby, white-haired man, he brought with him a portable record player that provided the occasion with tinny appropriate music. "Believe it or not, I do this from time to time," he told Gaboury. "Lots of G.I.'s get married over here!"

The chaplain moved some chairs aside, clearing a space in the middle of the living area. "This should do it," he said, removing his service cap and draping an elaborate shawl over his shoulders. He got out a well-worn bible, and motioned Brede and Jackie forward. Someone had given her a white silk scarf to cover her head. To Brede, she looked like an angel. Her radiant face at that moment would remain etched in his mind during the hard days to come. Everyone in the room became silent.

"Stand beside each other, right about here ..." the chaplain told them, looking from one to the other. Some weddings he'd officiated had been happy, he reflected—others sad. These two were brimming with love for each other, he could clearly see. "Dearly beloved ..." he began, donning his spectacles and opening his bible.

The ceremony was far from perfect. Neither Jackie nor anyone else involved had considered the need for rings. There hadn't been time. Major Rafferty found a ring for Brede. Seeing the problem unfold, he pulled a wedding ring from his left hand. "My Evelyn passed on several years ago," he said, handing the plain gold band to Jackie. "I've kept this around, never figured quite why. Now I finally know."

She slipped the just-borrowed ring on Brede's finger. Everyone waited for him to give something to Jackie in return. "Believe it or not, I thought about this," he said to her. "I didn't want to rush around and get you something you didn't want. Instead, please take this ..." he pulled the wolf's head ring from his hand, and put it on her wedding ring finger. "This ring has brought everyone in my family who wears it luck and protection from harm. Wear it for me—so it can protect you until we're together again." He kissed her tenderly.

"You weren't supposed to do that just yet," the chaplain whispered loudly, laughing. "Now that Jacqueline and Xabier have given themselves to each other by solemn vows," he continued, "with the joining of hands and the giving and receiving of rings, I pronounce that they are husband and wife, in the name of the Father, and the Son, and the Holy Spirit." He looked intently around the room. "Those whom God has joined together, let no one put asunder."

Then the old chaplain smiled. "God bless you both!" he said. "NOW you can kiss her all you want!"

Later on that evening, all the wedding guests had left. Gaboury had given Brede and Jackie the use of his quarters for the evening, "... as a wedding pwesent," he'd said. He had arranged to bunk with Major Rafferty until tomorrow.

Brede drained a flute of now-flat champagne, and sat staring at the empty glass in his hands, his thoughts muddled. He'd turned a corner in his life, he knew. It was time to stop thinking about "I" and "me," and begin "we" and "us." He smiled because that felt right and good. He looked around for Jackie, heard a rustling in the adjoining guest bedroom. She appeared in the doorway, wearing a big smile and a very small nightgown.

"You know," he said, rising from his chair, "if you keep parading around like that, Mrs. Brede, someone's liable to take advantage of you."

Her smile grew. "I was hoping that would be the case," she said, her eyes sparkling. "In fact, I had a very specific person in mind. Sadly, he is wearing far too much clothing at the moment."

"That can be corrected," Brede said, sliding his belt open as they moved toward each other. "Please understand that I'm saving myself for the one I love!"

"She feels the same way, and won't wait much longer," Jackie said, as they met and embraced. "I was afraid I'd have to start without you," she whispered in his ear, while opening his zipper and reaching past it. "Now it's obvious your timing is perfect!"

It was still dark when she felt him rise from the bed they had used all night. She had been filled with him, and hoped that somehow the overwhelming heat of their passion could continue longer. It was not to be. He stood before her now, his back to her as he put on his fatigues, then bent to lace his boots.

"Ex," she whispered.

He sighed. "I hoped you'd stay asleep, Jackie," he said, turning to her. "I didn't mean to wake you."

"How dangerous will this be, darling? How long …"

Brede shook his head. "Shouldn't be dangerous at all," he said. "Six weeks max. Don't worry. God wouldn't be cruel enough to keep us apart—now that we've found each other. We'll have a big party in San Francisco in September, just like we planned." He held and kissed her. "You own my heart," he told her. "You always will. Never forget that. Now lay down and get some more rest. Take care of my greens for me, will you?"

"Yes, dear," she said, "just like a good Army wife should. Kiss me once more before you go, Ex."

He did, and held her in his arms. "The ring will keep you safe," he said, staring into her eyes. Then he rose again from the bed, left the room, and was gone from her.

Jackie fell into a fitful, restless half-sleep for another hour, then dragged herself from bed. She sat on a couch and looked at the ring he had given her—his family's wolf's head, now shining on her wedding ring finger. It was heavy silver, she realized, carved as much as cast—and old, worn in places from many years of use. Even so, it glowed as though it had just been polished, and somehow fit her finger perfectly. She realized that by giving her this talisman, he had transferred whatever protective power it held to her—more proof of his devotion.

She showered, dressed in her Red Cross uniform, applied a little makeup, brushed her teeth, combed her hair—mechanically, without much thought. She stripped the colonel's spare bed of the much-used sheets for the mama-sans, memories of Ex from the night before still fresh in her mind. She gathered the few items they'd brought with them to take back to her quarters. Today, she determined to get herself a new nameplate to wear with her uniform until she left Korea and the Red Cross. "Brede," she thought. "What a wonderful name."

Major Caul was waiting for Brede in front of the now-empty tents, in the deep dark that precedes dawn. "It's good you're early," he told his newest team member. "I'd have hated to come after you on your wedding night."

Brede smiled. "Sir, I figure the best way to get this done with is to begin as quick as I can." He saluted.

They heard the truck pull through the Camp Pelham gate. Caul looked at his watch. "Right on time," he said, returning Brede's salute.

The team, including Brede, quickly loaded their gear into the duce-and-a-half that arrived, then climbed aboard and secured the tailgate. Caul opened the right side door of the truck's cab, swung inside. "Let's get out of here, driver," he said. "We've got a plane to catch."

The drive to Kimpo lasted more than three hours. Team members sat in the truck's cargo bay, facing each other on less than comfortable slat seats. Their only vision outside the truck was through the rear or frontally, through the small back window in the cab. Those in the truck found it dark, hot, dusty, and close. Poor road conditions only added to the discomfort.

Captain Beemer, the team's XO, had brought along large paper cups of coffee—which he shared with everyone on board. The officers sat at the front of the truck's cargo bay, the least pleasant seats. The coffee helped, even though it was the standard battery-acid brew found Army-wide.

Overwhelming noise from the truck's engine made conversation nearly impossible. Most of the men tried their best to sleep, with varying levels of success. In general, it was a bumpy, sullenly noisy journey that lasted well into morning.

Smoother roads and reduced honey-bucket odor alerted the team that the first leg of their journey was finally nearing its end. Sure enough, the truck made several maneuvers before backing to a stop in a parking lot near a hangar. The men in the truck climbed from it as soon as it stopped, glad once again to be on unmoving solid ground, breathing fresher air.

Major Caul climbed from the truck's cab, and it drove away. Captain Beemer spoke to him briefly, then walked toward the rest of the team. "Line up, single file," he said. "Smoke if you want. We'll be here a little while. Lieutenant Brede, come with me." He began walking into the hangar.

Brede caught up with the XO as they entered the structure. He wondered if this was the same hangar where he'd first set foot in Korea, a million years ago. "Where are we going, sir?" he asked.

"Turns out you need some shots, lieutenant," Beemer answered with a good-natured smile. "You didn't need protection against plague and some other nasty bugs here—but where we're going you will. I'm taking you to the medics. They'll fix you right up."

There was a midwestern twang to Beemer's speech. The tall, thin, sandy-haired captain wore thick glasses that sat heavily on his long nose. He always seemed to have a stick of chewing gum grinding between his blocky jaws.

A medic approached them, and Beemer nodded. "Come on back outside when they're done sticking you," he said, and walked off.

Brede counted four separate inoculations—two in each arm—before the medics sent him on his way. His arms ached afterwards, and he wondered if they'd hurt tomorrow, or if he'd feel the headache that sometimes follows such medication. He shrugged as he walked back outside the hangar. It didn't matter, really. He would be on an airplane for some time to come, going … somewhere.

He saw the rest of the team standing at the end of the parking lot, and joined their loose line, after picking up his duffle bag from where he'd left it. He pulled a cigarette from his pocket, lit it and inhaled a deep drag as he looked around.

"Got one to spare, lieutenant?" the soldier standing next to him asked. He wore an E-5 pin on his collar.

Brede dug out his pack again, offered it to the man, and gave him a light when he chose one. "Any idea where we're headed, sarge?" he asked.

The man smiled, staring at Brede's fatigues. "Hell, lieutenant, I was about to ask you," he said. "At least I know your name. The rest of us don't even know that much about each other. We were all warned not to talk about ourselves. I figured since you were our main instructor, you'd know something. What are you even doing here—if you don't mind my asking?"

"You had some drop-outs," Brede said. "I'm a replacement."

"Yeah, I notice three of the others haven't been around for a few days: that half-assed lieutenant and two of the other guys. Guess we won't be seeing them again, huh?"

"Your guess is as good as mine," Brede told him, grinding out his cigarette under his boot. He picked up his duffle and walked to where Major Caul and the XO were standing. "I don't suppose there's a phone around here I could use?" he asked them.

"Let's get a few things straight," Caul said, staring at him directly. "Watch what you say to the rest of the team, Lieutenant Brede. The three of us are the only ones who volunteered for this mission. The rest of these men are on orders. They're not even supposed to know each other's names. There's no reason to ask any of them questions. They don't know anymore about what's going on than you do."

"Yes, sir."

"There's no phone for you in that hangar, lieutenant—nor is there one for me. I know you're a newlywed—but you put your hand up, so live with it. We'll all have plenty of time to call our wives once we're done with the mission. Until then, no phones, no mail either. Is that clear?"

"Yes, sir."

"I can tell you this much, right now. There's a big Air Force transport jet due here for us—a C-141. Should touch down within the hour. It's going to take us straight from Kimpo to a place called Dong Ha, in South Vietnam. Once we're there, at a secure location, you and the rest of the team will be thoroughly briefed on our mission. Until then, don't ask about it. You'll only get me annoyed. Now, get back in line with the other officers. You don't have long to wait."

"Yes, sir. Thank you, sir." Brede turned to walk away.

"One thing more," Caul said, stopping him. "You made this mission possible. If you hadn't volunteered, I'd have had to scrub the whole thing. That counts with me, Ex."

Brede walked to his place in line, feeling better … but still wishing he could have made a phone call. A few minutes later, they were all alerted that the plane had landed. The team picked up their gear and moved into the hangar. Outside on the tarmac, a hundred yards away, was the sleek dark-green shape of their transport plane—high winged and t-tailed. A ramp had been put in place, but no entry was allowed until the aircraft had been refueled and inspected. While the men waited, they smoked and paced nervously, but said little to each other. When they were finally ushered aboard, they found seats, stowed their belongings, and settled down for their flight. Their destination, the U.S. combat base at Dong Ha, was almost two thousand miles distant—six hours away, even in the four-engine jet they were on. Most, including Brede, were able to sleep. He dreamed about Jackie and the life they were going to have, as the plane sliced across the East and South China Seas.

The new Mrs. Brede kept herself busy the rest of March, showing her replacement around the detachment's area of operations, introducing her to the ladies she'd be managing, making sure a mountain of paperwork was brought up to date. She began thinking about the degree she'd seek when she got back to college next fall. Would she study nursing, or some allied medical field—psychology or psychiatry, perhaps? Of course, much would depend on where the Army sent Ex on his next assignment. Still, there was a lot to think about. She got no word at all from her new husband, but he had warned her she might not hear from him for a month or more, so she didn't allow herself to fret over his silence.

As April continued, Jackie noticed a new lethargy in herself. She also became aware of a curious, subtle stretching sensation in her upper chest, and around her pelvis—like nothing she'd experienced before. She wondered if she'd somehow strained herself, hurt some muscles. Some of her love making with Ex had been exuberant, after all. As the month passed its midpoint, her menstruation—normally as dependable as clockwork—still had not come, and she began experiencing nausea.

Now certain something was medically wrong, she got herself to Seoul and an obstetrician at the bigger military hospital there. After several hours of examination and tests, she was gently advised there was nothing wrong. Her symptoms were perfectly normal for a woman in early pregnancy. Part of her counseling included cautions. Women her age, the doctors told her, experienced far higher rates of failed pregnancies than those younger. Dangers to both the child and the mother were real and severe. There was a higher probability of birth abnormalities, and older expecting mothers often suffered from preeclampsia and other serious prenatal conditions. The likelihood of cesarean delivery was also much greater.

As a college-educated nurse, Jackie was already well aware of the red flags raised. They didn't matter to her. Not now. She and Ex were having a child! She'd never considered the possibility, certain that her reproductive clock had run down. The new reality made her heart sing with joy. She knew he'd be thrilled when he found out. Their life together would be more blessed than they had ever hoped. She had never been so happy. All that remained now was to get ready for their baby, and to find a way to tell her new husband he was going to be a father.

CHAPTER THIRTEEN

QUESTIONS ANSWERED AND DENIED

As the big jet approached Vietnam, the sun was already reddened and sinking in the west. The pilot banked north, paralleling the coast below as he approached Dong Ha Combat Base. He circled the runway once for instructions, then lowered the plane's nose and dove for a quick landing. There were lots of weapons in the surrounding area—some hostile, others just loose in owners' hands. Either way, a stray bullet could prove deadly.

Coming in, the C-141 needed most of Dong Ha's available runway, and seemed to brake very hard to those inside. As they landed and taxied, they passed a varied collection of aircraft on the tarmac in the gathering dusk —helicopters, dual-engine transports, some small, high-winged observation planes, a couple of C-130's. In surprisingly little time, their plane turned, stopped, its engines powered down, and the cabin lights came up. They had landed. The men stood, grabbed their gear, and lined up as the hatch to their front right opened to admit warm, humid air. A man wearing a noise suppression helmet stuck his head inside, beckoning them through the exit. "Welcome to the Republic of Vietnam!" someone shouted, and received a ragged, half-hearted cheer. They moved down a low set of steps and walked into a lighted hangar on their right front, where Major Caul and Captain Beemer awaited them.

"Form around me," their CO told them. "A truck is on its way to pick us up. For those of you still wondering, we're in Vietnam—at the Dong Ha Combat Base, north of Danang. We'll be here a few days, while our equipment is delivered. Barracks have been made available for us, secluded

and out of the way—courtesy of the 108th Artillery Group. They've set up
a mess hall to feed us there, so we'll have all the comforts of home. By now
I shouldn't have to tell any of you that you're restricted to the barracks area,
but I will anyway. Please don't try to sneak off. You'll be apprehended, and
what happens after that won't be pleasant. For now, stay in the hangar if
you want to smoke. Stay close. There's a latrine out back if you need it. We
won't be waiting long."

A few minutes later, an anonymous truck pulled up to the open hangar.
The team piled in, and the truck took them to a small compound several
minutes away. There Caul was met by a trio of soldiers who handed him
keys to the structures around them and engaged in short, whispered conversation before fading into the growing darkness.

The major summoned his first sergeant, and the two of them opened
the doors to the buildings nearby, then called the rest of the team to join
them. "There are more than enough beds for all of you in these barracks,
sheets and pillows for you to use," he told them. "Both buildings have
electricity, working latrines, and running water, so you'll sleep in comfort
tonight. Be sure to put up your mosquito netting and use the Skin-so-Soft
that's set out. Take your malaria pills, please. First Sergeant will hand them
out. Tomorrow, we'll all get jungle fatigues and boots. We'll wait here for
our equipment and the gun crews to arrive. Day after tomorrow we'll road-
march to our destination. So relax and sleep in—once you've got your beds
in order. There will be no mama-sans here. I expect you men to keep these
quarters neat by yourselves. That means make your beds and stow what
you're not wearing. First Sergeant will set up details for the floors and latrines. They'll start serving breakfast in the mess hall at oh-seven-hundred.
See all of you then. Officers, please join me now."

While the noncoms and enlisted men filed into their new quarters,
Brede joined Beemer and the team's other two lieutenants around Caul.
"We've got two eight-inch howitzers and their support vehicles due here
tomorrow," he told them. "XO and I will inspect them before turning them
over to their crew chiefs. We'll also get some ammo to carry, including white
phosphorous and COFRAM rounds. Lieutenant Brede will pick up the
special rounds later—I'll let you know when and where, Brede. Get a good
night's sleep, gentlemen," Caul said and began to walk away.

"Excuse me, sir," Brede said, causing him to turn.

"What is it, Brede?" Caul asked.

"Months before your team showed up, my battalion in Korea got a shipment of COFRAM," Brede told him. "When it came in, it was so highly classified there were few around who could even guard it. I never found out exactly what it was."

Caul nodded. "COFRAM," he said, "stands for controlled fragmentation artillery munitions. Best anti-personnel round we've ever had, in my opinion. Some of our guys over here call them 'fire-cracker' rounds, because of the noise they make when they fragment. A shell ejects more than one-hundred separate bomblets. Deadly to massed troops. I hope we don't have to use them, because that will mean the bad guys are close. Even so, if we do, those rounds will stop a lot of them." He nodded again and continued walking.

The next morning, team members in the midst of their "chipped beef on toast" breakfast heard the rumble, whine, and clank of big machines erupt outside. As they sat in the mess hall, half-a-dozen vehicles arrived, parking themselves in the yard that fronted the barracks—their tracks churning up a small tornado of dust as they swung to a stop in the compound. Two were big M110 self-propelled eight-inch howitzers, fresh from the factory by their look, each crewed by a driver and two loaders. The guns were escorted by tracked M548 ammunition/crew carriers, already loaded with fifty howitzer rounds each and carrying crews of five. Behind them came two M577 command post carrier tracks, each manned by two men. A jeep brought up the rear of the procession.

A captain carrying a clipboard climbed from the jeep as it parked and walked to the first man he saw. "I'm looking for your CO," he said. "Got some equipment for him to sign for, and some troops to take under his wing." Directed to Caul, who walked from the mess hall to meet him, he saluted and handed the clipboard over.

"Sir," the captain said as his salute was returned, "here are the six vehicles I was ordered to deliver. Please sign for them once they've passed your inspection. The guns are brand-new, never fired a round, just got the cosmoline cleaned off 'em. They still have their auto-loaders. Let me know if you need those removed. The rest of the tracks have been depot maintained and repaired. Drivers have the logbooks. Both '548's are loaded up with ammo per your request. The personnel records for the gun crews and drivers are in the jeep for your review and sign-off. The fifty-cal machine guns you'll need are coming separately, should arrive later today. All the radios and scramblers are already mounted in the command tracks. You'll get a jeep and a driver later today."

"Very good, captain," Caul said, looking at the machinery sitting in front of him as the dust settled. "I'll send back the paperwork when our inspection is complete. Shouldn't take long."

"Sir, I need you to come back to group headquarters with me to see Colonel Jain and our S-3, Major Brill. You need to be briefed on the tactical situation in the area where you're headed, and on the rest of the support for the mission. I'll take you back with me if that's alright."

"Okay," Caul replied. "Give me a minute to get my XO out here, and we can go." He walked back into the mess hall, where Beemer was just finishing breakfast. "Jake, I need you to take charge of things while I'm at the 108th," he said, leaning over the table where his second-in-command sat. "Get the First Sergeant, the CFB, and the section chiefs rounded up. I want the section chiefs to give their equipment a thorough going-over, and get their gun crews squared away. Have the CFB supervise them. Use the lieutenants as you think best. I want you and the First Sergeant to inspect the command tracks, especially the radio equipment. Set up one as our FDC. Get up on the networks we'll use. The code books and call signs you'll need are all there, I'm told. I want a complete report of what you've found when I get back. Be tough, and don't go easy on the new men. We're going to be all alone out in Indian Country pretty soon. There won't be anybody to lean on if we need replacements—for the men or the equipment." He turned to Brede, who was sitting at the table. "Ex, you're with me," he said, then turned and left the small building.

Caul walked back to the jeep. "Let's go," he told the captain waiting for him, as Brede caught up. "Every minute we spend here from now on delays the mission. I'm bringing one of my officers with me. He'll need to know the logistics they're going to tell me about." They piled in the jeep's back seat and it circled, leaving their compound and picking its way over the soft, muddy gravel road before them.

Headquarters for the 108th Artillery Group sat on the side of a low hill, a mile from where Caul and his team had been put. The Headquarters Battery orderly room was positioned at the top of the hill, with various offices and barracks placed further down the hill's slope to either side. Group headquarters was on the upper right side of the slope, behind a high flagpole. Immediately below it, beyond a large water tank and a shed housing several enormous diesel generators, was the beehive-shaped operations bunker—where the jeep parked. Brede and Caul followed the captain, whose name-tag read "Englund," into the bunker's dark, sandbag-buttressed entrance.

Inside, fluorescent lighting glared over a narrow hallway, leading down to a large central room populated by men monitoring radio traffic and several large area maps of northern South Vietnam—some hung from walls, others laid out on tables. The room was cool—mildly chilly in contrast to the climbing heat outside. From time to time, one or more of the men would rise from their seats to annotate the maps with markers. A colonel and a major stood by one of the maps. Englund approached them and saluted. "I have Major Caul and one of his officers, sir," he said, as his salute was returned. "That's all for now, Captain Englund," the colonel told him, "we'll take it from here." The captain nodded, turned on his heel and left.

"Good to see you again, Caul," Colonel Jain said, extending his hand, which Caul shook smiling. He nodded to the man standing next to him. "This is Ed Brill, my S-3. He's been working on your mission since we got the go order. You are now officially 'Task Force Tollbooth.' There's a lot to get through, and time's not on our side. I see you've brought someone along …"

"Lieutenant Brede will be in charge of special weapons, sir. We picked him up in Korea. He was our primary instructor, the man who volunteered when we had that unfortunate incident."

"Good to meet you, Brede," Jain said, shaking his hand. The colonel was a very tall, extremely thin man, Brede noticed—whose coffee skin was offset by unexpected grey eyes. His deep voice carried no discernable accent. "I'm told you made this mission possible. It's good to meet you."

Seth Jain had run the 108th Artillery Group for almost six months. His replacement would arrive soon. Then he'd move down to Saigon and promotion to flag rank. His heavy guns supported the volatile northern border war, while his anti-air units protected convoys and bridges from Danang to the DMZ. The 108th also supervised many shadowy Command and Control North (CCN) activities, which continued to try and move South

Vietnamese agents north of the border—among other highly sensitive efforts. The effort had turned his hair from dark to salt-and-pepper, and tested his nerve like no assignment he'd had before. The Tet Offensive—only now finally settled—and the continuing action at Khe Sanh had pushed his men to the edge of their capacity to fight. Still, they had won. Perhaps this "Tollbooth," this end-run, would bring the North to the negotiating table in Paris and finally end this lunatic war.

Jain ran a hand through his short hair, and took a long look at the young lieutenant in front of him. "Hardly more than a boy," he thought, picturing his own sons—one of whom would soon begin West Point. Just married the day before he came here, Jain had heard—yet willing to volunteer for a mission that would surely put his life on the line.

"I'll let Major Brill get you current on the tactical situation," he said.

"Please look at the map," Brill said, gesturing to the large map laid out on a table behind them. "Khe Sanh Combat Base is no longer in jeopardy. Operation Pegasus forces have relieved NVA pressure to the south. The engineers have gotten Route Nine open from here to as far west as you'll need to go—to the river beyond Lao Bao." His hand traced the road, well known since the French had fought here as "The Street Without Joy," all the way from Dong Ha to an area south and west of the embattled U.S. base.

"You'll be part of a supply convoy to Khe Sanh," Brill continued," but you'll move south to an area near the old prison at Lao Bao, right on the banks of the Sepon—Hill 213. The engineers have already carved out firing positions on the hill for your howitzers, on the reverse slope of a bluff overlooking the beach. They've put in some culvert for your team's quarters."

"What about security?" Caul asked.

"Your ammo carriers mount fifty-caliber machine guns," Brill said. "A light company of infantry from the 101st will climb on your tracks as you pass south of Khe Sanh—about sixty men. A South Vietnamese infantry battalion is positioned between you and Khe Sanh. You're only supposed to be in place a week or so. That should be sufficient."

"Any word on the enemy?"

"The NVA got their noses bloodied pretty badly at Khe Sanh," Brill said. "There are still elements of at least four divisions—the 304th, 308th, 320th, and 324th—somewhere to the north and west of Khe Sanh, but they've all suffered heavy casualties. Our estimates are that fifteen to twenty thousand of their men were killed in the past month—by our forces, close air support, and Arclight strikes. We don't know how well organized the remaining troops are, but their tanks are gone. The prisoners we've captured say they're pulling back toward the border. The Third Marines are chasing them. *Muscle Shoals* sensors confirm their direction. They're all moving away from where you'll be, trying to regroup further north. Your major problem, if you have one, will be NVA artillery. They have one-twenty-two and one-hundred-thirty millimeter cannons that may be within range, or close enough to get there if they want to. Get done quick and get out, that's the best solution. Don't give them time to find you and react."

"Will the special weapons move with the convoy?" Brede asked.

"Good question, lieutenant," Brill said. "No, they won't. Too much risk. The 'Tollbooth' rounds—along with their assembly kits and spotter rounds—are sitting on an aircraft carrier in the South China Sea right now. When your guns are in place, Major Caul, they'll be flown straight out to your position by chopper. We estimate the whole operation will take about half a day."

"Observation support?" Caul asked. "What's available?"

"You'll get an aerial observer, in an O-1 Bird Dog flying out of here," Brill said. "He'll adjust the spotter rounds until you're on target. Then you'll have to give him time to get out of range before you fire anything else. We've also got some other eyes in the sky, but they won't help you—except for BDA. The observer's call sign is in your code book."

"That should do it," Caul said. "If you don't mind, sir, I'd like to get back to my team. They're inspecting all the vehicles you sent over this morning, and I'm anxious to see what they've found. I've also got some personnel records to look through."

"You shouldn't have any trouble with the equipment," Jain said. "It's all new or good as new. The men should work out well. They're straight off the line, from five good batteries. We're hoping they'll be back at their old jobs pretty quick. A couple of 'em were going to get their own gun sections."

"I'm sure we'll be fine, sir," Caul said as he saluted. Captain Englund was waiting for them outside the bunker. In a few minutes, they joined the rest of the team—now "Taskforce Tollbooth."

The Chief of Firing Battery approached Caul as he climbed from the jeep. "I'm ready with my report, sir," he said.

"Let me have it, 'Smoke,' and don't be kind," Caul told the E-7, a heavy-set, wide-shouldered man—as bald as a queue with a mahogany complexion. His name, the major knew, was Betancourt. "We've got to fix any problems now. In another day or two, we'll have to live with them."

"Major, the carriers look fine, and the guns both look good to me. Hell, they're just out of the factory. Only possible problem is the rammer-loaders. You and I both know they go bad quick around here. Their 'cherry juice' doesn't hold up in this heat and humidity. Sure would be nice if we could keep 'em, though. Ramming those rounds by hand gets old in a hurry."

"Take 'em off if you have to," Caul advised, "but consider this. We're going to be near the border, in the high sawgrass. Gets cold at night—we'll need sweaters. We're going to fire a hundred, hundred-fifty rounds max. If you think we can get away with it, let me know. If you don't, let's yank 'em off now—while we've got more hands to help us."

"How about a compromise, sir? Let's take the rammer off one, leave it on the other. We can save the one with the rammer for the special rounds."

Caul smiled. "Good thinking, sarge," he said. "Give the idea some more thought, and let me know your decision in half an hour. In the meantime, you and a section chief can get to work taking one of them off. Anything else?"

"We've got three or four men I'd like to give a closer look, sir. The section chiefs agree. They're showing all the signs."

Caul sighed, shrugged. "If they look hinky, search their gear," he told Bentancourt. "Understand, we'll get rid of them whether we find any drugs or not." He looked around. "Have you seen the XO?" he asked.

"He's with Top, over in one of the command tracks, sir."

"Okay, I'm headed that way if you need me."

Walking toward the vehicles, Caul smiled. It was good to be headed for action again.

As she waited to leave Korea, Jackie struggled to deal with the surprise of her pregnancy. Quitting smoking cold turkey was hard for her. She'd smoked since her teen-age years, and found the calming comfort of a cigarette enjoyable. Holding a cigarette, pausing to think while drawing on one, had become part of how she met the world. Besides that, almost everyone around her smoked—making the desire to have one ("Just one more …")

nearly irresistible. Even so, she knew that she could take no chances that might lower her baby's weight or otherwise compromise the child's health. At her age, ending her enjoyable addiction might make the difference between the infant's survival and death. So she forced herself through weeks of withdrawal with grumpy, jittery constraint.

Ending the social drinking she'd become used to at Camp Pelham was also tough. Jackie soon realized that, for her anyway, smoking and drinking were intertwined compulsions. Having a cigarette while sipping a martini made both more enjoyable. She stopped going to the Officer's Club so often, and had Kwan fix her "club soda-tinis" when she did.

A few weeks after Ex departed, Jackie paid Will Gilliam a visit. The Thirty-seventh's heavyset S-1 took a few minutes from an obviously hectic workday to see her. "Have to take the time," he said through his southern drawl, "you're the only dependent the unit's got right now—this side of the Pacific, anyhow. What can I do for you, Mrs. Brede?"

"Thanks for seeing me at all, Will," Jackie said. "You must be busy. That poor man out front is buried in manila files. If you'd like, I'll come back later on."

Gilliam shook his head. "Won't get no better 'til the day I leave," he said with a wry grin. "Ol' Carter, that boy papers himself in personnel files every damn day! Can't open one without opening 'em all. Ex is my buddy, so you'll never have to wait, Jackie. Just tell me what you need."

"Two things really," she told him. "Thanks for all the help you gave me getting the ID card and all the paperwork done. I'd still be wading through those forms without you, Will. As you may know, I'll be heading stateside soon. I want to make sure the paychecks and the other information concerning Ex follow me. The problem is, I don't have a good stateside address to forward them to yet. What can I do?"

Gilliam frowned. "That is a problem, Jackie," he said. "The only advice I can give you is to get settled as soon as you can, and head to the nearest military finance office quick after that. Every piece of paper in the Army takes time to move around, like an old man walking. It's going to be a month, maybe two, until your checks start coming like they should. No way around that. I can get you an advance before you go, should soften things up some. I'll get to work on that right now."

"That's going to help a lot, Will. Thanks."

"What else can I do for the prettiest bride on Camp Pelham?"

Jackie sighed. "I know Ex is still assigned to the Thirty-seventh, Will. He's TDY, wherever they've sent him. I don't expect you to tell me where he is or what he's doing. I know that's all classified. Even so, have you heard about him? Do you know how he is? Is there anything, anything at all that you can tell me? I miss him so, Will." she said. "More than I ever thought I would." She turned her head and quickly wiped away a tear.

Gilliam looked at her, his own heart softening with sadness. "I'd tell you something, if I knew anything," he said softly. "Promise, Jackie, I'll let you know if I hear something. Right now, there's nothing." He smiled. "We all expect that rascal back here soon enough, though. Hell, ol' Kwan hasn't sold any scotch since he took off. By the time you're settled back in the states, he'll be on his way home to you."

Two weeks later, checks in hand, Jackie Brede climbed the steps to an airliner that would take her back to the United States—and a future swirling with both doubt and promise.

CHAPTER FOURTEEN

STREETS WITHOUT JOY

A resupply convoy left Dong Ha Combat Base for the Khe Sanh area at oh-five-hundred on April fifteenth, a seasonably hot and overcast Monday morning. The Taskforce Tollbooth vehicles were easily inserted—a small, unremarkable segment in the large caravan of vehicles moving like an enormous caterpillar west on Route Nine. As the convoy wound its way toward Vietnam's embattled northwest edges, it expanded and contracted like a huge accordion, as vehicles within it sped up or slowed down in a vain attempt to maintain the proper interval between themselves and those in in front of them. Hectored military police buzzed up and down the convoy's length in jeeps, trying to keep the motorized beast's ponderous momentum from fracturing into chaos through villages and road junctions.

From his command track, near the rear of the procession, Major Caul focused his attention on the seven vehicles under his control. As the starts and stops of the convoy around him multiplied, he wished he'd demanded his own path west. Based on progress so far, they'd have to laager overnight at Ca Lu before going further west. A full day would be lost before his team could reach their firing positions on the Sepon. Every extra day compounded the risk they faced. Caul knew that secrets are fragile things, easily shattered. A word, a whisper, can be enough. Once even a hint becomes known, death, failure, or ignominious retreat can quickly become the only rational outcomes. Success is no longer possible.

Caul refused to allow this mission to fail, after all the work and effort that had taken it this far. He knew this was his chance at the brass ring—the difference between ending his career as a light colonel and pushing forward to wear stars. He would lead the taskforce out of Ca Lu tomorrow without the dragging anchor of a convoy slowing him. They'd depend on speed and the confusion around them to get to Lao Bao unnoticed. Decision made, he sent the necessary messages.

Brede was unaware of his commander's travails. The morning the convoy had left Dong Ha, he had been put on a C-130 an flown to Danang. From there, a Navy C-2 took him to an aircraft carrier in the South China Sea. A Navy lieutenant named Alford took charge of him there, after an abrupt and terrifying landing (the ship looked enormous from the air, but far too small as his twin-engine aircraft charged up its deck).

"First landing on a carrier?" Alford asked as he guided a pale Brede off the flight deck. "Don't bother to answer. I can see it in your eyes. Kind of startling, huh?"

Brede could only nod as he was led through a nearby hatch, down several decks on companionways, into a narrow hall. "Welcome to *Bonne Homme Richard*," his guide boomed, slapping his back. "You're about fifty miles off Vietnam's coast right now. The goodies you're here to pick up are stowed below. I'll take you to see them later. Here's your cabin, right near the Officer's Mess. We're taking good care of you, Mr. Brede. With any luck, you and your stuff will be gone tomorrow. Three heavy-lift choppers will take you straight where you're trying to go. Until we get word to transport you, stay in your cabin and don't talk to anybody except me. Understand?"

Brede nodded dully.

"Good!" Alford said, shoving him into the cabin. "There's a bunk there, and some shaving gear, if you need it. I'll come back by when it's time for chow. Until then relax and enjoy your quiet solitude, compliments of the U.S. Navy." The big, blonde naval aviator closed the hatch door and left. Still a little dizzy, Brede collapsed on the narrow bottom bunk, closed his eyes, and thought of Jackie.

Jackie was thinking about her husband, that day, too—as the big jet she was on touched down at Lindbergh Field, in San Diego. The Red Cross had sent a car to pick her up. She was checked into the famous Hotel Del Coronado, and spent the next day at the Red Cross Regional Headquarters, where she turned in her uniforms and completed her resignation. The following day, she took a cab downtown and bought a car, using some of the money she had saved while in Korea. The car she chose, a three-year-old Ford Falcon, was hardly a luxury ride. Even so, it had low milage, plenty of room in back for a future baby seat, and the light blue color appealed to her. She found it easy to drive and shift, plenty fast enough for her needs. The bucket seats in front were comfortable. Suitcase in the trunk, she was checked out of the hotel the next morning and on her way up the coast to begin her new life.

Jackie made it through L.A.'s sprawl and north on the 101 on her second day out of the Red Cross, and decided to get as far north as possible. As the sun set, she stopped in Santa Barbara, tired and light-headed. She pulled into the first decent motel she saw along the highway, a large place with a colorful Mexican motif. As she stood at the counter checking in, she briefly felt her legs collapse beneath her as she sank to the floor …

Jackie regained consciousness briefly in what seemed to be an ambulance, but the world soon went away again. She regained her senses wild-eyed in a hospital bed. A nurse came to her side in a few minutes, to ease her confusion. "You're in Santa Barbara Cottage Hospital," the nurse explained. "You collapsed while you were trying to check into a motel down the hill from here."

Jackie rose in her bed, frightened and frowning. "What's wrong?" she asked. "Do you know? I'm pregnant! Is the baby alright?"

"You're fine, and so is your baby, as far as we can tell," the nurse assured her. "We've run some tests, and we're running a few more, but nothing serious seems to have happened to you. It looks like you just tried to drive too far without stopping to rest and eat. You should be fine to go on with your travels, once you've gotten a good night's sleep and some food in you."

Relieved—and suddenly, exhausted—Jackie sank back against her pillows. "Thanks," she said. "I feel so weak …"

The nurse nodded. "You probably haven't eaten all day. Tried to make it up the 101 too quick. It happens more often than you might think." She came to Jackie's bedside, and poured her a glass of water. "Here," she said, "drink this. I'll bring some food around for you in a little while. Try to eat what I'll bring, even if you're not hungry. Your body really needs it, and so does the little life inside you. My name's Rachel, by the way. Rachel Parris. I'll be on this ward all night. Just hit the switch on your side table if you need anything, anything at all."

Jackie forced herself to eat most of the soup the nurse brought her, and even consume the crackers in their hard-to-open cellophane packets. She cursed herself for failing her child. She had to remember, she told herself, she was eating for two now. Afterward she fell into a deep, dreamless sleep—awakening when light from the room's window and increased activity around her signaled the arrival of a new day. A doctor named Singer gave her a thorough examination the next morning, after she'd made herself consume some breakfast. "There's no reason to keep you here," he told her, "but I'd advise you to stick around town for a while, to get your strength back. I'd like to see you again in a few days, just to make sure everything's alright with you and your pregnancy. Santa Barbara's a beautiful place. There's plenty to see and do. Relax, stay off the road, and enjoy yourself."

Jackie agreed to a follow-up appointment with Dr. Singer in four days, on the following Friday. She settled her hospital bill, and took a cab back to the motel where she'd collapsed the night before. Happy to see that they'd kept her suitcase secure, she decided to get a room there.

"Let's try this again," she told the day clerk, and was handed the key to a bright, first-floor room near where she'd left her car. She cautiously lugged her suitcase to the room, unpacked, hung up her clothes, and collapsed on the bed, suddenly ready for a nap. When she awoke, it was mid-afternoon. Too late for lunch, really—too early for dinner, so Jackie contented herself with coffee and some toast at a diner near the motel. While there, she bought a copy of the local newspaper and read through the "help wanted" classifieds. To her surprise, the hospital she'd been rushed to last night was looking for nurses.

She certainly needed to find a job, Jackie decided as she sipped her coffee. The town around her was beautiful, right on the ocean with the mountains of the Santa Ynez range towering to the east. The climate was a wonderful relief from the sultry heat and frigid winters of Korea. Could she afford to live in such a nice place? The classifieds "for rent" section said she could if a reasonable job was at hand.

In the past, this would have been the time to smoke a cigarette while she thought matters over. Jackie's need for tobacco was suddenly demanding, but she fought the impulse—shaking her head to clear her mind. Any decision she made now had consider three people, not just one. There was Ex to think about, and their child. She decided to take the paper back to her room and look through it further. At the diner's counter, she purchased a city map as she paid for her coffee. She looked at her wristwatch as she left. It was just before three. There would be plenty of time to think things over. No decisions needed to be made until she saw the doctor again.

In the meantime, Jackie explored the town, on foot and by car. She discovered shops and restaurants she loved, a wonderful department store downtown—and, across from that, a big, magnificent bookstore. As she walked from it with two new books on a bright Thursday afternoon, she ran into Rachel Parris.

"Looks like you're up and about," the nurse said. "How are you doing, Mrs. Brede?"

"Much better than when you saw me last, Rachel," she said smiling. "Please, call me Jackie. Is there somewhere around I can buy you a cup of coffee?"

The two spent the rest of the afternoon talking. Jackie shared her situation with her new friend, and got some much-needed advice. "There's a military program for you and the baby, Jackie," Rachel told her. "It's called CHAMPUS. It will pay for your medical bills while your husband is overseas, at the hospital where I work. I can help you start the paperwork when you come in for your exam tomorrow. There's no reason why you should have to pay for your care and treatment out of your own pocket. I'm surprised you husband didn't tell you about this."

"We didn't spend a lot of time discussing military benefits," Jackie said with a wistful smile. "CHAMPUS—that would be marvelous, Rach. Even so, what I really need right now is a job. Ex said he'd only be gone six weeks or so, but it's the Army. God knows how long he'll end up being away—wherever it is they sent him. I won't really know he's home until he steps through the door. Until whenever that is, I have to find a way to make ends meet."

The next morning, Dr. Singer pronounced both Jackie and her child in good health, ready to move on with her travels if she saw fit. "Where are you off to, if you don't mind my asking?" he inquired.

Jackie smiled. "My original plan took me farther up the coast, to San Francisco," she told him. "But now I wonder if I haven't found my journey's end—at least for now. Santa Barbara is a beautiful place, and I'm already beginning to make friends. If I could find a job, I'd probably just stay here."

"What are your skills?" Singer asked her. "What do you want to do? There are some limitations, with the pregnancy, but you have several months before they'll become severe—as long as you're not looking for construction work or logging."

"I've got a nursing degree from the University of Maryland," Jackie told him, "and I'm surgically qualified. For the past five years, I've worked overseas for the Red Cross as a supervisor in one of their programs."

"Sounds impressive. I don't suppose you'd consider a position here? We're always short of nurses—and people with your qualifications are rare indeed."

"What about my condition?"

"That might be a problem," Singer told her, "if you were walking in off the street—but with a physician on staff to vouch for you, it shouldn't be an issue. Come back on Monday, with your resume and references. In the meantime, I'll talk to my supervisor, and the people in personnel. I think if you want a job here, you can have one."

Jackie's eyes filled with tears of relief. "If I knew you better, I'd hug you," she said. "Hell, I'll hug you anyway." She did, with a big smile on her face. "Thank you, Dr. Singer. you've helped three people today, not just one. Believe me, you won't regret it."

CHAPTER FIFTEEN

LANDING ZONES

The loud drone of the big helicopter's engines was mind-numbing, but Brede was far too keyed up to feel drowsy. As Vietnam's coastal fields and rice paddies turned to forest beneath him, he remained actively observing the changing scenery outside—as well as two more big choppers flying with his in formation, ten thousand feet above the war-torn nation spread before him. All were CH-53 Sea Stallions, heavy lifters loaded to far less than their typical capacity, since only a maximum of four nuclear "bird cages" could be safely carried by each one. The third aircraft carried only two of the ten being transported, along with spotting rounds and assembly equipment. He had personally supervised and checked the securing of each component.

Finally, after almost three hours in the air, the formation banked and abruptly lost altitude. Below him, Brede could see the banks of a river, fronted by hilly, grassy terrain, the ruins of an old structure nearby. Scarlet smoke billowed from a nearby field, where vehicles and men were gathered. His morning journey was over. They were settling for a landing.

The impact of ground contact had scarcely registered as crew members opened the large hatch behind Brede and began pushing four coffin-like crates from within the cargo hold to waiting hands outside. The sound of the engines remained a high-pitched thin wail that filled the air around him. He was unceremoniously unstrapped from his seat and pushed out the hold as well. The big chopper lifted up and away from him, quickly disappearing from sight to the northeast. He was on solid ground once more, shaken and confused.

As Brede adjusted his steel pot and fought to clear his head, men worked around him to load the rounds he had delivered to ammo-carrying tracks, four to each vehicle. He barely heard Major Caul shout his name, his ears stilled deadened from the engine noise he'd just endured. Caul shouted his name again, and grabbed his shoulder. Brede turned, wide-eyed, then realized where he was and nodded.

"Still having some trouble hearing, sir," he said in apology, careful not to salute in the field. "Good to be back with the team."

The major nodded, gestured, and led him to a jeep. "You're right on time," he said. "Come on. I'll take you up the hill to our position." Brede nodded, his hearing now beginning to return. He slid into the back of Caul's jeep, which drove toward the river on a narrow trail apparently beaten down by tracked vehicles through the high sawgrass around him.

At midmorning, the sun was an unwatchably searing ball set in a pastel sky. To Brede's right, mountains filled the horizon. The jeep headed up a promontory, allowing him to see a broad blue river to his front, edged by dark, sandy beach. "That's the Sepon," Caul told him, pointing. "Laos is on the other side. The pile of bricks to the north used to be a French penitentiary, where they kept political prisoners. Hold on to your seat. The road gets steep from here."

It did indeed. Tilted upwards as though he were on a roller coaster, Brede was slammed into his seat. As the jeep's motor whined, its driver furiously worked clutch and accelerator, trying to preserve traction and forward motion on a radically steepening path. Just as suddenly, the horizon fell and the jeep jerked to a stop. Wherever they had been going, they'd arrived.

Brede climbed from the jeep and looked around him. He found himself on a flat, almost circular earthen pad about two hundred yards wide. Pieces of large concrete culvert had been haphazardly placed around the pad's perimeter. Men could be seen crawling in and out of them. Behind them sat the two command tracks, now sporting a small forest of radio antennas and tented at their rear hatches. To their left about twenty yards sat two excavated trenches, in which a pair of howitzers were parked, their big gun tubes pointed out over the river. Ammo carrier tracks were backing up behind them. A crew of men was hard at work, digging a bunker nearby to protect unloaded ammunition and powder. "Welcome to Taskforce Tollbooth," Caul said from behind him. "Come on, let me show you around."

Brede was led to the command tracks, while Caul explained what was going on around them. "The engineers punched this space out of the hill we're on. It's almost like we were in a volcano," he said. "They left most of the rock face up to our front, to give us some counter-battery protection. There's most of a company from the 101st dug in on the ridgeline below us and to the east. They're here to protect us from unwanted visitors, but the chances we'll get any are low. There's a battalion of ARVN infantry positioned between us and Khe Sanh. We shouldn't get any unexpected company." He continued walking, entering the tarped area behind the closest track.

"You'll bunk here, with the rest of the officers," Caul told him. "Your cot's already set up. This track is set up as our command post. We have secure radio communication with everybody from 24th Corps down, including the aerial observers who will direct the spotting rounds for us tomorrow. That means we should be able to do what we're here for Wednesday night, if you're ready. I'd do it sooner, but we have to clear the air of any aircraft. Khe Sanh is still a hornet's nest, so that will take a while. We need at least fifty kilometers around the target area free from all flying."

"Ready any time you say, Major." Brede said with a broad smile. "I'm anxious to get done with this and back to my life." He threw his backpack on the cot he'd been assigned, went to find the Chief of Firing Battery, to explain the M424 spotting rounds they'd be firing to him.

"We've got ten rounds of M424 here," he told Sergeant Betancourt. "They won't look or feel much like the nuclear round to your gun crews, but they'll act the same ballistically and aerodynamically. Once we've found the target with them, our next round can be the real thing."

"Any special loading problems?" the CFB asked.

"None that I'm aware of," Brede told him. "Are you using both guns?"

"Nah. We're going to use the gun with the autoloader, for a more consistent ram. That is, if the damn thing holds up. So far, it hasn't been super-hot up here. Maybe we'll get lucky."

Later on, after the spotting rounds were uncrated and set by the howitzer, Brede took a break to scan the land beyond their position to the east and north—back toward Khe Sanh. He could see intermittent the flashes of artillery on the horizon, and hear the heavy "crump" of mortar fire. The action around him may have calmed some, he decided, but it was not over.

He walked to the areas where the nuclear rounds themselves had been placed, still in their birdcages and crates (they'd set up one of the ammo carriers to use as an assembly area, but the weapons wouldn't be moved there before assembly). Since the day he'd been introduced to these weapons, Brede had always wondered what it would be like to actually detonate one—as he imagined most men who worked with them did, from time to time. Now he would find out. Though mildly excited by the prospect, his primary emotion was anxiety. More than all else, he wanted to finish this mission and get back to the woman he loved.

The day ended without incident, night falling suddenly as a curtain over the men on the riverside hill. All was quiet as they ate their c-rations and settled in for the evening. Morning would come early.

The sun had yet to rise when Brede was awakened. Beemer and Caul were already working the radios in the command track, talking to 108th Group. The observers would soon be airborne, in their fragile O-1 "Bird Dog." The little plane, really no more than a civilian Piper Cub, would take more than two hours to reach its station after take-off, even flying as fast as it could. It would fly a track paralleling the Sepon River, looking into the heavy forest to the west where the Ho Chi Minh Trail lay. At an altitude of a thousand feet, the observer would be able to direct fire to the broad trail easily enough. Though equipped with two radios—one for the pilot to talk to ground control, and one for the observer to talk to the firing unit—only one could draw power at a time, so aerial observation missions took a while. Enemy gunners would try their best to shoot the little aircraft out of the sky while this was going on. Brave men flew these missions.

Brede listened as Beemer contacted the observer: "Tiny Doorstep five-two, this is Rapid Student zero-six, over."

"Student, Doorstep, Go."

"Checking in, Doorstep. Come back when you're at the target area, over."

"Roger, Student. We're just up. Back in a while, out."

While they waited, Brede walked to the gun that would be firing. Bentancourt was standing beside it. "What's the word, Smoke?" he asked.

"Looks good, sir," the Chief of Firing Battery replied. "Rammer's working like we was in Grafenwöhr. I'm hoping for a good day."

"How does the powder look?"

"Not too damp, lieutenant. So far, anyhow. If metro cooperates, we should be okay."

Brede made his way back to the command track, hoping the metro news was good. Eight inch artillery shells traveled at altitudes high enough to make them subject to meteorological influences. Severe winds or variation in air pressure could affect the accuracy of trajectories. He was relieved to hear that FDC saw no big problems with the air they were shooting through. He got himself a cup of awful coffee and waited through an hour that seemed far longer.

Finally, the voice of the observer was heard again: "Rapid Student zero-six, this is Tiny Doorstep five-two. Estimate in position in five, over."

These were the days before earth satellites and GPS had accurately mapped the world. Exact geodesic locations remained unknown in many parts of the planet, and maps in remote areas were often based on surveys conducted decades ago. Yet the placement of artillery rounds demands precise location determination. U.S. Army units used teams of surveyors to provide them with correct position information. These men often risked their lives to lay chains forward from precisely known locations. Even their heroic efforts were not enough in many undeveloped areas, like those faced in southeast Asia. Here target map coordinates were at best approximate, many from nineteenth century French surveys. Rounds fired by artillery had to be directed and adjusted to find actual target positions. The process, carried out by forward observers who could see the desired target, radioed changes in range or deflection necessary for the gun's rounds to strike meaningfully. No more than four or five rounds were needed for an experienced observer to adjust fire to strike a specific target. Whether in the air or on the ground, the forward observer's job was dangerous. Those being targeted frantically tried to find and silence him. Many hateful eyes would watch "Tiny Doorstep five-two" as the eight-inch rounds he directed fell closer to their target, meter by meter.

A few minutes later, ten miles away and a thousand feet above the deep forests of Laos, the little fabric-winged airplane carrying "Doorstep" banked to fly parallel to a wide. gently sloping path below it. People could be seen walking the path in large groups, flanked by squadrons of heavily loaded bicycles. They had found the Ho Chi Minh Trail. The observer, a veteran of twenty previous missions, focused his gyroscopically compensating binoculars and contacted the waiting guns. "Student, Doorstep: in position, over."

Back at Taskforce Tollbooth, gun two's chief of section sealed the howitzer's breech and pulled the lanyard. As he heard the thunderous report that followed, Beemer contacted the observer. "Doorstep, Student: shot one round, over."

An eight-inch artillery shell, specially designed to share the aerodynamic profile of a nuclear round, arced its way toward the approximate target position calculated by the men in the fire direction center—the FDC. Moving at supersonic speed, reaching as high as 31,000 feet in altitude, the round exploded fifty meters above the ground in less than two minutes. "Tiny Doorstep five-two" estimated the impact was at least two-hundred meters beyond the trail and a hundred meters right of it. "Student, Doorstep: drop two-hundred, left one-hundred."

The FDC recalculated target coordinates and passed them to the gun crew. Within a minute, a second round was fired. "Doorstep, Student: shot one round."

Banking to make another pass, the little plane was able to watch the second round's impact, which the observer judged low by a hundred meters and left by fifty meters. "Student, Doorstep: add one-hundred, right five-zero," he radioed.

In the meantime, the gun crew lowered, opened, and swabbed the big howitzer's gun tube while they prepared another round for firing. When corrections from the FDC reached the gunner, the next round was rammed and quickly fired. "Doorstep, Student: shot one round," Beemer reported.

Two minutes later, the observer on the little plane—now under fire from the ground—gave his final corrections. "Student, Doorstep: add five-zero, left two-zero, fire for effect." The Bird Dog banked and dived to avoid a sudden burst of machine gun fire.

There'd be no more rounds fired today. Before a nuclear round could hit the now-verified location, all aircraft flying within fifty kilometers of the area would have to be warned from the sky. "Doorstep, Student: end of mission." Beemer broadcast.

The little plane banked again, scrabbled for altitude as enemy fire sang through its fabric wings, and made its way back across the Sepon River.

"Roger, Student. See you on the other side, out," the observer concluded, ending the radio conversation.

"We'll fire our first rounds this evening," Caul told Brede, "as soon as the sun goes down and everybody gets out of the air. You'd better start to set up."

Jackie was happy. Dr. Singer had found the baby healthy and developing well—and had also given her a clean bill of health. Just as important, she had landed a job, a nursing position at Santa Barbara Cottage Hospital. She'd be on call at first, working odd hours to fill in if another nurse was unavailable, but the head of nursing assured her that she'd be on regular shifts before too long. With the job and Ex's pay, she'd be able to handle the bills and also put some money away for college.

There was even more good news. She'd found a place to live. Upon leaving the hospital Monday morning, she'd decided on a whim to cruise the streets nearby just in case some "for rent" signs popped up. To her surprise, a small, rusty yellow sign hung in front of a pair of what looked like cottages—on Prospect Avenue, about a mile up the hill from her new place of work. She pulled off the street into a long driveway, surrounded by a grove of avocado trees. The steep hillside dropped away to her front, with a view over what looked like a park. She left the car, climbed a wooden staircase surrounded by garden, rang the doorbell of a narrow old house.

She heard no sound for a long time, and was about to turn away when the high red door in front of her suddenly opened. A small woman leaning on a cane looked out at her from the depths of the cottage's interior. Her long, pale, heavily lined face was framed by slate grey hair. She wore thick glasses and spoke in a loud, clear voice. "Why have you rung my bell?" she asked.

Jackie was taken aback, even more so as a large parrot landed on the woman's shoulder in a torrent of colorful feathers. "I ... I saw the sign on your lawn," she stammered.

"*Saw the sign!*" the parrot squawked, focusing on her with one gleaming eye.

"That old sign!" the woman scoffed, shaking her head. "Been up for years. You're the first to notice in ages. Probably should take the damn thing down."

"So you have no cottages for rent?" Jackie whispered, as she began to back away from the door.

"Didn't say that, did I?" the woman responded. "Don't let Imogene scare you. She's docile enough once she gets to know you."

"*Didn't say that!*" the multi-hued bird echoed, flapping its big wings.

Jackie decided to stand her ground. "I'm new in town, ma'am," she said as calmly as she could. "I'm a nurse. Just got work with the hospital down the hill. I was looking for a place to rent …"

"A nurse, is it?" the woman interrupted, cocking her head even as her parrot did the same. "Might have something. Want to look?"

"*Want to look!*" the bird squawked, launching itself back into the house in a flurry of red, green, and blue brilliance. The little woman sighed, walked forward and shut the door behind her, gesturing for Jackie to follow. Heavily favoring her cane, she slowly made her way down the steps and across the driveway to another, smaller structure, reaching into the pocket of her sweater to produce a large brass key.

"The place has been empty for a long time," the woman said over her shoulder as she walked. "Apologies for the dust. It cleans up bright enough." She stopped and turned. "Before we go in, tell me a little about yourself."

"My name is Jacquelline Brede," Jackie said, gaining back some confidence now. "I'm a service wife, just married. My husband is overseas. He'll be home in the fall. I'm hoping to take some courses at UCSB while I'm waiting for his return. Along with the job, they should keep me busy. This location is wonderful—quiet, great views, I could walk to work."

The woman nodded. "The exercise will do you good, as long as you're up to it," she said. "When is the baby due?"

Jackie blushed. "In October. I hadn't realized it was so obvious," she murmured.

The woman's lined face softened. "It's not, my dear," she said. "Old women like me who have been mothers ourselves can often tell. Are you new to southern California?"

"Yes," Jackie said, "mostly here by accident, I'm afraid. Trying to pull a life together from loose threads."

The woman looked at her intently, nodding. "The place is furnished, but we can put away any pieces you don't need." She hefted the big key, using it to unlock and open the cottage door. "Come along then," she said as she guided Jackie inside.

They entered what had to be the cottage's main room, wood-floored with high plaster walls, framed with windows on three sides. Two of the windows featured built-in seats, and craftsman-style cabinets lined the rear wall. A wood-framed entry led to a small kitchen. The room was furnished with a couch and two upholstered chairs, covered with sheets and facing each other over a long coffee table. A larger table with three wooden chairs stood adjacent to the kitchen. Two radiators across from one another provided heat—not needed on this, a beautiful late spring day.

"The furniture comes with the place unless you've got your own. My name's Ava, by the way. Ava Whitehouse. My family's been in Santa Barbara a long, long time. We used to own the entire hill. Now this is all that's left. This, me, and Imogene of course." She led Jackie into the kitchen.

The small kitchen was brightly lit with ceiling lamps and a big window facing the driveway. The tiled counter featured a two-tub sink set in a waist-high cabinet that included space for two high stools set against it. Shelves holding plates and glasses lined the facing wall, next to an aging gas stove and a small refrigerator. "The appliances all work," Ava told her. "Everything here is yours to use. What you don't want, you can bring over to my place."

"I'll need everything, at least to start," Jackie told her. "All I have with me are some clothes in a suitcase."

There were two doors on the back wall. "The door on the right leads to a laundry room," Ava said. "There's an old washer in there that still works, a sink and an ironing board. A clothesline's been hung out back."

She opened the left-hand door. "Here's the bedroom," she said as she stepped through. The room they entered spanned most of the width of the cottage, with a large, curtained window overlooking a grove of Avocado trees. A high, wide wooden bed with nightstands to either side took up half the space. A mirrored wardrobe stood against the far wall. The door to a small bathroom stood ajar, showing the leg of a claw-foot tub. Her first vision of the room, as sunlight dappled by the swaying leaves of the trees outside kissed its walls, convinced Jackie she'd found a home. Still, she spent the next half hour going through the little cottage, walking from one end to the other, trying to envision what living here would be like—alone, with Ex, and with a baby.

"There's room here for a crib when you need it," Ava said. "Plenty of sheets and blankets in the wardrobe. The plumbing in the bathroom's all good. No leaks. There's another bedroom below, with its own bathroom. Have to go outside to get in. I won't charge you rent for that, unless you have a guest who needs to use it. Any questions?"

Jackie had none. She saw no reason to hesitate. This little cottage fit all of her needs. It was a place she could make her own. "I won't bother to haggle over price, Ava," she said. "This is exactly what I'd hoped to find. If I can afford it, I'll move in this week. How much do you want for rent?"

The small woman remained quiet, looking at her intently as she leaned on her cane. "The cottage has remained empty for a while, a long while," she finally said. "Others have stopped to look, but I never found any among them I wanted nearby. Imogene and I live quietly, and enjoy our privacy. Will you be a good neighbor?"

"There will be a baby in October, and my husband will be here a month before that. He and I aren't loud, but the baby may fuss from time to time. I'll try to be the best neighbor I can, Ava. I feel drawn to the cottage already. It's truly a beautiful little jewel—a great place for us to start our family."

"I'll charge you $250 a month, plus utilities," Ava said, "all due the first of the month. You can bring the check to my door. One month's rent as deposit. Bring the deposit and the first month's rent with you when you move in."

She handed Jackie the big brass key. "Welcome," she said, holding her new renter's hand. "I'm glad you found us."

CHAPTER SIXTEEN

FIRST IMPACTS

As a bloated red sun sank below Laotian hills to their west, the tempo of activity among the men of Taskforce Tollbooth increased. The howitzer which would fire the nuclear rounds was thoroughly inspected. In the fire direction center, coordinates and firing solutions for tonight's mission were checked and rechecked. Infantry at the base of the hill were put on high alert. No intrusions could be allowed now. Soon, all aircraft would be warned from the skies within fifty kilometers of the target—a wide, smooth strip of beaten dirt track descending a gentle hill, ten miles beyond the Sepon River beach they sat above. That path itself saw heavy traffic now. Evening brought the trucks out in force, headlights dimmed, pushing bicycle and pedestrian traffic aside. They were a mixed automotive collection, some Russian, some Chinese, some ancient Fords and Studebakers from World War II lend-lease—rumbling south, their transmissions grinding.

Within one of the ammo carrier tracks, Brede and his assembly teammate—a three-stripe sergeant named Pickering—worked to assemble the fourth of six nuclear rounds planned to be shot tonight. It was hot and close inside the canvas-covered track bed. Both men were stripped to the waist and perspiring heavily. The wiped their hands often on towels draped over their shoulders, careful to keep the metal parts they worked with dry and clean. The sweet, caustic odor of degreasing tri-chloroethylene pervaded their space.

Having trained together in Korea, each man knew well what he had to do, and what his partner must do in turn. Both men were armed with pistols—not because of enemy threat, but due to the compulsory paranoia of the "two-man rule." The rule, still observed when nuclear weapons of all varieties are handled in any way, is simple. It assumes that at least one of two equally knowledgeable men working with such a weapon is not a traitor. If that person's team-mate shows treasonous activity or intent, his partner is required to disable or kill him immediately. Neither Brede nor Pickering paid overt attention to the rule, but it remained in the back of each man's mind—as it always must for those who work with these terrible instruments of destruction.

After half an hour of hard work under bad light, the men lowered the titanium sheath over the assembled round, making it ready to rain kilotons of irresistible nuclear fire on its target. They dropped from the track bed to the ground, glad to have fresh air and a breeze around them. Brede slapped his partner's shoulder. "Good work, Pick," he said. "Go tell the section chief to haul this one over to the gun, then take a break. I'm going to have a smoke and get some coffee before we start working on the next one."

As the sergeant hurried off, Brede stretched and shrugged into his fatigue shirt as he looked around the area. Twilight was bringing cooler air to the hilltop. By midnight some would look for light sweaters against the evening's relative chill. Stepping to a safe area, he lit a cigarette and silently studied the activity around him, as his unit worked to perform its mission. Four men arrived with a loading pallet, carefully hefting and moving the assembled round to the waiting howitzer. The gun's loader-rammer still worked perfectly. Soon the breech was closed. The first nuclear weapon used in anger since 1945 was ready to find its target.

An initial "no-fly" warning was transmitted unencoded over several frequencies to all aircraft and aviation units in or near Quang Tri Province at eighteen-thirty hours local time, demarcating a fifty-kilometer circular zone centered on Lao Bao prison's coordinates. The ban on all air traffic within the zone would remain in effect from nineteen-hundred to twenty-four-hundred hours. After twenty additional minutes were allowed to verify the airspace was cleared, permission was transmitted to Taskforce Tollbooth to commence firing. One minute later, the first W33 round thundered from its howitzer's gun tube.

The men on Hill 213 raised a subdued, ragged cheer as the howitzer boomed with overwhelming noise and dustily recoiled. There were no friendly eyes directly on the round's impact, though an orbiting Corona spy satellite captured the event for later examination—once its film canister was recovered over Canada. An experimental Vela satellite, designed to watch for nuclear explosions, recorded the event as well. Other robotic eyes may also have glimpsed the brilliant flash.

An impossibly bright almost-star lived briefly where the round detonated, one hundred fifty feet above Laotian forest. Vehicles, trees, dirt, and people within four-hundred feet of that event instantaneously dissolved, completely disintegrated. Anyone closer than half-a-mile away died from burns and blast concussion. A glowing, writhing gold-to-purple cloud rose from the initial explosion, carrying with it particles of metal, wood, and flesh. Some of these—the heaviest—would soon fall back to earth. The rest would coalesce into the emblematic mushroom shape that would climb more than two miles as it moved northeast, morphing into a glowing, writhing pyro-cumulus cloud as it drifted.

Those near the target zone who escaped annihilation may have turned north or south on the trail to escape the horror confronting them. Some may have survived, at least until radiation exposure killed them—but most were caught by the second, third, and subsequent nuclear rounds which impacted the area during the next two hours. By midnight, when the no-fly order was lifted, six large craters cut the trail and its western subsidiary. Each was more than forty feet deep and almost two-hundred feet wide. To airborne reconnaissance cameras that photographed them the next day, they looked like giant steps down the slope of the hill where they'd been aimed, now filling like small lakes due to the region's high water table. Months—if not years—of work using heavy construction equipment would be needed to make the trail usable again once background radiation had subsided. At the crater perimeters, blasted, fused sand replaced underbrush, and fitful, winking fires added smoke and haze to the opaque air. Trees and foliage in what had been dense surrounding forest were destroyed or wrenched from their roots, leaving barren, glassy soil behind. Further up the trail, the remains of destroyed vehicles still smoldered and burned, consuming the dead who lay around them. Those attempting to enter the area later without protective clothing soon found themselves poisoned. Many died. Operation Tollbooth had succeeded. The date was April 24, 1968, and the Ho Chi Minh Trail was now closed.

Soldiers on the hill above the Sepon ten miles distant had been cautioned to look away from the monstrous eruptions they caused that night.

Those few who disregarded that warning suffered blindness and corneal burns. Everyone in the task force heard the enormous explosions and felt the ground beneath them heave furiously as each round detonated. They watched the eerie clouds that rose, spread and climbed away to the northeast—each glowing, roiling, and flashing as it moved. The Moon rose as a decaying crescent that night. Hellish clouds scudded above it as they rose, turning the evening sky otherworldly.

Even though he'd thought himself more prepared for what he witnessed, Brede was as shocked and shaken by the horrifying aftermath as those around him. He would never wonder again what the effects of the weapons he worked with could be—nor would he want to cause them, he decided. He looked to his left as the last blazing cloud began drifting away, and saw Caul standing nearby. "What happens now, sir?" he asked.

"Now we wait," Caul said. "We'll have recon in the morning, once the planes are up. If we're lucky, we'll get some radio traffic intercepts we can use on top of that. If the mission's completed, we'll head back to Dong Ha—probably drop off the guns and their crews along the way. If there's still work to do, we've got four more rounds on site, and as many more as we need in the pipeline. Go get some sleep, Ex. It's been a long day. You did a good job."

Brede got to his cot, sat down, and lit a cigarette. He looked around him, at foliage sprayed with Agent Orange on the nearby perimeter and wondered at their demise. When exposed to the defoliant, plants didn't merely wilt and die, he'd noticed. Instead, they bloomed brilliantly for a while, as if using up their life force in one last spasm—then quickly fell away to dust. He wondered idly what effect the chemical had on people, stubbed out his smoke and lay down.

Sleep was difficult for Brede to achieve that night. He tossed and turned on his narrow cot. In his mind's eye, he watched a never-ending procession of roiling, incandescent mushroom clouds move across his line of vision, their cancerous light bathing the world around him.

The morning after renting the Prospect Avenue cottage, Jackie set out on a sixty-mile drive up U.S. 101. Her destination was an Air Force base, just outside the small town of Lompoc. Vandenberg was enormous and still growing, the place where the nation's huge intercontinental rockets were perfected. It was the closest military facility of any size to Santa Barbara. Her hope was that the finance department there could get her husband's pay sent to her now that she'd established a permanent address.

She filled the car's tank with gas and got on the road early, aiming to reach the base before late morning. The air around her was fresh and cool, the sky blue with few clouds apparent. The highway climbed along California's Pacific coast, above pretty beaches. Half an hour into her journey, Jackie left the 101 for CA 1—a less scenic road that arced inland as it climbed the surrounding hills to the picturesque flower farms around Lompoc. She'd been driving a little more than an hour   by the time she approached Vandenberg, which spread out in front of her. The Air Police at the gate listened to her request, examined her military ID card carefully, and directed her up California Street to Washington—where the base finance office was located. She parked in front of the big, square sand-colored building she found behind the large sign, grabbed the file folder Will Gilliam had given her what seemed so long ago now, and walked through the double glass doors to put her immediate financial life in order.

Jackie went to the information desk, explained her needs, was given a numbered card and told to wait until that number was announced. She sat in the building's waiting area for about twenty minutes until being called forward. Her needs were addressed quickly, thanks to Gilliam's preparations. A sergeant told her she'd begin getting her husband's regular allotments in May and gave her a phone number to call if she had any problems. Within an hour, she was driving through the base gates again, her business concluded.

Jackie had intended to return to Santa Barbara, but stopped to reconsider when she glanced at her road map. Solvang, where Ex had wanted them to spend their honeymoon, was less than an hour away—and she had the rest of the day off. On the spur of the moment, she decided to take a side trip to the place he'd found so enchanting.

She'd driven half an hour on CA 246 when she reached the town of Buelton. A big, high sign to her left proclaimed she was passing the home of "PEA SOUP Andersen's." Since she'd never been fond of that thick, green broth she drove on. Three miles down the road, she found herself passing Hans Christian Andersen Park and entering the colony of Solvang—Danish for "sunny field." Her first impression of the town explained why Ex wanted to honeymoon here. Solvang was adorable! She parked the Falcon and wandered through the village streets, stopping to investigate fascinating shops with displays that caught her eye. Realizing she was hungry, she got brunch at one of the town's restaurants—delicate Danish pancakes with sausage—delicious! She treated herself, purchasing an "Aebleskiver Cookbook," a good start she thought to a collection she planned to begin. As she walked through the jewel-like little town, Jackie tried to imagine being there with Ex. What fun they'd have had! She realized Solvang would always have a special place in her heart, and promised herself to return soon.

By the time Jackie got back to her car and headed down San Marcos Pass Road to Santa Barbara, it was late afternoon. She needed less than two hours to make it back to the narrow driveway on Prospect Avenue, unlock the door to her cottage, and stand in her new home. She decided she and Ex would take a trip to Solvang as soon as he came back to her. September couldn't come quickly enough.

The next day, Jackie drove to her first day of work at Santa Barbara Cottage Hospital. She'd made up her mind to walk to work as long as she could, but realized she'd have uniforms and other items to bring home today. After an hour in the personnel office filling out forms, she was issued her uniforms, escorted to her ward and introduced to one of her shift supervisors, an older woman named Jean McGill. Jean was short, with silver-grey hair and intense blue eyes. Her seamed face was proof she laughed more than she frowned. When they shook hands, her grip was firm and dry. "I'm glad for the help," she said. "Lord knows we need it here. Santa Barbara is twice the size it was when I got here. I'm told you have plenty of nursing experience."

Jackie nodded. "I've been working as a nurse or an administrator for almost twenty years," she said. "I'm glad to get back to nursing. I've missed it."

The older nurse laughed. "We'll keep you plenty busy," she said, nodding. "This is a general ward. We get patients of all kinds, from people going into surgery to injury recovery. I'll show you around, but before I do we have to talk about your own medical condition."

"I'm expecting the baby in October," Jackie said. "My health is good, at least so far. I should be fit for duty until August at least."

"You look great," Jean told her. "As long as you're up to the work, there won't be a problem. I'll leave it to you to let me know when you think you have to slow down. We can put you at a desk after that. Come along. Let's take a walk through the ward."

That evening, as she sat in the cottage's living room wishing silently for a martini (or at least a cigarette), Jackie considered the day she'd been through. She would walk to work from now on, she decided. The exercise would do her good, until August at any rate. She was hardly showing any "baby bump" yet, and didn't expect to for another month at least. Jean seemed like a good supervisor, and her first day on the ward had held few surprises. She realized the past few years—her years in Korea before she met Ex—had been a neutral waiting time. Now, she was coming back to life. The curtains were slowly parting. She had no idea what would eventually be revealed, but she felt ready to meet her future.

CHAPTER SEVENTEEN

OLD TRAINING

B rede felt as though his eyes had only closed a second when he awoke, neither rested nor refreshed. He sat on his cot for a time, rubbing sandy itchiness from his bleary eyes, trying to make sense of the world around him.

He looked at his wristwatch, discovering it was past oh-seven-hundred— far later than he'd wanted to sleep. He saw others around him still asleep, but decided to rise and meet the day. Sleep could wait until he saw Jackie once more. Brede grabbed a clean t-shirt, his shaving kit, a towel and took his empty steel pot to a nearby lister bag. Filling the helmet about half full of water, he washed his face and upper body, toweled himself dry, shaved and brushed his teeth before emptying the water off the side of the hill and shrugging into the t-shirt. Returning to his cot, he stowed his kit underneath it, dried the helmet's interior, put it and a helmet liner on, donned his fatigue shirt, changed his socks, and went to get coffee to begin his day. His preparations took him less than fifteen minutes, from the time his eyes blinked open until he sat on his cot once more, cigarette and coffee in hand.

As he sipped his awful coffee, Brede's thoughts wandered back to the time he'd spent hitchhiking through Europe, just two years ago. He'd often awakened outdoors back then, in a farmer's field or beside a road, part of an ever-changing troupe that included Australian, Canadian, and European quasi-adults wandering roads from Brittany to Barcelona— pooling funds cajoled from parents and friends to buy cigarettes, wine, drugs, and bread. Some of the Americans were avoiding draft notices ineffectually seeking them through the mail. From time to time, a few would tire of thrill that became drudgery as the road stretched before them. They fell away from the group, quickly replaced by fresher faces in their wake. Brede lasted nearly half a year—before a minor row with his German girlfriend woke him to the grubby pointlessness his life had become.

The military encampment he was in had much in common with his bohemian roadside stops, Brede suddenly recognized. Both were purely temporary, and offered barely minimal levels of personal privacy or comfort. Of course, the Army was far better organized and directed than a gaggle of wandering college drop-outs. Still, similarities abounded. He allowed himself a wry smile. The more things changed, the more they stayed the same, he decided.

Shaking his head to clear his mind, he rose and walked to the command track, eager to know whether the Tollbooth mission was concluding. As he entered, Caul was ending an encrypted transmission. The task force commander smiled when he saw Brede. "I was just on the horn with group," he said. "Initial recon is in. The Ho Chi Minh Trail is out of business. Our rounds cut it decisively. Nothing's going to get much further south than Tchepone on that road for a long time. Maybe years."

"That's great news, sir," Brede said. "So, are we done?"

"Group wants us to stay in place for a couple more days, just to make sure the bad guys don't try anything," Caul said. "We've got enough conventional rounds with us to help out the local situation, if that needs to happen." He saw Brede's frown. "Don't worry, Ex. It's only a precaution. Plans are for you to be in the air going back to Korea by the weekend."

Brede nodded, feeling somewhat better. "Any news from the world?" he asked.

"Both the North Vietnamese and the Chinese are accusing us of using atomic weapons or poison gas—or both," Caul said. "The Soviets say their analysis points to natural causes. Nobody's certain, and that's the way we like it. It will be a while before any physical evidence gets out of Laos. The area is fairly remote, and we're not letting anybody in from this side. Meanwhile, we're keeping our mouths shut. Must have been an earthquake, as far as we know."

Brede made a "zipped lips" gesture and began to walk away, just as a high, droning whistle announced incoming artillery fire. A round detonated at the northern base of the hill the task force sat on. Four more followed quickly, marching up Hill 213's face. Six subsequent explosions damaged Tollbooth's left howitzer, killing a soldier and wounding two more with whining shrapnel.

"Incoming!" Caul yelled. "Everybody down!"

The explosions ceased. The major rose and ran to a shallow, still-smoking crater nearby. Beemer joined him. The major pulled a slim stick from his pocket, stuck it into the crater, then pulled out a compass. "My azimuth reading's three-four-seven," he said. "Check me, Jake."

Beemer nodded. "I concur. The size of the hole, the shrapnel, looks close to our one-oh-five. I'll call it a one-twenty-two, Major."

"Get over to FDC," Caul told his XO. "Let's get some counter-battery started before they hit us more. Assume five to seven mile range along the azimuth." Beemer hurried off. "Get down to the infantry," the major called to Brede. "Tell them we've got an observer somewhere around, directing fire on this hill."

Three men lay near the damaged howitzer, already getting aid from the task force medic. He looked up when he saw Caul hurrying his way. "One dead, two need dustoff," Caul was told. "I don't give either man a day if we don't get them out of here."

Caul nodded. "I'll call it in now. Get Sergeant Betancourt over to the command track when you see him." He darted away without waiting for a reply.

Brede got himself to the hill's base as quickly as he could, and found a sergeant peering from a nearby foxhole. "We just got some incoming ..." he said.

The trooper nodded. "No shit!" he said. "We got patrols out to find the observer. Get back up the hill and tell your CO we're doing what we can. He should contact the ARVNs up the road, see if they're getting hit. We tried, got no answer."

Brede nodded and scrambled back up the hill. He made his way to the command track, where Caul and the First Sergeant were on the radio—calling for medevac, aerial observers and ARVN support. The First Sergeant signed off. "We'll have a dustoff chopper coming in quick, Major," he said, "down in the flat to our south. I'll get some men to help me get the stretchers down there and give us security. I'll be laying smoke."

"Get to it, Top," Caul said over his shoulder. He'd been trying to contact the ARVN battalion to the north. So far, he'd gotten no response. He looked at the silent radio and cursed. Where were those guys?

Switching frequencies, he radioed Group Headquarters again, and immediately asked to "go green"—slang of the time for switching to encrypted transmission.

"Long time no hear," Brill responded once the signal was secure. "What's the problem?"

"We've been hit," Caul told him, "just now. Looks like one-two-twos, eight klicks north, probably firing from Laos. One KIA, two wounded, one gun out. Dustoff is on the way. I need some fire support. Also need to know the status of the ARVNs to our north. Tried to contact them several times, no response, over."

"I'll get to work on counter-battery," Brill replied. "Can the gun be repaired? I'll contact Fourth ARVN, see what's going on, over."

"Starting to feel kinda lonely out here." Caul said. "I'll let you know about the gun. Get back to me when you hear from the ARVN, out."

Caul turned from the radio to see Bentancourt, the chief of firing battery, standing before him. "Tell me about the gun, smoke," he said.

The sergeant shook his head. "Gun one took three hits," he said. "The turret motor's out, and the traverse pump. Cherry juice all over the damn place. Pneumatic equilibrator's shot too. Can't move her very far—a road wheel's gone. She's scrap, sir, unless we can somehow tow her to depot."

"Can she fire at all?"

"Maybe one or two rounds, wherever she's pointing now. I wouldn't want to be close by if we tried it."

Caul grimaced. "Shit!" he said, shaking his head. "Strip her then, and get ready to spike the gun tube. We'll leave her when we go, but I don't want anything useful left on her." Betancourt nodded, and quickly moved away.

By now Brede had climbed back up the hill to report what he'd heard from the infantry below. He watched the dustoff Huey land noisily in a field of stunted sawgrass to the south, where red smoke billowed in the wind as an escort gunship orbited above. In less than a minute both helicopters were retreating into the sun—only dissipating smoke and the sound of their engines left behind.

The first sergeant pushed by him to report to Caul. "The wounded are gone, sir." He said. "Pilot reported ground fire as they came in, about five klicks north at the tree line."

The major nodded, and turned to face Brede. "I know they taught you how to direct fire in OCS," he said. "Put those skills to work now. Get back down to the infantry, get some radio equipment, and find me some bad guys to shoot at. Your call sign will be Rapid Student three-one. Take an M-16 with you. You might need it. Get going."

Startled by the order, Brede could only nod wide-eyed.

"Get going, lieutenant!" Caul repeated. Brede hurried from the command track, wondering how well he'd remember what he'd been taught all those months ago. As he loped down the hill, he grinned at the irony. He always assumed he'd end up a forward observer. Now he finally had.

Two hours later, he and two other men walked a path through a field of sawgrass, approaching a line of trees in the distance. The soldier to his front signaled for the trio to stop, and all sank to the ground.

"I'm seeing movement at the tree line," said the soldier, a corporal named Tremaine.

Brede lifted the binoculars he carried and scanned the area Tremaine had noted. "I see them too," he said. "Looks like a squad or better. There may be others behind them. I see more movement in the grass, further back." He nodded to the radio operator, who knelt beside him. "Get the radio on my freq, Johnson. I'm calling it in."

When the mike was handed to him, Brede contacted the task force, logged into the network, and established his estimated location—roughly two kilometers north-northwest of the hill where the taskforce sat.

"Activity to my direct front," Brede radioed the command track. "Looks like a squad or better with more movement behind them in the grass, five-hundred meters north of my location. Fire mission, over."

"On the way, over," came the almost immediate reply.

"Left one-hundred, add two-hundred," Brede transmitted as soon as the round hit.

"On the way, over."

"Right five-zero, add five-zero, fire for effect," was Brede's final adjustment.

"One round COFRAM, on the way." Brill replied calmly.

Brede watched the men in the tree-line, as a loud popping noise that might have come from a gigantic firecracker assaulted his ears. The enemy soldiers he saw began to dance and scream, as hundreds of explosions erupted among them. A second COFRAM round detonated, and the screams abated.

"Cease fire," Brede radioed. "There's movement behind these guys, in the sawgrass. Recommend Whiskey Papa to light them up. Add one-hundred, fire for effect."

"Roger three-one. On the way, over."

Three white phosphorus rounds detonated in quick succession as Brede watched through his binoculars. The sawgrass was enveloped by explosions of thick white smoke, which quickly set the area ablaze. More yelling could be heard, and forms stumbled through the smoky, toxic fog that now pervaded the area. Several more large explosions erupted. Apparently, the approaching enemies had carried supplies of ammunition or explosives, now ignited by the phosphorus.

Brede watched the bombarded area for several minutes, searching for signs of movement among the scorched, burning grass and splintered trees before him. He found none.

"Targets eliminated," he reported. "Returning to base."

As he stood to brush himself off, Johnson grabbed his shoulder. "What the fuck is that?" the trooper asked, pointing at the field in front of them.

Brede raised his binoculars to get a better look. Five-hundred meters from where the three soldiers lay, an apparition had slammed through the tree line and now roared toward them. The narrow black shape, its bed and tires aflame, bounced and crashed through the field fronting the target they had just destroyed—igniting small fires around it as it came.

"That's a logger's truck," Tremaine told them. "We know some of them are VC, but they're allowed to cut down trees in this area. If it gets much closer, I'll take it out."

He reached in his pack and withdrew a dark green plastic tube about two feet long and four inches wide. "Stand to my side," he told Brede and Johnson. The trooper crouched and pulled the tube to his shoulder, as its sight clicked into place. "LAW's good for about six hundred meters" he said. "Let me know when you think that truck's close enough, sir."

Brede looked through his bino's at the truck, which continued to labor toward them through the field of high sawgrass, igniting fires behind it as it came. By now it was so near that he could see the NVA soldiers in the cab. He tapped Tremaine's shoulder. "Close enough," he said.

A smoky arc erupted from the tube as the trooper pulled its trigger. It hit the oncoming vehicle almost instantaneously, ripping the black shape to wreckage with an enormous explosion. Momentum kept the shattered bed of the truck coming closer, until it finally slid and crumpled to rest about half a football field away from Brede and his companions. Incredibly, a fiery shape staggered from the still burning hulk, lurching a few steps before sinking to the smoldering sawgrass. Then silence reigned, punctuated by the snap of flickering fires. As the sun reddened and began to set, the trio made their way back to the hill as quickly as they could. Night in the fields around them would not be safe.

Jackie carefully backed her Falcon up the narrow driveway on Prospect Avenue, stopping several feet away from the chromed bullet nose of Ava's venerable Studebaker. The large parrot, Imogene, had perched herself on the old car's roof. She squawked as she saw Jackie pull in. "*Careful!*" she shrieked, "*Mind the paint!*" As the car stopped she flew away, into the avocado trees.

Jackie laughed as she slid from the car's seat. The old bird was as cantankerous as her owner, but meant no harm. Ava was quickly becoming a friend. After only a few days here, Jackie knew she was adjusting to this place, where her instincts told her she was meant to be—at least for now.

As she stood from the car, Jackie stretched. She'd finished her shift at Cottage Hospital, marveling at how quickly her old skills and knowledge returned. Afterwards, she had stayed for a scheduled check-up with Dr. Singer. He pronounced her in great shape, and treated her to an experience she'd never had before. For the first time, she got to hear her baby's heartbeat. It was strong and sure, filling her with wonder. Her child—hers and Ex's—a miracle she longed to share with him. She hugged herself, laughing out loud at the joy of it. What a family they'd be! She wondered how many more days would pass before she could tell him the news. Surely not too much longer, she hoped. He'd said it would be six weeks. She looked up, wondering if somewhere around the edge of the world he looked at the same sky.

CHAPTER EIGHTEEN

GHOSTS AND SHADOWS

While Brede revived his forward observer training, others spent several hours trying to find the ARVN battalion that had been positioned north of Taskforce Tollbooth to shield the small unit from possible enemy attack. When communications were eventually reestablished, that unit was found back in its barracks in eastern Quang Tri, where they had been for two days—on orders from their regiment. An unfortunate misunderstanding, everyone agreed. The truth was more complicated.

The war in Vietnam, like those since, was fought beside local allies whose devotion to our vision of victory was decidedly mixed. Some units—especially those buttressed and motivated by U.S. or Australian advisors—fought hard and well. Others were far less aggressive. Compounding the problem, desertions were high among local draftees, whose loyalty seldom expanded beyond village boundaries to include some vague national concept. Even so, ARVN unit payrolls were largely subsidized with U.S. funds. The money kept flowing as long as paperwork verified the rosters of soldiers to be paid. Clever officers, long since unconvinced of their side's eventual triumph, saw no reason why their morning reports had to mirror stark reality—especially when the difference could so easily be invested to underwrite a comfortable postwar future in some more peaceful part of the world.

The "ghost battalions" brought into semi-existence by this administrative sleight-of-hand were never entirely mythical. Most were truly at half strength or better, though actual headcounts varied from month to month. They could perform many duties adequately, but failed when confronted by real, flesh-and-blood opponents in battle. Then they seemed to melt away, quickly leaving the field to their enemy. Suspecting the imminent arrival of NVA opposition, ARVN officers thought it wiser to evacuate a paper battalion, and keep a useful cash cow in operation.

The unexpected gargantuan explosions that broke the Ho Chi Minh Trail had propelled North Vietnamese intelligence to frenzied activity. What had the Yankee Devils done? Could the massive destruction be repeated elsewhere? Could the weapon they used be destroyed or—better yet—captured and turned against them?

That old saying, "a secret is safe with two people, as long as one of them is dead," proved true once again. A few too many senior officers at MACV became aware of Tollbooth. One was a drug addict who confided in his Vietnamese mistress, supplier of the poison he pumped into his veins—who was also a North Vietnamese agent. Within two days, planners in Hanoi knew enough about the mission to evaluate their next steps. They decided to send a few hundred troops on a lightning raid to overwhelm the unit that had fired the monstrous shells—destroy it utterly, and capture some nuclear weapons for their own use if they could. South of Khe Sanh, their way was clear. The ARVN forces charged with defending that area had left the field. Three-hundred NVA troops hurried forward, unopposed and unseen, through the area where a ghost battalion should have been.

Brede had no sooner climbed back up the hill than he was confronted by Major Caul. "We got trouble coming," Caul told him. "There's a strong NVA force coming down from our northwest, probably crossed the river south of Khe Sanh. Get the nukes we have left in an ammo carrier, along with any associated equipment. We'll take 'em down to the LZ after dark, and get 'em the hell out of here. Can't risk their capture."

"We'll need two choppers to carry the four," Brede replied. "I'll get right on it."

Caul put his hand on Brede's shoulder. "Get yourself on one of those choppers tonight, lieutenant," he said. "I can't risk leaving you here, in case things go sideways."

Brede shook his head. "I'm a pretty good FO, it turns out," he said. "I can help."

The major laughed. "There's half a dozen men on this hill can direct fire as good as you," he said, "and I'm one of them. You've volunteered enough, Ex. Time for you to go home. That's an order."

For the next hour, Brede and two of the gun crew loaded the four remaining W33's into an ammo carrier track, carefully secured with quick release tie-down straps. Manuals and other equipment were also packed and loaded. The fifty caliber machine gun the vehicle mounted was loaded and checked. "We're as ready to go as we'll get," he reported to Caul. The sun was setting. Night would be upon them soon.

"A squad from the 101st guys is already waiting at the LZ," Caul told him. "They'll come back with the carrier. The choppers will come in low, dropping flares. If we're quick enough, the bad guys won't have time to react. Start up when you see my signal. See you back at Dong Ha, lieutenant."

Brede sat in the carrier track, waiting what seemed a long time for Caul's signal. It finally came, and he told the driver to start his engine and proceed down the hill to the LZ, on a path well-worn into the sawgrass. They reached the field just as the evacuation Huey's came in low to their front on their first pass over the field. Machine gun fire erupted immediately from a tree line at the field's edge.

The gunner in the carrier's ring turret immediately poured fire on the tree line. For a few seconds it seemed as though the fifty caliber fire had neutralized the enemy. The lead copter began to drop toward a landing. Then, a flash of rocket fire lit up the field as if daytime had returned. An RPG round hit the Huey as it descended, breaking the aircraft in two. The second helicopter veered away, clawing for altitude as it took machine gun fire. The 101st troopers advanced into the field, trying to locate any survivors from the downed and burning chopper.

Brede shook the driver. "Back up!" he yelled. "Get back up the hill!" The track slewed left, then accelerated off the field and back up the hill it had just left. In a few minutes, they were back in relative safety.

"What happened?" Caul asked as Brede flung himself from the track.

"They were waiting for us," Brede told him, shaking his head. "Must have figured we'd try to evacuate. At least platoon strength, by the flashes from their weapons. We won't get out from that field unless we clear it first. Looks like they're south of us."

"North of us, too." Caul said frowning. "Brill tells me Corps is trying to scrape together some help, but things are still too hot around Khe Sanh to break loose forces from there. The Marines can't get to us for a day or so. Until then, we'll have to hold out here with what we've got."

"How bad is it?" Brede asked.

Caul took off his steel pot, scratched his head as he scowled. "The front of the hill's too steep to climb, and we'd easily kill anybody who tried it. The only way to get to us is up the road you just took. Between the men we have and the 101st people, we should be able to hold that. We've got plenty of ammo and good cover. I'd like to know how close the NVA is, how many of them are out there. We'll find out later tonight."

"How's that going to happen?"

The major smiled. "Basketball," he said as he walked away.

Brede decided to leave the W33's loaded on the track in case another opportunity to fly them out arose. He watched as men from the 101st climbed the hill toward him, bringing with them two survivors from the downed Huey. One was a medic, in good shape—his burns treated. The other, who had been a Huey gunner, was more severely injured and lay on a stretcher. In all, fifty-five of the sixty infantry who had been assigned to defend the taskforce now made their way to new positions on the hillside. The rest lay dead in the field below, near the brightly burning helicopter wreckage. A patrol would be sent out later to retrieve them. The arriving soldiers laid down their gear and immediately began digging foxholes to improve their positions. A few stopped by a pot of hot water nearby to grab warm c-ration tins from it, or to look for coffee.

The night grew dark, as clouds occluded the moon. Captain Beemer walked over to Brede. "We're going to try to reposition the damaged gun," he said. "Can you help, Ex? We'll need all the muscle we can get."

In theory, the plan was simple. The damaged howitzer couldn't move on its wrecked carriage, but it could probably still be fired. If a big enough berm were built behind the damaged gun, it could be aimed straight down the hill, providing defenders with powerful direct fire against enemies trying to attack up the road. To accomplish this, the berm would have to be expanded, enlarged, and solidified. The wreck could then be manhandled to rest on it. Twenty men worked with shovels and picks to enhance the berm, building a slope high enough to give plenty of cover to defenders positioned behind it. That effort took several hours to complete. Then, the two ammo carrier tracks attached cables to the damaged howitzer—pushing and pulling it down the hill. The men of the taskforce worked until almost dawn, through frustration and several injuries. Finally, the howitzer's breech rested high on the berm, pointed straight down the narrow path climbing the hill.

In the meantime, more had been learned about the enemy around them. Shortly after twenty-one-hundred hours that evening, the drone of aircraft engines above them made several taskforce soldiers look up from their digging. A large aircraft was invisibly flying overhead. Beemer put his hand on Brede's shoulder. "Get as high as you can up the hill," he said. "Take some bino's and a radio with you. You'll have more fire to direct in a few minutes."

Without pausing to wipe the dirt from him, Brede did as he was told. Quickly scrambling to a point near the pinnacle of Hill 213, he could clearly see in every direction—though little was visible in the dark. Suddenly, he heard a loud popping noise. Out of the clouds above drifted scalding light, too intense to look at directly. A large flare floated toward a field to his north, hanging below a parachute. Its light momentarily returned daylight to the area, casting giant shadows from a large group of NVA soldiers about five-hundred meters north, and another smaller group about the same distance to the south.

The hair on the back of Brede's neck stood as he saw enemies so close. The flare that had discovered them faded in a few minutes, but another took its place. "Rapid Student zero-six, this is Rapid Student three-one," he rasped into the radio's mike, his throat suddenly very dry. "Student zero-six, go," came the immediate reply.

"Three-one, I have enemy troops, platoon or better, five-hundred meters north of our position, over."

"Roger, three-one, wait."

As Brede watched, an artillery shell exploded two-hundred meters from the enemy soldiers north of him.

"Zero-six, drop two-hundred, fire for effect. Break. Enemy troops, five-hundred meters south our position over."

"Roger three-one, wait."

A third flare swung from its parachute as the NVA north of the hill were enveloped in artillery fire. At the same time, a single shell exploded over the enemies to Brede's south.

Zero-six, repeat, break, fire for effect, over."

Brede watched more annihilating fire engulf the NVA to his north. Less than a minute later, a similar fate befell those to his south. "Zero-six, both targets neutralized," he reported.

"Roger, three-one," the reply came. The voice he now recognized as Caul's. "Climb down and report to me, over."

When Brede got to the command track, Caul was waiting for him. "Nice work, Ex," he said. "Those flares came from a C-119 we got for half an hour. They're pretty busy around here right now. The code-name was 'Basketball,' in case you were wondering. We'll get them tomorrow night as well if we need them. Right now, I'm thinking we will. The support fire came from Camp Carroll. Everybody did a good job. We may get out here alive yet. Go get yourself some sleep. Tomorrow's going to be busy."

After fortifying himself with coffee, Caul walked from the command track to the berm his soldiers had spent the night digging, just as the sun began to rise. He stood by the wrecked gun's breech, siting the path shells from this hulk would follow down the hill they would soon have to defend. Captain Beemer soon joined him.

"You guys did a great job, Jake," Caul told his XO. "As long as this howitzer fires, nothing's going to come up the hill at us. We'll set the fuses on 'contact.' I figure if we can hold out a day—two on the outside, we'll be home free."

Beemer smiled, shook his head. "Nothing's free in this place," he said. "We've already lost eight, not counting the chopper crew. This was supposed to be a clean mission, in and out before the bad guys knew what hit them. Remember? I wonder what went wrong."

"I'm guessing the NVA know what we have here, and they're coming to get it," Caul said. "Either they figured out themselves or somebody told them. It really doesn't matter. If I'm right, they'll send in as many men as it takes to get themselves one of our nukes. If we don't make it out soon, we won't make it out at all."

The major found the first lieutenant in charge of the 101st soldiers, met with him and his first sergeant. "We're not going to get much help for another day or so," he told them. "We have to hold this hill with what we've got. See what you can do to improve our position. My XO, Captain Beemer, will be your contact. He'll get you whatever you need that we can supply. I'll give you as many of my men as we can spare to fill your foxholes. What else do you need?"

"Just chow and fire support, sir," the lieutenant replied. His nametag read Alvarez.

"OK," Caul nodded. "If you think of anything else, let us know."

"We're going to send patrols out, north and south, to probe the tree lines." Alvarez said.

"Can you plant some claymores while you're at it?" Caul asked. "We've got some if you're running low. I think we'll need them approaching the hill, places that look like cover." The infantrymen agreed and left to start their day.

An hour later, the hill was bracketed by more enemy artillery fire. The shelling continued intermittently for the rest of the day, answered by counter-battery fire. Two soldiers suffered shrapnel wounds, but by now the men on the hill had dug enough cover to prevent severe casualties. All continued work to improve and deepen their protective positions. Most agreed their enemies wouldn't appear in strength during the day. Any attack would come up the hill after dark.

Patrols sent out found evidence of large-scale enemy presence in the area, all around the hill. The 101st troopers engaged in several firefights with small NVA units, and four claymores set around the hill earlier were tripped. The level on tension felt by everyone rose with each incident, heard or reported. In the afternoon, Brede returned to his hilltop observation post to scan the area for enemy movement. On Caul's instruction, he preset targets and adjusted fire on them. Artillery strikes on these could be called up immediately, should enemy movement take place. The crew of the damaged howitzer practiced loading it. Aiming was impossible. The damaged beast would simply fire where it was pointed, nothing more. Betancourt, the experienced chief of firing battery, wondered how many rounds could be fired before its ruined carriage fell apart. He kept silent, praying the lash-up would hold together through the long night to come.

Brede left his foxhole high up the hill for a few minutes in late afternoon, to get some chow and a cup of coffee. He saw Caul pass by. "Will we get more flares tonight, sir?" he asked his C.O.

Caul nodded. "Look for Basketball around twenty-hundred. Might get more than that, too. I've requested Shadow."

Brede had no idea what "Shadow" might be, but Caul walked on without continuing the conversation. He'd have to wait until nightfall revealed the meaning behind the code word.

As she walked her ward that morning, Jackie felt inexplicably on edge—as if something bad were about to happen. There was no reason she should feel so nervous. Both she and the baby were healthy. She'd long since gotten over the worst of nicotine withdrawal. None of the patients she passed showed any need for concern, and yet … and yet she felt jumpy and tense. Every shadow loomed at her, every noise heard caused her to stop and investigate the source. "Too much coffee," she decided, and promised herself to wait a while before having any more. Still, the unsettled feelings continued.

CHAPTER NINETEEN

THE TWENTY-
THIRD PSALM

The sun set abruptly, almost like a light turned off—or so it seemed to those on Hill 213. Silence prevailed. There was little radio chatter from the command track. Conversation between the men in the foxholes was whispered and terse, as they peered downward into pools of gathering gloom. Spare ammo magazines were stacked close at hand, caressed often by anxious fingers. Feeling their presence brought a small comfort. Everyone surmised this would be their final night on the hill. Either they'd last through it until relief arrived the next morning, or they'd die here.

A sliver moon eventually began to climb a dark, cloud-crowded sky. Only the drone of a multi-engine aircraft soaring high overhead eased the evening's oppressive silence. Parachuted flares suddenly popped, swinging as they slowly fell—their hellish parody of daylight slowly fading as they descended. Now the fields around the hill were mowed by gunfire from above—bright tracer-defined lines that wove through the sawgrass to the windy roar of airborne mini-cannons. This was "Shadow," a big transport aircraft converted to a gunship. Orbiting above them, its weapons stitched bright deadly patterns in the fields close to Taskforce Tollbooth's position. The continuous whine of fire went on for minutes, and seemed to those watching to last even longer. As the noise abated and the sound of the aircraft engines faded, the men on the hill felt renewed hope. Surely nothing alive had survived the unleashed hell they had just witnessed. Desultory fires started by tracers smoldered beneath them, casting impossible shadows eventually consumed by murk.

Any confidence gained was shattered in less than an hour, with the tinny screech of a megaphone from somewhere below. "We're still here, Major Caul," a baritone voice calmly stated in perfect English. "You'll get no relief, not tonight. There are enough of us here to take the hill. We know everything about your mission, Taskforce Tollbooth. Our demands are simple: leave the W33 rounds you have where they are, with all their associated equipment. If you do that, Major Caul, you and your men can come off the hill, and walk back to Camp Carroll. We won't stop you. If you fight, we'll kill you. It's now twenty-one-forty hours. You have until twenty-three-hundred to make up your minds. If you agree to our terms, come to the bottom of the hill and meet me. I'll see you soon, one way or another." The unseen megaphone screeched again, then fell silent.

A hand shook Brede's shoulder as he crouched behind the berm. "Major wants to see you," the first sergeant whispered. Both men hurried to the command track, now lit only by the glow of radios against its metal wall. Caul moved to the center of the tented area when he saw them, nodded as Brede came close. "I need a technical opinion," he said, his voice low.

"What can I do, sir?" Brede asked.

"These W33's, the nukes ... can they be set off without firing them?" The words spat from the major's tongue, as if he hated to speak them.

Brede thought back, to a conversation he'd had in Korea—at D Battery, with prickly Lieutenant Farr. It all seemed so long ago now. He nodded slowly. "It can be done, sir," he said. "It's tricky, but the clocks can be rigged."

"If you set a round that way ... how long before detonation?"

"Detonation would be immediate—within seconds, sir."

Caul sighed, then nodded. "Ex, you're going to have to volunteer one more time," he said.

"Yes, sir," Brede answered, as profound grief welled up within him.

"I think we can hold on, I really do," Caul said, after a long silence. "It's going to be hard getting up this damn hill. Relief will be here by morning."

Brede could only nod. Tears formed in his eyes.

"Even so, we can't risk the chance that the bastards could lay their hands on what we have here. You and I know that, Ex."

"Yes, sir," Brede said, dreading the words he knew must come next.

"There's no easy way to say this, Ex. I want you to jury-rig a round to go off. We'll put you in back of the command track. Will you do it, lieutenant? No one else here can."

Brede threw off the overwhelming sadness that now cloaked him, the truncation of a life he would now never know. "Yes, sir," he said. "Better get a round and the tools back there. I should start assembly right now." He sat on a nearby metal crate, took off his helmet, stared at the ground as he lit a cigarette.

Caul nodded, and gave the orders required to put Brede's last volunteer assignment into motion. He remained alone in the command track for now. Top and the FDC crew were in foxholes on the perimeter.

Time seemed to slow on the hill. Minutes felt like hours to the men watching the dark below them, sensitive to even the slightest noise. Even so, no one could tell who started speaking the powerful words. They rang out from one of the perimeter fox holes, loud and clear:

"The Lord is my shepherd, I shall not want ..."

As the words continued, more voices joined in. Some knew the verses by heart, while others could only mumble along:

"Yea, though I walk through the valley of the shadow of death,
I will fear no evil for Thou art with me,
Thy rod and Thy staff they comfort me."

By the time the psalm concluded, almost everyone had joined in. Atheism fades on places like Hill 213.

"... and I will dwell in the house of The Lord forever."

A few minutes later, at twenty-two-thirty hours, Captain Beemer walked to the half-wrecked howitzer resting on the much-enlarged berm facing down the dark path. He called Sergeant Bentancourt to his side. "No reason to operate on their schedule, smoke," he said with a smile. "Put a round down the hill and let's see what we hit."

Bentancourt grinned and nodded. "Okay, you gun-bunnies," he growled, "let's find out if this wreck still shoots!"

With some difficulty, the gun crew rammed a shell into the damaged howitzer, added powder, and sealed the breech. Once the crew was under cover, Betancourt pulled an extended lanyard. The round fired without destroying the gun's carriage, though the grinding of tortured metal was baleful. Detonation occurred almost immediately, not far from the base of the hill. In the flicker of the explosion, shapes could be seen flying—people who had massed in its path. "Repeat!" Bentancourt yelled.

Within a minute, another shell was loaded and fired. Meanwhile, Caul requested artillery within range to begin firing on the targets he and Brede had preset earlier. The battle for Hill 213 had begun.

Explosions mingled with the firecracker snap of COFRAM rounds as the supporting artillery at firebases within range responded. Howls of desperation and anguish could be heard as the lethal bomblets detonated. The sounds of rifle and machine-gun fire added to the overwhelming cacophony, as jangling tripwires signaled the advance of enemy troops up the hill. It seemed impossible to the men in the foxholes that anyone could survive the volume of death they sent down the path. Yet flashes of returned fire proved their enemy continued toward them. The men could see those coming to kill them now, as the flat thump of mortar rounds and the sizzling flash of RPGs began to cause defenders casualties as well. Cries for "Medic!" went largely unanswered, as the men who uttered them began to fall where they had stood. The enemy took awful losses, but there were hundreds of them—and they were determined to take the hill at any cost.

One round too many was attempted from the wrecked howitzer. Recoil snapped the gun's barrel from its battered undercarriage, killing three gunners and several more in the area, friend and foe alike. The final shell exploded still lodged in the ruined gun tube, flinging deadly shrapnel as it rolled heavily down the hill.

In the command track, Caul yelled to Brede, as bullets began whistling blindly around him. "How close are you, Ex?" he cried. "They're coming!"

"Ready now!" Brede shouted through the canvas tenting. "Give the word. Good serving with you, sir."

The major nodded, wishing he could give the younger man more time, a few more seconds of life—knowing he could not. "Do it!" he yelled. "Do it now!"

Caul lowered his head. "I'm sorry, Ex," he muttered, pulling his pistol from its holster, chambering a round, then walking from the track to meet his fate. He watched Bentancourt fold to the ground in front of him, and killed the Asian man who had shot the chief of firing battery. To his left, he saw Jake Beemer's head dissolve to pink mist as an NVA soldier slowly turned a rifle toward him. He fired twice more, felt breathless pain, and died.

In the alcove between the command track and the hill's face, Brede finished the work in front of him and set the clocks in motion. Time seemed to slow down. He wondered if he'd done something wrong, and began to rise. He heard a noise, looked to his left, and saw a pair of NVA soldiers move in his direction. At once an immense glow filled his world, then abolished it.

Brede, the command track, everyone on Hill 213—indeed, a large part of the hill itself—all became loose atoms, wrenched violently from their previous bonds by inexorable energy. They rose skyward, buoyed by a small star which briefly destroyed the local night sky with raw, blinding radiance.

As the conflagration continued to rise, it coalesced into a pulsing cloud, which would find mushroom configuration as it continued to cool and drift northeast, eventually climbing to an altitude of more than ten thousand feet. No one remaining alive near the hill, now far less prominent than milliseconds before, attempted to watch the seething metamorphosis. Those few uninjured by blast or heat and not blinded by the detonation began wandering away from the destroyed area. Radiation exposure would soon murder most of them. As the poisonous cloud drifted, the heaviest particles flung skyward within it would soon begin drifting back to earth as irradiated fallout.

Profound silence settled over the fields around the blasted hill. The next morning, cautious reconnaissance would warn relieving troops away, pending return to less hazardous levels of radiation. Aerial inspection showed little left to save or salvage in any case. Taskforce Tollbooth had erased itself entirely. No evidence of it remained, beyond the devastation left behind: a scorched black scar like punctuation on the injured land, centered on the knob of a low hill.

As she walked the ward that afternoon, Jackie suddenly felt so faint and dizzy that she had to sit down. An unused wheelchair sat nearby and she sank into it. She gasped as the world around her spun. Another nurse ran to her side.

"Are you alright, honey?" the nurse asked. "Is it the baby?"

"No," Jackie replied through hands still held to her head. "No, it's not the baby." She exhaled slowly and looked up. "I just felt a little off balance for a second there. I'm fine now." She looked around, forced herself to smile.

"I'll get you some water," the nurse said, and hurried off.

Dropping her hands to her lap, Jackie looked around the dim hallway where she sat. The weakness, the disorientation she'd just felt was gone now—replaced by a sense of loss and emptiness she could not explain.

"Funny things happen to pregnant ladies," she said to herself, and rose shakily from the chair. She felt better now, she decided. Whatever had come over her was gone. She shook her head. Perhaps "gone" was the wrong word, she realized. "Changed" would be more accurate. Right now she felt as though a valuable aspect of her life was suddenly absent—a part that could never be replaced.

The other nurse returned with a paper cup. Jackie sipped the water gratefully. "Thanks," she said, "I'm fine now." She steadied herself and continued her rounds, but the feeling she'd experienced refused to dissipate. It lingered at the edges of her consciousness for the rest of the day.

Walking home after work through pretty Santa Barbara neighborhoods usually calmed and lifted Jackie's spirits—but not tonight. Reaching her bungalow, she didn't pause to watch the sun settling beautifully over the Pacific behind her. Instead, she hurried inside, quickly changed from her uniform to slacks and a sweater, rushed next door and rang the doorbell—hoping her neighbor and landlord was at home.

Imogene the parrot could he heard shrieking at the noise, crying *"At the door! At the door!"* as she swooped through the house. Eventually, Ava Whitehouse opened her door, looking skeptically at her renter. "Problem with the house?" she asked, as Imogene fluttered to light on her shoulder.

"Oh no, it's not that," Jackie told her, shaking her head. "I just needed to talk to someone—if you don't mind listening. I hate to bother you, but I don't know many people in town yet. If you're too busy ..."

As she saw the look on Jackie's face, Ava's countenance softened. The woman was upset. That much was obvious. She needed a kind ear, at least. She could not be turned away. "Yes," she said, "of course. Come in, dear. Sit down." She led Jackie to an overstuffed chair in her small living room.

"Give me a moment. I'll get us some tea. I always have some this time of day. It will be nice to have company. Make yourself comfortable." She darted to the kitchen, put some water in the teapot, turned on the stove, and hurried back to sit near her new neighbor's side. "Do you like sugar or cream in your tea?" she inquired.

"Both, please," Jackie answered. "Don't go to any trouble, Ava. I'm probably just being silly." She glanced down at her stomach. "Most likely it's only a panic attack," she said, trying unsuccessfully to smile. "Pregnant women get them."

"Just a second, while I bring the tea around," Ava said as she returned to the kitchen, where she filled two big mugs and set them on a tray. Carrying it carefully, she set the tray on a coffee table between them. "There's cream and sugar, dear," she said. "Please serve yourself. I take mine as it is." She lifted her mug and took a sip, as Jackie sweetened hers, poured some cream, and drank as well.

"Now then," Ava said, looking into Jackie's eyes, "what's brought you to my door this afternoon?"

"It's probably nothing ..." Jackie began, putting her mug down to wring her hands.

"Nonsense. If you were some flighty twenty-year-old I might agree. You're not. Something serious is on your mind. You came here to share it. I'm listening."

Jackie nodded, sighed deeply. "This afternoon, while I was on my rounds at the hospital, the strangest feeling came over me," she said. "Suddenly, I felt a terrible sense of loss—as if something important had been taken from me. Ava, the feeling was so overpowering that I had to sit down. I thought I was going to faint."

"Has this happened before?"

Jackie shook her head. "Never. I can't remember feeling this way before. Ever."

"This feeling, has it gone?"

Jackie began to answer, then stopped herself and sat silent for a period. "It hasn't gone ..." she finally said haltingly, "but it has changed."

"In what way?" Ava asked, cocking her head, trying to listen more closely.

"It's hard to explain, Ava. It's almost as though there's an emptiness now, where something important used to be—like a hole that can never be filled." Jackie put her head in her hands.

Ava took Jackie's hands and held them in her own. "I've had the feeling you describe myself," she said. "Like you, I was a young bride, expecting my first child, my new husband off to war—he was in submarines, you see, in World War II."

Jackie looked up, a big round question in her eyes. "What happened ... in your case?"

Ava laughed. "Oh, my dear, everything worked out for the best. Until just now, I'd forgotten all about it. I think strong women—and you are a strong woman, Jackie—I think strong women get frustrated when the world around us seems out of our control. It's like a teapot boiling over. This feeling you have, it will fade, the same way it did for me. I promise! Just wait and see."

Jackie sighed deeply. "You've made me feel better," she said, blinking through tears of relief. "Just knowing someone else has felt the same way, been through it, helps more than you can know."

"Now drink your tea, dear. It's good you're here. I've needed to talk to you. It's high time your cottage got some new paint. It's been years, and the place is looking a little dingy. We should brighten it up before your husband arrives, not to mention the baby! Do any colors come to mind?"

The two talked about paint for almost an hour. By the time she left, Ava assured herself that Jackie was in a better frame of mind. Even so, she knew the younger woman would continue to feel a sense of loss and emptiness, just as she had, twenty-seven years ago.

She hadn't told her tenant the whole truth—a truth that would have broken her heart. Ava knew the same terrible feeling that had flashed through Jackie. It had upset and disoriented her just as fiercely. Others around her had tried to calm and soothe her, but the feeling persisted. Then the telegram arrived, announcing the death of her husband, Gene Whitehouse, whose submarine had been lost off Guadalcanal. Crumpling the terrible message in her hand that day, Ava became certain she had felt Gene's death flash through her soul, days earlier.

Though she hoped she was wrong, Ava believed Jackie would soon receive some very bad news about her new husband. She wondered if she could help soften the hard blow she feared was coming.

CHAPTER TWENTY

TERMINAL DETAILS

A mixed force of Marines and calvary from Fifth Mech reached the area near what had been Hill 213 on April 29th—a day after the battle. They were ordered to form a perimeter no closer than two miles north of the hill, search for and detain any US or NVA survivors in the immediate area, prevent further enemy infiltration, and await further orders.

While they waited, searchers found the remains of more than thirty enemy nearby. Those whose units were identifiable were from the 308th and 324th Divisions, both of which were known to be operating in the general area. Half had died from severe burns. The rest had succumbed to what was later determined to be radiation exposure. A dozen living NVA soldiers were also discovered. These men suffered from acute burns. Several were blind from corneal scaring. All were sick and weak. They attempted no resistance, surrendering immediately when found. Half died soon after capture. The rest were evacuated to Danang.

A day later, a Chinook helicopter brought a team from DASA to the area. The team donned protective clothing and breathing apparatus before taking a pair of jeeps to the site of the battle, the hill itself. The 108th Group's Major Brill accompanied the DASA team, who brought photographic, radiation measurement, and soil sampling equipment with them.

Years later, dying from cancer in a Virginia V.A. hospital, Brill could still remember what he'd seen. "There was nothing there, really," he told those around him, his eyes wide. "Just scorched earth around that knob of a hill. At its crest, the hill was like a bowl, you know, indented in the middle. The soil was crunchy, like rice paper. There were rocklike blobs of radioactive metal—maybe the remains of the guns? Who could tell? No people, though. No people at all. No bodies, no bones, no shadows of where they'd been, nothing—like they'd never been there at all."

Before departing, the DASA team verified that radiation levels in the area had subsided sufficiently to allow limited, timed access to areas immediate to the hill. A subsequent search discovered the remains of more than sixty additional NVA soldiers in the immediate area.

U.S. troops soon left. The land beside the stunted hill along the Sepon lay quiet, further undisturbed for more than a year. In the meantime, reports and accusations of what had occurred there echoed through the capitals of the world, from Beiping and Moscow to Washington, DC— even reaching the halls of the United Nations. North Vietnam and the Lao Democratic People's Republic, supported by China, accused the United States of using nuclear weapons to bombard the Ho Chi Minh Trail, citing both soil samples and seismic evidence to prove their case. U.S. diplomats supported by the Soviet Union refuted the charge, while Europe's leaders remained neutrally silent. After a few news cycles, other issues intervened and the charges were tabled.

Unreported, but just as interesting to those aware of it—a furious air battle occurred soon afterward over northwestern China, in the Tarim Basin. A squadron of Soviet bombers was turned away from targets there by massive Chinese opposition. When whispered accounts reached the press, spokesmen from both nations categorically denied that any such confrontation had taken place, noting that conferences soon to begin were aimed at strengthening ties between the world's communist giants.

Two years later, the area near Lao Bao saw U.S. artillery set up once again—this time in support of ambitious ARVN strikes against extensive NVA logistics bases near Tchepone. The attacks were blunted and repelled, sending the survivors from some of South Vietnam's best fighting forces staggering back across the Sepon, setting the stage for full scale invasion of the south.

Sadly, repercussions from Taskforce Tollbooth's mission continued. The 1971 release of "The Pentagon Papers" in *The New York Times* brought clandestine U.S. use of nuclear weapons in southeast Asia to the headlines of newspapers around the world. Kissinger's negotiations with Le Duc Tho in Geneva were damaged, forcing a weaker settlement then Washington had hoped to achieve, laying the groundwork for the Communist conquest of all Vietnam in 1974.

Although the Soviet side of the agreement that led to Tollbooth was never publicized, Chinese leaders became aware of its terms. Perhaps the greatest immediate casualty of the whole incident was the failure of Kissinger's "Ping Pong Diplomacy" initiative to broaden relations with the Chinese Communists. Tensions between the two nations remained palpable.

Even more destructive was the signal to many world leaders that the nuclear genie was clearly out of the bottle. Nations possessing nuclear weapons immediately realized the need to buttress and improve their deadly arsenals. Others reconsidered decisions against acquiring weapons of their own. Within ten years, the list of nations holding nuclear weapons had doubled, and a dozen more were actively developing atom bombs of their own—or attempting to buy them from others. After all, most of the necessary basic technology was by now publicly available, and no nation that had ever tried to develop the bomb had failed. Treaty after limiting treaty was put forward by diplomats at the United Nations and other world bodies, to little avail. Tollbooth had made the world a far more dangerous place.

April slowly crept into May, with no word from Ex. Without alternatives, Jackie willed herself to patience. She convinced herself daily that "no news is good news," forcefully concentrating her efforts on work, fixing up the little cottage, keeping her mind occupied, and staying healthy as her pregnancy advanced. She was visibly with child by now, needed looser uniforms and shoes half a size larger than just a few months ago. Still, she felt good and made the walk to and from work at the hospital without undue effort or complaint. As she passed through the pretty neighborhoods around her, she imagined her husband's reaction upon seeing them for the first time. He'd be thrilled, she was sure.

Tea with Ava after work had become a regular event—a part of Jackie's day she enjoyed. The older woman was full of stories about Santa Barbara, California, and the world in general. She'd seen a lot, been through a full life, Jackie realized. Although reserved by nature, Ava showed a warm sense of humor and unexpected kindness as the women came to know each other better. She seemed to look forward to their tea-side talks as well. Even so,

Jackie sometimes sensed a hesitation in her, as if Ava wanted to tell her something but couldn't or wouldn't bring herself to do it.

May had almost ended when the dark green government car pulled up the driveway by Jackie's cottage. It was late morning. She had slept in since her shift at the hospital wouldn't begin until after five. Her plans for the day included planting flowers around the place, some bright and pretty blooms to make the place more cheerful. She idly wondered what kinds of flowers Ex liked best.

Jackie heard car doors open, then shut. Two men in green Army class A uniforms walked up the steps toward her door. Her breath caught as she heard her doorbell ring. For a timeless instant she froze, then hurried to the door to find out why they'd come. Surely, she told herself, surely it couldn't be what she feared.

She opened the door to the little cottage, to find the them standing in front of her—a young infantry captain and an older major. "Are you Mrs. Jacqueline Brede?" the captain asked. She could only nod as she stared at him. He was a tall, thin man with a prominent jaw and large hands, she noticed—and he smelled vaguely of cigars. There was sadness in his brown eyes.

"My name is Jeremy Ritter, Mrs. Brede," the captain said, his voice soft. "This is Major Bullard from the Chaplain Corps. May we come in?" Nodding, eyes wide, she opened the door so they could pass and led them to the living room couch, though they remained standing.

Jackie slumped to a chair. "Please ..." she started to say.

The captain stiffened and faced her. "Mrs. Brede," he said slowly, "The Secretary of the Army has entrusted me to express his deep regret that your husband, Lieutenant Xabier Brede, was killed in action against hostile forces on April 28th, 1968. The secretary extends his deepest sympathy to you and your family for your loss."

Even though she'd expected to hear those dreaded words the moment she saw the men before her, Jackie was still overcome with the weight of terrible loss. A deep, empty moan of sadness and anguish welled up from the depths of her soul. The room seemed to spin around her. For a moment, she thought she would faint. Instead, she straightened in her chair. "How did it happen?" she managed to gasp. "Where?"

"I'm afraid that information has not been provided to me, ma'am," the captain said, shaking his head. "It's classified. I'm sorry."

Stunned even further, Jackie put her face in her hands and wept. The two officers stood silently, waiting for her tears to abate. Her wracking sobs filled the room for a long time. Finally, she looked up, rubbing her tears aside. "Please ... sit down," she sighed, rising suddenly from her chair. "Give me a moment. I'm sure you've both traveled a long way. Let me get you some coffee, at least."

Both men raised their hands in protest as she moved unsteadily by them, but Jackie was not to be deterred. They sat, as sounds from the nearby kitchen—percolating coffee, clinking cups—followed her progress. No words were spoken. She returned in a few minutes, holding a tray with three steaming mugs of coffee, as well as spoons, a creamer, and a sugar bowl.

"There we are, gentlemen," she said firmly as she set the tray on the coffee table in front of them. "Please, grab a mug and fix it as you like. I'll take mine black today," she continued, raising a mug to her lips as she sat, holding it in both hands.

"Thank you, ma'am," Bullard said, as he added sugar to his mug and lifted it to take a sip. "It's a long drive here from Fort Hunter-Liggett— nearly three hours." Ritter nodded in agreement.

"Please accept my personal sympathy for your loss, Mrs. Brede," Ritter said.

"Mine as well," Bullard added. "At times like these, God is close to all of us. I can offer you the comfort of prayer ..."

Frowning, Jackie shook her head. "Perhaps later," she interrupted. "Ex and I were not much for religion. Right now, I want to know more about what happened to my husband. The last time I saw him, he told me there was no danger at all where he was going."

"Did he tell you where he was being sent, or what he'd be doing?" Ritter asked.

"No. No, he didn't," she said, shaking her head slowly. "He was a good soldier, captain—a good officer. The Army should be proud." More tears formed in her eyes. She angrily wiped them away. "If he had, I'd have begged him not to go. He volunteered, you know. Volunteered! He was a big idiot—always raising his hand."

"Ma'am, I ..."

Jackie looked down, touching the child growing inside her. "Now his son will never know his father. The life we'd hoped for will never happen," she said slowly, frowning. "I guess the 'where' and 'how' don't really matter, do they?" She raised her head, looking skyward. "Oh, Ex!" she cried. "My wonderful Ex! What have they done to you?" Her eyes clouded once more, and she wept inconsolably again.

When she recovered, Jackie spent the rest of an interminable afternoon going through forms and details, the clerical minutiae of military casualty. Most passed through her without comprehension—talk of medals and compensation. She felt battered, as though she'd been hit. Her consciousness ebbed. She nodded blankly when papers were put in front of her to sign or read. "Where will the remains be sent?" she finally murmured.

The two officers looked at one another, silent for a time. "There will be a ceremony at Los Angeles National Cemetery," Bullard finally said. "It's scheduled for June 15th."

Jackie was puzzled. "Isn't that a long time … to keep …"

"There are no remains, ma'am," Ritter explained, "for your husband, or any of the other members of his unit. They were all completely destroyed."

Ex's memorial service took place as scheduled. Ava drove Jackie to Los Angeles in the old Studebaker Commander, down the 405 to Sepulveda and the quiet, peaceful fields within the gates of the place, which she was told had served American soldiers since the last century. The pleasant, sunny day seemed somehow inappropriate, as did the calm silence that surrounded them.

The guard at the gate directed them to the chapel, an attractive white building with a ceramic tile roof. They parked and walked inside, ushered to their seats in the first row of pews by blank-faced attendants. To her surprise, they weren't the only people attending. She noted two older people (near her own age, really)—a man and woman who sat distantly apart from one another. Ex's parents, she guessed. Neither made any effort to approach her.

Several high ranking military officers she'd never seen before, gathered at the rear of the nave, caught her attention. All wore full dress uniforms and conferred among themselves, waiting for the service to start. Another man, in civilian clothes, rose from their midst and came to her side as she entered. As he stood and walked toward her, she recognized Colonel Gaboury from Camp Pelham—though he looked out of place in mufti. She stood to meet him.

"Colonel," she said as he came near, "I never expected to see you here. How did you ..."

The small man held her hand. "The Army has a gwapevine, like any other big institution," he told her. "Word reached me, just as I was wetiring from service. So, I stuck awound here. When this is over, I'll head back to Vermont—where my family is fwom." He smiled sadly. "Ex was the best young soldier I ever knew. Pwease accept my sympathy."

"I'm glad you see you here," Jackie told him. "Ex thought a lot of you. Who are the men you were with?"

"They're all high wanking bwass from the pentagon," Gaboury said. "They're the men who sent your husband on that mission." Seeing the look on Jackie's face, he cautioned her. "Don't twy to confwont them," he warned, shaking his head. "They won't talk to you. They're here because their boss ordered them to come." He looked up into the sanctuary. "We should sit down. They're about to start. God bwess you and the baby, Jackie." The little man darted away.

A silver-maned older man wearing an Army uniform with Chaplain Corps insignia strode toward the pulpit. The susurrus that had echoed through the high-roofed room ceased. "Let us begin with a prayer," the man at the pulpit said, raising his hands in resonant voice.

The service was short—almost abrupt, basically a re-reading of the transcript for Ex's Silver Star, which Captain Ritter had presented to her. There was no casket, but a soldier brought a folded American flag to Jackie and presented it. She clutched the flag to her, and could not hold the tears back any longer. She lowered her head and wept. When she looked up, she and Ava were the only people left in the nave. The pews behind them had emptied. She had hoped to meet Ex's parents, but they had already left—along with the enigmatic colonels and generals who had been sitting in the back. "It's time for us to leave too," Ava said softly, helping her rise from her seat.

Jackie dried her eyes and walked from the chapel to the old purple car, aware that the last vestiges of her life with Ex and all that had led to it were behind her now. Her new beginning, the life of their child, had dawned.

CHAPTER TWENTY-ONE

THE RING CONTINUES

The baby didn't wait until October. Complications not uncommon to older mothers made cesarean delivery necessary several weeks sooner. Alexander X. Brede opened his eyes to the bright confusion of the world around him late in the day on September 7th, 1968, and promptly cried out against the injustice at the top of his lungs. Though premature, he weighed six pounds, two ounces at birth, and showed a healthy head of auburn hair. Jackie adored him at first sight. Alex was her dreams come true, her terrible worries and doubts erased, her love for Ex made real.

Ava brought her home from the hospital to a surprise—a crib, a changing table, a bassinet, and enough children's furniture to half-fill the bedroom in her little cottage. "Where ..." she began, all but speechless. She'd worried about how to shop for what she needed, much less pay for it all.

"It's not new," Ava explained, "but it's all well-made, serviceable. It was bought for my own child, my Joseph. I've kept it around, in storage, for ages. Never knew quite why." She nodded. "Now I do."

A tear formed in the older woman's eye as she touched the crib. "My little Joe," she said. "Died of polio before he saw three. I hardly speak of him anymore. The pain of his death still hurts too much. His furniture will find use now. That makes me feel a little better, after all these years."

Alex was a good baby, who slept regularly almost immediately, gurgling and smiling when fed, eyes bright, perfect little hands caressing Jackie as she suckled him. He began crawling early and walked before his first birthday. His eyes stayed grey-blue, his auburn curls quickly became a mop.

Ex's G.I. insurance allowed Jackie the luxury of staying with her baby for six months without concern about money. Even so, as March approached she knew she'd have to get back to work. The hospital was happy to have her back. The only problem was finding someone to care for little Alex while she was away.

"I'll not have strangers disturbing Imogene," Ava insisted, "nor my privacy either. I'll watch the boy myself. He still can't move that fast." She'd hear no arguments against her decision. "Go! Get back to work," she said. "Alex and I will be just fine."

She set up a small folding chair next to one of the Adirondacks in her garden, at the edge of the Avocado grove. That's were Jackie usually found them upon returning home, both in sun-hats against the sky's brightness. Ava would lean from her chair and talk to Alex, who would look up and gesture back—as though the two were in real conversation. Imogene usually hovered nearby, making the gathering an offbeat convocation.

Even though they'd both avoided any contact at his ceremony, Jackie hoped one or both of Ex's parents would want to see his child. She kept up a one-way correspondence with both of them, sending photos of their grandchild along. His father never responded, but in August she received a letter from his mother, Cora. By now Alex was tottering around the garden and joyfully uttering the first noises that could sound like words.

"You've been far more gracious than I have," Cora wrote her, "and the photos you've sent have become dear to me. I can see some of Xabier in each of them. If you agree, I'd like to visit. I want to know my grandson and his mother better."

Cora Brede arrived a month later, flying into the local airport from her home near Phoenix. Jackie put her up in the cottage's spare room, which she'd thoroughly dusted and cleaned beforehand. Careful politeness soon melted to genuine affection between the two women, who were roughly the same age. Cora visited often after that, and seldom missed spending holidays and birthdays with her grandson. Alex loved her more as he grew, paying rapt attention to her stories of his father.

The boy grew to be a thin, handsome youngster with grey-blue eyes and an unruly mop of russet hair. He read early, was good in school, and enjoyed playing baseball with the other neighborhood children. He adored the women of his family—Aunt Ada, his mom, grandma. Alex also kept a special place in his heart for his father, never present but always nearby in his mind. His mother sent him to the San Raphael School, a parochial institution where any tendency toward his father's left handedness was thoroughly discouraged (though he remained a baseball switch-hitter).

Jackie went back to work at Cottage Hospital, and soon resumed her specialty as a surgical nurse. She considered quitting to go back to college but dismissed the thought, deciding to save the remaining balance of Ex's G.I. insurance for unexpected emergencies and Alex's future education. Her search for another man to fill her life was half-hearted at best. After a few tentative dates, it became obvious that Ralph Singer preferred men for his companionship—though he remained a good friend and like an uncle to Alex. Other men came forward (the hospital was full of handsome doctors), but none caught her heart's attention the way Ex had so effortlessly. Though Jackie remained a handsome, attractive woman, she took no lovers to the little Prospect Avenue cottage.

Ava Whitehouse passed away suddenly in 1979, after suffering a massive stroke. Several friends from the neighborhood attended her funeral, but no family was present. A month later, Jackie was called to the offices of a local attorney, where Ava's will was read to her. To her shock and surprise, Ava had left her the cottages and land, as well as over half a million dollars' worth of stocks, bonds, and cash—with the proviso that she care for Imogene. "I have never met two finer people than you and your wonderful son," she had written. "Please accept what I have left, small recompense for the joy you both brought into my life."

Jackie immediately contacted Cora, who enthusiastically agreed to move into the smaller cottage. She sold the old Studebaker and the aging Falcon (to her surprise, the older car was worth a good deal more) bought a new car, had the place repainted, and bought some new furniture. A year later, Jackie climbed the hill from work to find Imogene lifeless in the avocado grove she had loved to fly though. The old bird had become far less active and vociferous since Ava's death. Even so, her death was a sad surprise. At Alex's insistence, she was put to rest beneath the trees where she died.

Jackie kept her job at the hospital and was eventually promoted to a senior nursing position. Alex went through high school at Bishop Diego Garcia, where he lettered in baseball. At eighteen, upon his graduation, he remained slim, of medium height, quiet. He had a girlfriend, and Jackie had thought they planned to stay in town for college, at UCSB. He surprised her by applying to West Point. As the son of a veteran killed in action, he was accepted for the class of '90. "I'm not sure I'll make it a career, mom," he told her. "I think it's something dad would want me to do. Besides, I want an engineering degree anyway, and it's free."

All those thoughts were running through Jackie's mind that morning in 1990, as Alex packed his duffel bag before leaving for the airport. He would be travelling to Fort Sill, for final training before joining his unit in Germany. He had graduated high in his class at West Point, and had made the Field Artillery his branch of choice. Standing there in his uniform, he looked so much like his father had, two decades ago—butter bar, mustache and all.

When he held her at the door to say goodbye, she looked into his eyes and saw his father. The same grey-blue eyes looked back at her. "Wait a minute," she said, backing away.

"Mom, I've got a plane to catch …"

"This will only take a minute," she insisted. Looking down, she pulled the wolf's head ring from her left hand.

He saw what she was doing, shook his head. "I can't, mom," he said.

She put the ring in his hand, nonetheless. "Your father gave me this ring to protect me, to keep me safe—and it has, all these years. Now you must wear it, Alex. Your father would have wished it." She closed his hand around the ring.

"Now keep this until you pass it on to someone you love, to guide them and keep them safe," she told him. So he put the ring on his right hand, surprised that it fit so well.

She reached behind her neck to unclasp the guardian angel she'd worn since that winter day in Korea. "You must take this too, Alex," she said, handing him the delicate golden necklace. "Give this to the woman you will marry, for her protection. It has been in your father's family for generations." He took the tiny angel and looked at it in his hand. Then he stuffed it in his pocket, kissed her, and left for a cab waiting outside.

A few months later, Alex rolled through the Brazilian pampas with his artillery brigade. Argentine admirals had recently floated an aging tanker converted to hold a large, crude atomic weapon into Port Stanley. Its detonation killed half the population of the Falkland Islands, triggering a harsh NATO response. This was the third use of nuclear weapons the world had endured during the past five years. Port Stanley joined Grozny, Chechnya and Luanda, Angola on a terrible but growing list—the continuing legacy of Operation Tollbooth.

Six months after Alex left, Jackie was struck by a car in the street facing the hospital as she hurried to work. A man rushing his pregnant wife to the emergency room drove far too fast to avoid her. The ER staff worked hard to keep Jackie alive, but she had been badly injured. The car that hit her had been traveling more than fifty miles an hour. She remained unconscious and unresponsive while they tried to save her life.

As she lay in the hospital's emergency room, waves of pain and terrible distress passed through Jackie's mind. At one point, she regained consciousness to look down upon a group of people in surgical greens bent over a still form on a blood-spattered gurney. When a nurse moved aside for a moment she realized she was looking at herself—as if from above—while others struggled to save her life. Sound and light suddenly overwhelmed her. She heard music—a few notes at first, that gathered coherence as they grew louder. A clarinet?

She moved through a long hall or tunnel of some kind, toward welcoming light. She recognized the song. Moonglow. A warm hand held hers, as she found Ex by her side—so handsome in his uniform. "Come on, Jackie," he said laughing, "don't be a sleepyhead. You and I have to make up for lost time. I have so much to show you, darling."

"Ex!" she said. "How I've missed you. It's been so long …"

"Don't worry," he said, smiling. "We'll never be apart again."

Jackie took his hand. They walked into the light, together. The music swelled. By the time the ER surgeon admitted his defeat and called it, they were far, far away.

THE END

GLOSSARY

Some of the terms used in **Operation Tollbooth** may not be familiar to those without military experience or knowledge of Korea. These definitions may help. They are presented in alphabetical order.

1-A During the Vietnam War era, the draft card rating that made induction into military service virtually inevitable. College students who were deferred were rated "4-A," while those unfit for service due to medical or psychological limitations were rated "4-F."

24th Corps During the Vietnam War, the headquarters in charge of U.S. forces in the northern five provinces of South Vietnam.

101st Refers to the 101st Airborne Division, a unit which fought in the northern provinces of South Vietnam during the Vietnam War.

Aerial Observer An artillery forward observer who operates from an aircraft. During the Vietnam war, the aircraft of choice was often an O-1 "Birddog."

AR 380-5 The principal Army regulation covering security, including the assignment of security classifications, the storage of classified documents and materials (including their destruction), and reporting breaches of security.

Arclight During the Vietnam War, the code designation for bomber strikes on tactical targets utilizing U.S. Air Force B-52 heavy bombers, which typically flew from bases in Guam or Thailand.

ARVN	Acronym for South Vietnam's Army during the Vietnam War: **A**rmy of the **R**epublic of **V**iet **N**am.
ASA	Acronym for the **A**rmy **S**ecurity **A**gency—a top-secret military organization that existed between 1945 and 1977. The ASA intercepted and analyzed enemy communications, and also oversaw the security of Army communications. ASA was under the direct supervision of the National Security Agency (NSA), and NSA operatives oversaw all ASA activities.
Auto-loader	The M110 eight-inch howitzer featured a hydraulically operated rammer/loader to automatically chamber the projectiles. These rammers broke down frequently, especially in the hot, humid climates of southeast Asia. Because the gun tube had to be completely lowered prior to its use, firing rates using the rammer were typically slower than when a manual rammer was used. Trained crews could achieve higher rates of fire using a manual rammer, basically a steel rod tipped with a hard rubber pad—even though ramming force was not as consistent.
AXO	At an artillery battery, a lieutenant junior to the XO— typically assigned to the FDC or vehicle maintenance.
Background Investigation (BI)	The FBI investigation required before a higher security clearance (Top Secret, or above) can be issued. A BI requires in-depth interviews with family and other associates, and may take three months or more to complete.
Basketball	The code name given to C-119 aircraft modified to deliver large, parachute-suspended magnesium flares over combat areas at night during the Vietnam War.
Battalion	A military unit made up of a headquarters and two or more companies, batteries, or similar units. Battalions are typically commanded by a lieutenant colonel (O-5) and may have as many as 1,000 troops. They are capable of conducting limited independent operations.

Basque   Descendants of people who originated in a region that
                      reaches from sections of north-central Spain across
                      the Pyrenees to Southwestern France. Their distinct
                      language is unrelated to any spoken elsewhere in the
                      region. A large Basque population emigrated to the area
                      around Boise, Idaho in the nineteenth century.

Battery   The designation for a company-sized unit in a field
                      artillery battalion. Typically commanded by a captain
                      (O-3), a battery has four to six gun sections, each run by
                      a section chief sergeant who reports to the Chief of Firing
                      Battery. A battery has between one-hundred and two-
                      hundred soldiers.

BDA   Acronym for **b**omb **d**amage **a**ssessment.

Birdcage   Jargon for the caged protective carrying container for
                      nuclear weapon materials.

Blue House   South Korea's equivalent of the white house—the
                      residence of her president.

Brigade   A military unit composed of three or more battalions,
                      typically the size of a reinforced regiment. Brigades are
                      the primary maneuvering unit of an Army division,
                      commanded by a full colonel (O-6) or a Brigadier
                      General (O-7).

Butter Bar   Slang for a brand-new second lieutenant (O-1), recently
                      commissioned, typically on his or her first assignment.

C-119   A twin-engine, propeller driven obsolescent cargo aircraft
                      modified during the Vietnam War to deliver large flares
                      ("Basketball") or—as replacement for the older, less
                      powerful "Spooky"—to strafe ground targets with a bank
                      of GAU-2/A miniguns. Later versions also mounted two
                      M61 Vulcan cannons.

Camp   Army jargon for a semi-permanent base, which may
                      contain permanent structures.

Captain   In the U.S. Army, the highest junior commissioned officer rank (O-3)—higher than lieutenant, lower than major. In the U.S. Navy, the highest field grade rank (O-6), equivalent to a U.S. Army Colonel.

CFB   In the field artillery, acronym for "Chief of Firing Battery."

Chaebol   The English transliteration of the Korean word 재벌, which means plutocracy, rich business family, or monopoly. The chaebol structure can encompass a single large company or several groups of companies. South Korean chaebols linked powerful military leaders, politicians, and rich families to create that nation's largest industrial businesses.

Chaff   A radar-confusing countermeasure composed of thin strips of aluminum, ejected from an aircraft.

Cherry Juice   Slang for the hydraulic fluid used in many forms of U.S. military equipment, due to its watery red color. Well-suited for temperate climates like Europe or North America, the fluid worked far less well in the hot, damp air in Southeast Asia.

Chief of Firing Battery   the non-commissioned officer (NCO) who oversees the actual firing of the guns during an artillery battery mission; in the US military, this position is often informally called "Smoke."

Chinook   A twin-rotor heavy lift helicopter introduced to the U.S. Army during the Vietnam War.

Chopper   Army slang for a helicopter.

CINCPAC   Acronym for **C**ommander **In** **C**hief **Pac**ific—the commander of all U.S. military forces in the Pacific Ocean and eastern Asia.

Class A Uniform   During the 1960's, a formal uniform that included a dress jacket, dress pants, and insignia indicating level of authority and experience.

Claymore	An anti-personnel mine used to defend perimeters. The Claymore mine has a curved, rectangular case filled with plastic explosive and hundreds of steel ball bearings, propelled forward in a 60-degree arc when detonated.
CO	Acronym for **C**ommanding **O**fficer.
XO	Acronym for Executive Officer: the second in command of a military company, battalion, or brigade.
Comm Officer	At battalion or higher echelons, the officer in charge of the maintenance and use of all unit communications equipment—both wire (telephone) and radio. The comm officer is typically a captain with communications training. Because of their nuclear support mission, artillery battalions like the Sixth of the Thirty-seventh also employed cryptographic radio transmission equipment, mounted in special trucks.
Command and Control North (CCN)	During the Vietnam War, the secret operation that attempted to infiltrate agents and surveillance devices into North Vietnam.
Command Track	A tracked vehicle used by the commander of a unit. The vehicle houses the radios, maps, and any other equipment needed to oversee unit operations.
Corfam shoes	Corfam was an artificial leather material created by the DuPont Company that appeared similar to patent leather. During the 1960's corfam shoes became popular in the U.S. military, because they kept a high gloss with minimal care—when compared to natural leather.
Cosmoline	A brown, waxy, petroleum-based rust inhibitor, used to preserve machinery during shipping or storage.
C-rations	Personal rations given to soldiers during the Vietnam War, when mess facilities were unavailable. They replaced the K-rations used in World War II, and were superseded by MRE's (Meals Ready to Eat). Each twelve ounce container held some kind of canned meat and vegetables,

hard bread (with peanut butter, jam, or cheese), crackers, fruit or cake, coffee, sugar, salt, chocolate or candy, as well as a portable trioxane heater for warming the food. In more settled situations, the canned meat/vegetable containers were often warmed collectively in a vat.

Counter-battery   Artillery fire that attempts to silence rounds from a hostile artillery unit.

Culvert   A concrete pipe or box structure used to carry water under roads to prevent flooding or erosion. During the Vietnam War, large culverts were sometimes used as housing/shelter for troops in the field.

DASA   Acronym for **D**efense **A**tomic **S**upport **A**gency—the Cold War Department of Defense organization that oversaw military nuclear weapons programs. DASA was later replaced by the Defense Nuclear Agency (DNA).

Dependent   In the military, members of a soldier's family—typically wives and children.

Deuce   Army slang for the S-2, G-2, or J-2 officer.

Div Arty   Army shorthand for "Division Artillery," the headquarters for division-level artillery operations. This level of command has been discontinued.

DMZ   Acronym for **Dem**ilitarized **Z**one—a buffer zone between belligerent nations where both parties agree not to emplace or deploy weapons, troops, or facilities. In reality, such zones are often heavily mined, targeted by artillery, and systematically patrolled—as was the case in Korea.

Domang-Gada!   Korean for "flee," or "run away."

Dress Blues   Slang for the Army formal dress uniform, which includes a dark blue jacket and trousers.

Dustoff   Slang for a medical evacuation by helicopter.

E-5	A three-stripe sergeant, the second lowest rank for a noncommissioned officer.
E-7	Sergeant First Class (E-7) is a senior noncommissioned rank, who may hold the position of First Sergeant or Chief of Firing Battery in an artillery battery.
EAM	Acronym for "Emergency Action Message"—a preset code printed within a sealed plastic "wafer" or "cookie." If the EAM code matches the code sent by secure communications (encoded tropo-scatter radio, for example), the nuclear weapon employment orders on the message must be followed.
Ersatz	An inferior substitute for something else.
Fatigues	The Army's daily work uniform, normally made of treated cotton. They may be supplied in a variety of camouflage patterns, depending on the part of the world where the soldiers wearing them operate.
FDC	Acronym for "Fire Direction Center." During the Vietnam War, a section of four soldiers commanded by a lieutenant, who calculated the firing solutions for an artillery battery's guns—using maps, logarithm books, and specialized slide rules. Nowadays, these functions are accomplished by a single soldier using a hand-held computer.
Fifth Mech	Slang for the Fifth Infantry Division (Mechanized), a unit headquartered in Quang Tri, which fought in the northern area of Vietnam.
First Sergeant	The highest ranking noncommissioned officer in an artillery battery or infantry company. He or she reports directly to the battery or company commander, and manages most of the personnel and logistics matters within the unit.
Fizzle	Slang for a nuclear weapon that does not completely detonate, creating dangerous radiation but far less blast than intended.

Forward Observer/FO	An artillery junior or noncommissioned officer who is sent close to enemy forces to direct and correct artillery fire toward them. Typically the first job a "butter bar" lieutenant is assigned.
Fourragere	A braided cord worn over the shoulder of a military uniform as a decoration. The Fourragere was first used by the French and Belgian armies in 1919. The word derives from the French "fourrager" ("of forage"). It is awarded to military units that distinguish themselves in battle.
French 75/ *Milimetré Soixante Quince*	Slang for a French-designed 75 millimeter howitzer used by the French, Belgian, and U.S. armies in World War I. The "French 75" was renowned for its exceptional mobility and high rate of fire.
Freq	Slang for radio frequency.
Grafenwöhr	In West Germany, the training area used by U.S. Army artillery units for annual battery and battalion tests.
Hamilton	Slang for a U.S. ten-dollar bill.
Hanoi	During the Vietnam War, the capitol city of North Vietnam. Now, the capitol of the entire nation.
Hanbok	Traditional Korean dress, it consists of a jeogori (jacket-like top), baji (trousers), and chima (skirt).
Hangul	(Korean: "Great Script") The written language of Korea. Invented during the fifteenth century, *Hangul* is the alphabetic system currently in use for writing the Korean language. The alphabet is comprised of twenty-four letters—fourteen consonants and ten vowels.
Headquarters Battery	In a field artillery battalion, the unit that includes the battalion commander and his or her staff—as well as other battalion level operations, such as communications, survey, and air defense.

Ho Chi Minh Trail	During the Vietnam War, a major North Vietnamese supply line that brought food, munitions, medical supplies, and replacement troops into the south. The trail, in reality a system of broad roads, ran through eastern Laos and Cambodia.
Honey Bucket	In many less-developed nations, the container for the excrement from a farmer's family and animals, saved to use as fertilizer.
Hooch	G.I. slang for any quarters with a roof and walls. In Asia, "hooch" can also refer to the place a G.I. sets up housekeeping with a prostitute.
Howitzer	A widely used type of field artillery cannon. The ratio of bore to barrel length for a howitzer is more than that of a mortar, less than that of a gun. In the late 1960's, the U.S. Army deployed four sizes of field artillery: the 105-millimeter howitzer, the 155-millimeter howitzer, the eight-inch (203-millimeter) howitzer, and the 175-millimeter gun.
Huey	Slang for the HU-01 Iroquois utility helicopter, widely used during the Vietnam War. More than 16,000 were produced for the U.S. armed forces between 1956 and 1988.
Hwangudan Shrine	(Korean: 환구단) was a shrine complex built in Seoul, South Korea in 1897. The complex consisted of two main buildings: a coronation site for Korean kings and *Hwanggungu* (황궁우; 皇穹宇; the "Imperial Vault of Heaven"). The coronation site was demolished by the Japanese in 1913, to make room for a hotel. *Hwanggungu* still stands today.
JAG	Acronym for **J**udge **A**dvocate **G**eneral—the Army's legal branch.
JCS	Acronym for Joint Chiefs of Staff—the U.S. Military's highest headquarters.

Jung-wi	Korean for "second lieutenant."
KATUSA	Acronym for **K**orean **A**ugmentation **T**o **U.S. A**rmy—South Korean Army soldiers assigned to U.S. Army units, in order to bring their manpower up to acceptable levels.
Laager	A temporary overnight encampment for a convoy.
MACV	Acronym for **M**ilitary **A**ssistance **C**ommand **V**ietnam—the Saigon-based headquarters that oversaw all U.S. military operations in Vietnam between 1962 and the war's end.
Makkoli	A Korean rice beer.
KIA	Acronym for **K**illed **I**n **A**ction—referring to U.S. military personnel killed in combat.
Klick	Slang for kilometer. By the 1960's, the U.S. Army had converted distance measurement from imperial to metric. A kilometer is roughly six-tenths of a mile.
LAW	Acronym for **L**ight **A**nti-tank **W**eapon. The M72 LAW was developed to replace the World War II-era bazooka. It is a portable, one-time use, unguided rocket launcher that fires a sixty-six millimeter explosive projectile.
Logger's Truck	The South Vietnamese people carried on their lives and commerce, even during the war in their nation. The forests of northwestern Quang Tri Province were heavily wooded, and people in towns and villages depended upon wood and charcoal for cooking and other purposes. Logger's trucks worked the forests, even while fire-fights occurred nearby. Some of the loggers were in fact Viet Cong agents themselves.
LZ	Acronym for **L**anding **Z**one: an area designated for helicopter landings, sometimes marked with colored smoke.

M-16	The standard U.S. Army rifle during most of the Vietnam War. It weighed 6.8 pounds, and fired 5.56 x .45 millimeter rounds from a standard 20-round magazine. More than eight million were manufactured.
M424 Spotting Round	The ballistically matched artillery round designed to allow adjusted fire for the M33 nuclear round from an M110 eight-inch howitzer.
M548	A tracked ammunition and crew carrying vehicle used to support the M110 eight-inch howitzer.
M577	A modified M113 armored personnel carrier, fitted out as a mobile Tactical Operations Center (TOC). The interior included fold-out tables, radio racks fitted along the left wall, as well as wall-mounted map boards and storage facilities for maps and code books.
Mama-san	G.I. slang for an indigenous women hired to maintain the barracks for U.S. troops in Asian nations—including South Korea and Vietnam. Also, any older woman found in a village.
Military Time	The military keeps time on a twenty-four hour clock, so two P.M. becomes fourteen hundred hours, six-thirty P.M. becomes eighteen-thirty hours, and so forth. Local time zones are adhered to, though some communications may refer to "Zulu" or mean Greenwich time—which is unchanged worldwide.
Mimeograph	A hand-operated duplicating machine used to make copies prior to the development of xerography. The machine forced ink though a stencil onto paper cranked through it—often a messy, time-consuming process.
Metro	Slang for the meteorological data transmitted to all artillery units regularly, which provides air temperature and pressure, wind speed and direction, and humidity information critical in properly calculating firing solutions for the FDC.

MP	Acronym for **M**ilitary **P**olice, the U.S. Army's police force.
MPC	Acronym for **M**ilitary **P**ayment **C**ertificates. In post-war South Korea, merchants did not trust the just-established national currency (the won). Preferring a more stable currency like U.S. dollars, they accepted payment in dollars for less than the accepted conversion rate. As dollars became more favorable to hold, the won became inflated, frustrating plans to stabilize the South Korean economy. Soldiers paid in dollars discovered merchants were happy to convert unlimited amounts of U.S. banknotes to won at the floating (black market) conversion rate—which became far better than the government fixed rate. To reduce profiteering, the U.S. military devised the Military Payment Certificate (MPC) program—paper money issued by the Department of Defense. MPCs were fully convertible to U.S. dollars when servicemen left South Korea, and convertible to won when servicemen went on leave (though the reverse was not allowed). In order to eliminate U.S. dollars from local economies, it was illegal for unauthorized personnel to possess MPC. Even though US greenbacks were not circulating, most local Korean merchants accepted MPCs as though they were U.S. dollars, since they could still trade them on the black market. To prevent MPC from eroding the won, Eighth Army frequently changed MPC banknote styles—in an effort to defeat black market hoarding. A "conversion day" or "C-day" was a soldier's only chance to trade in his old MPC's for the new issue, after which any old MPC lost all its value. Foreknowledge of the date of an upcoming "C-day" became valuable information in every Korean ville.
***Munsani*, or Munsan**	A South Korean village, located near Camp Pelham.

Muscle Shoals sensors	Air-dropped, battery-powered acoustic, magnetic, and seismic sensors deployed in strings at known points along the Ho Chi Minh Trail as part of Operation Igloo White—between early 1968 and 1973. Once in place, the sensors alerted U.S. forces of any movement near them.
Nbyeong	Korean word for "soldier."
NCO	Acronym for **N**oncommissioned **O**fficer. In the U.S. military, an NCO is an officer who does not hold a commission from Congress. He or she is authorized to lead and give orders, having earned rank and authority by promotion through the enlisted ranks. NCO ranks run from Corporal (E-4) through Sergeant Major (E-9).
NOFORN	In document security, an acronym that stands for "**no** **for**eign **n**ationals." When indicated on a document, it means the information contained cannot be released to non-U.S. citizens..
O-1 Bird Dog	A two-passenger, fabric-winged, single engine aircraft used during World War II, the Korean War, and the Vietnam War for observation and liaison—the military version of the famous Piper "Cub."
OCS (Officers Candidate School)	In 1967, a twenty-two week U.S. Army program, completion of which awarded commissions to successful candidates. Participants were selected from within noncommissioned and enlisted ranks, based on test scores, recommendations, and the decision of an evaluation board. All the combat arms (infantry, armor, artillery, engineers) ran separate OCS programs, similar only in their harsh discipline and strenuous physical training. Attrition rates for those who entered the program averaged sixty percent or more. Roughly one in five commissioned Army officers were OCS graduates during this period.

Officer	In the military, an individual authorized to give orders to subordinates, lead troops, and perform other command functions. Commissioned officers are granted their commissions by act of Congress. Noncommissioned officers earn their authority by promotion through the ranks.
Officers Club	The commissioned officers of most Army units in garrison (permanent quarters) formally establish an "Officers Open Mess" (OOM) for their use. OOMs serve alcoholic beverages and meals, and provide off-duty entertainment for members. Noncommissioned officers organize similar messes (NCOOMs), and enlisted messes may be established as well. All are supported by monthly dues levied on members.
Operation Pegasus	During the Vietnam War, the drive to relieve the Khe Sanh garrison and re-open Route Nine in western Quang Tri province. Spearheaded by units of the 1st Air Cavalry, the 3rd Marine Division, and the 3rd ARVN Task Force, the forces fought elements from the 304th, 308th, 320th, and 324th NVA divisions from April first through April fifteenth, 1968. Arclight strikes were also employed. More than sixteen thousand NVA were killed around Khe Sanh during Pegasus.
OP-Plan	Military slang for an operations plan—a document that describes in detail movement of units during an operation under a stated contingency.
Oralloy	Acronym for "Oak Ridge Alloy," the standard uranium explosive in a U.S. nuclear weapon.
Ozark Airlines	A regional airline that operated in the central U.S. during the 1960's. Ozark was purchased by TWA in 1985, and subsequently became part of American Airlines.
PFC	Acronym for "Private First Class," the single-stripe (E-3) enlisted rank given most soldiers who successfully complete training and are sent to duty.

Pit	The explosive fissile material in a nuclear device, usually stored in a protective cannister called a "birdcage."
Platoon	In the U.S. Army, the smallest component of an infantry company commanded by a commissioned officer—normally a lieutenant, with the aid of a sergeant (E-6). An infantry company usually contains four platoons, each with thirty to forty soldiers.
Pogey Bait	G.I. slang for a personal stash of "store-bought" treats or candy, sometimes used to lure prostitutes.
Powder	In the field artillery, the propellant used to send a shell through a cannon to its target. Powder is provided in bags, labeled according to explosive power. The bags needed for a fire mission are communicated to the gun section chief by the FDC. Unused powder is burned later on in a fire pit.
PX	Acronym for "Post Exchange"—the store at which personal goods, liquor, cigarettes, clothing, and other sundries can be purchased. Variations in other services include "BX" (Air Force) and "Ship's Store" (Navy).
Quonset	Corrugated, galvanized steel structures prefabricated with semi-cylindrical cross-sections, derived from the British Nissen hut design. Hundreds of thousands were produced for the U.S. military during World War II. The name comes from their first use, at Quonset Point, Davisville, RI. Quonset sides were corrugated steel sheets. Ends were covered with plywood, and included doors and windows. The insulated interiors were lined in plywood and had wood floors.
RPG	Acronym for **R**ocket **P**ropelled **G**renade. An unguided rocket and firing container, descended from the German World War II *Panzerfaust*, produced by the Soviet Union and popular with NVA and Viet Cong forces in Vietnam.

S-1	In a U.S. Army battalion or brigade, the staff officer responsible for administration and personnel.
S-2	In a U.S. Army battalion or brigade, the staff officer responsible for intelligence and security.
S-3	In a U.S. Army battalion or brigade, the staff officer responsible for operations and training.
S-4	In a U.S. Army battalion or brigade, the staff officer responsible for supply and maintenance.
SAM	Acronym for "Surface to Air Missile." During the Vietnam War, the Soviet Union supplied North Vietnam with large quantities of radar-guided, rocket-propelled antiaircraft missiles.
SASP	Acronym for "Special Ammunition Supply Point." Depots where the Army stored and maintained nuclear and other "special" weapons. Because of unique security and storage requirements, these categories of ammunition could not be stored with other ordnance.
Scrambler	Army slang for NESTOR KY-8 equipment. By the mid-1960's, it became apparent that the NVA was intercepting most U.S. radio transmissions. NESTOR equipment (developed by the NSA), which could be mounted on radios in use on jeeps or in other vehicles, was designed to "scramble" radio transmissions and prevent their interception. In use, a radio operator would signal his intent to use the equipment by telling those receiving his message he was "going green," because the device showed a green light when operating. In practice, NESTOR was prone to failure in the field, and most radio communications continued to be sent "in the clear."
Scuttlebutt	Army slang for rumor or gossip.
Shadow	A heavily modified C-119 cargo aircraft, designed to deliver fire from a bank of mini-cannon to strafe enemy troops; the replacement for the C-47 "Spooky."

Short	Army slang for being close to the end of a tour of duty. Tours in South Korea lasted thirteen months, which considered the projected time to leave and return from Korea by ship—even though transportation was always via aircraft by the 1960's. A tour in Vietnam lasted twelve months. A "short-timer" was generally thought to be a soldier with less than three months left on his or her tour.
Short-timer calendar	A line drawing, usually depicting an attractive young lady, whose body was subdivided into numbered segments—one for each day of a soldier's tour. By the time he came home, the drawing's segments would all be filled in.
Skin-So-Soft	A bath oil marketed by Avon, popular with soldiers in Vietnam because it deterred mosquitoes.
Slicky-boy	G.I. slang for South Korean thieves, many of whom were children or adolescents. These accomplished pillagers were able to remove mounted spare tires from vehicles driving through villages, burglarize tents and buildings, and pick pockets.
Smoke	Army slang for the Chief of Firing Battery. Historically, firing entire batteries at the same time produced a large cloud of smoke.
SOP	Acronym for **S**tandard **O**perating **P**rocedure. The taught or recorded instructions for properly operating equipment or behaving in certain situations.
Space heater	A self-contained appliance, usually electric or oil burning, used for heating an enclosed area.
Spec-Four	Army slang for "Specialist, fourth class," a rank roughly equivalent to a corporal (E-4), but having no command authority. Spec-fours are usually clerks or mechanics.
Squad	The subdivision of a platoon, with four soldiers, commanded by a corporal or a sergeant (E-5).

SRAO/ "Donut Dolly"	Between 1953 and 1973, 899 women participated in the Red Cross Supplemental Recreation Activities Overseas program in South Korea, designed to boost troop morale with refreshments and entertainment activities. They worked in the field, visiting units of the Second and Seventh Infantry Divisions, providing what they hoped was "a taste of home" to soldiers in trenches south of the DMZ.
Survey Section	In the days before lasers and GPS, artillery battalions determined precise locations using survey teams equipped with measurement chains, ranging rods, and theodolites. Measurements were taken from the nearest verified location, and often subjected survey parties to enemy fire. The survey section officer (typically a lieutenant) commanded a survey section of two teams— roughly twenty soldiers.
Taps	The plaintive bugle call played at U.S. military installations around the world, at the end of every working day, and also at military funerals. Its twenty-four notes honor soldiers who have fallen.
TDY	Acronym for "**T**emporary **D**uty Assignment."
TOC	Acronym for **T**actical **O**perations **C**enter—an artillery battalion's operational nerve center, where communications with firing batteries and information about their locations and capabilities were kept. The FDC was located here, as was the bulk of battalion-level communications equipment.
Top	Army slang for a first sergeant, the highest ranking noncommissioned officer (NCO) in a company-sized unit.
Top Secret/TS	The military issues three basic levels of security clearance: classified, secret, and top secret. Most enlisted troops will be cleared for classified materials unless their jobs specifically demand exposure to documents

or equipment requiring a higher clearance. Most NCOs and officers will hold secret clearances unless their jobs require exposure to documents or materials demanding a top secret clearance. A top secret clearance requires evaluation of a full personal background investigation (BI), performed by the FBI. There are specific clearances above top-secret, including "Q" clearances for special weapons and "SI" (signal intelligence) clearances for exposure to certain types of intercepted foreign documents or messages, among others.

TOT Acronym for "Time on Target." During the time before computers, the feat of timing fire from artillery at several different locations to hit the same target at exactly the same time was considered a measure of remarkable professionalism.

TPI Acronym for "Technical Proficiency Inspection." The detailed evaluation of nuclear weapons management conducted among U.S. military units by higher authorities. Failure to perform adequately can result in ruined careers.

Track G.I. slang for any vehicle that runs on tracks, like a tank, instead of tires.

Tri-chloroethylene Sometimes called "Trike" by those who have to use it, tri-chloroethylene is an industrial solvent and degreaser, used in nuclear weapons assembly to clean human residue from parts and surfaces.

Ujeonbu A town in northwest South Korea. *Ujeonbu* was important to the North Korean invasion of the south in 1949. North Korean troops initially travelled by railroad to the town at the beginning of their assault on the South.

VC Acronym for **V**iet **C**ong—South Vietnamese militias that supported North Vietnam during the Vietnam War.

Ville	G.I. slang for a village or town where soldiers procure liquor, drugs, or prostitutes.
W33	A U.S. nuclear artillery shell, designed to be shot from an eight-inch howitzer.
W48	A U.S. nuclear artillery shell, designed to be shot from a 155-millimeter howitzer.
Waiver	A formal application to consider a soldier for a duty who has not yet met specific required standards. A waiver is not automatic, and each request must be considered individually.
Warrant Officer	In the U.S. Army, experts in a specific technical area throughout their military careers. There are more than forty warrant officer specialties, ranging from aviation to harbor master. Chief warrant officers take the same oath as commissioned officers, and may command aircraft, small units, or detached teams.
Yangkiseu	Korean derogatory word for "Yankee."
Yield	One measurement of the explosive power of a nuclear weapon, often expressed in kilotons (thousands of tons) of TNT equivalence.
Zippo™	A metal cigarette lighter with a hinged top, manufactured by the Zippo Manufacturing Company, extremely popular with soldiers during the 1960's.

As you read this book, if you find terms that remain unclear or need further clarification, please contact the author at *www.kipcassino.com*.

APPENDIX A

U.S. Army Nuclear Cannon Artillery
During the Vietnam Era

By the mid-1960's, the U.S. Army's demand for atomic artillery was fully realized. Nuclear-armed battalions were deployed in South Korea, West Germany, and Guam—as were M28/29 "Davy Crockett" rounds, fired from modified recoilless rifles on jeeps by infantry. With a range of less than three miles and a yield of only one-hundredth of a kiloton (ten tons), the M28 was possibly the smallest yield nuclear indirect fire weapon ever put in service by this nation. The blast effect from these rounds was considered only secondary, however. Far more important was the hard neutron radiation they generated. "Davy Crockett" was designed primarily to kill people, even those buttoned up in tanks or other vehicles. More than two thousand were produced before the system was retired in 1971.

Some M28's were modified to become SADM—"Special" Atomic Demolition Munitions, sometimes called suitcase nukes. For this purpose, the eighty-pound "Davy Crockett" warheads were divided into paired forty-pound packs, which elite Special Forces "Greenlight" teams were trained to man-carry to specific objectives behind enemy lines in the event of war. In 1988, the remaining three-hundred SADMs were retired from NATO inventory. The following year, both SADMs and "Greenlight" teams were officially removed from U.S. service.

Atomic artillery had been in U.S. Army inventory since the Eisenhower administration, with the introduction of the M65 atomic cannon—sometimes called "Atomic Annie"—in 1953. Twenty of the gargantuan 280-milimeter cannon were manufactured after the Knothole Grable nuclear test at Frenchman Flat, Nevada proved the W9 gun-type warhead's efficacy. The M65 could fire its six-hundred pound, fifteen-kiloton yield projectile twenty miles. Carried to war by an eighty-five foot tractor steered from both ends (like a ladder fire-truck), the whole apparatus weighed more than eighty tons, was eighty-four feet long, sixteen feet wide, and twelve feet tall. Even so, a crew of five to seven men was sufficient to operate "Atomic Annie"—though rates of fire were low. M65 batteries were deployed to both West Germany and South Korea until the system was retired in 1963.

Even though "Atomic Annie" gave the U.S. Army its own nuclear punch, the system was not agile enough to meet many tactical needs. The huge carriers were incapable of traversing rough, off-road terrain, and the cannon took more than ten minutes to set up before a round could be loaded. More compact nuclear rounds that could be fired by field artillery weapons already in service were needed.

Since 1953, efforts to reduce the weight and dimensions of a nuclear artillery shell resulted in a "double-gun" mechanism code-named *Fleegle*—which reduced the needed velocity of the oralloy fissile components shot toward each other by half, since each would be propelled toward the other simultaneously through an annular bore. By making other parts of the projectile from titanium, overall weight was shaved to 243 pounds—light enough for handling by a howitzer crew in the field. The W33 was designed to be fired from eight-inch howitzers already in use, with a range of eighteen kilometers (eleven miles) and a yield of between five and ten kilotons (depending upon the model and pit choice).

First detonated in 1957, in the Laplace test of the Plumbob series, W33 rounds began entering U.S. stockpiles in 1955. Two-thousand rounds were manufactured by 1965, when production ended. They could be fired by all U.S. M115 and M110 eight-inch howitzers. The shells were retired from service in 1992, as the artillery that fired them was phased out in favor of the M270 tactical rocket system.

Success of the W33 program piqued Army interest in an even smaller nuclear round—one that would provide division and brigade commanders close nuclear fire support. In 1957, design work started on what would become the M48 nuclear artillery round. A new form of implosion was developed to shrink weapon size to meet Army needs.

The new design required only two implosion detonators—one at either end of a tube—which simultaneously push shock waves against an oblate spheroid (egg-shaped) fissile plutonium "pit" within the tube, using detonation fronts formed by wave shapers. The shock waves condense the egg to a spherical shape with critical explosive mass. Christened two-point linear implosion, the design allows smaller, more aerodynamic atomic shells to be constructed, as was proven by the success of the W48 round.

> **Author's Comment.** My instructor explained it this way: "Think of two bowling alley lanes, one facing the other, pins in the middle. When both get a simultaneous strike, you have fission."

W48 testing commenced in1962, and production began in late 1963. Delivered rounds were thirty-four inches long, weighed one-hundred twenty pounds, and produced yields of one-tenth of a kiloton (one-hundred tons) at ranges up to fourteen thousand meters (almost nine miles). A total of one-thousand sixty were eventually manufactured. The W48 was removed from service in 1992, as nuclear artillery shells were replaced with rocket systems.

Note: the information in this appendix was largely gathered from Wikipedia and my own recollections.

APPENDIX B
The M110 Eight-inch Howitzer

Howitzers firing the eight-inch (203-milimeter) artillery shell have been used by the U.S. Army since World War I. Design work on the M1, the howitzer that would eventually become the M115 towed eight-inch howitzer, began shortly after the end of the Great War, but was interrupted by lack of funding during the Great Depression.

Nevertheless, M1's were in production when World War II broke out, and remained in use throughout hostilities, towed by Mack 6x6 trucks or M4 tractors. Fifty-nine battalions using the howitzer were trained and fielded in northwest Europe, Italy, and the Pacific.

In the 1950's, development of the W33 nuclear round spurred M1's adoption by several NATO allies—under the NATO nuclear sharing concept. In 1962, the M1 became redesignated the M115.

By that time, development of a self-propelled version of the weapon was underway. Utilizing the chassis and engine of the M578 tracked light recovery vehicle as its basis, the whole vehicle weighed more than thirty-one tons, was thirty-five feet long, ten feet wide, and ten feet high. Rear-mounted spades allowed the thirteen-man crew to emplace the weapon, minimizing movement between rounds when fired. The whole assembly was designated M110. Its range was twenty-five kilometers (roughly sixteen miles), firing a high-explosive shell weighing two-hundred pounds (ninety-one kilograms or more).

The M110 entered service with both the U.S. Army and the Marine Corps in 1963. The last units were retired in 1994.

Author's Comment. With its four-hundred horsepower engine, the M110 could road march at speeds up to thirty miles an hour, even on the rough dirt roads of Quang Tri Province. The units we supported loved its heavy shells and its accuracy. We often went on "shoot and scoot" missions, taking the howitzers to unexpected locations to hit targets not thought to be within range. On these we were typically accompanied by Rome Plows from the Engineers and some infantry for security.

At the firebase, the M110 firing positions were fenced by sunken telephone pole-sized timbers, to allow accurate multi-round fire from any position of the compass. To our consternation, the poles began to sink into the earth, and eventually had to be replaced. The reason, when eventually discovered, was that the powerful detonations when the weapon was fired momentarily liquified the earth beneath it, allowing the poles to sink.

Note: the information in this appendix was largely gathered from Wikipedia and my own recollections.

Printed in the United States
by Baker & Taylor Publisher Services